# A Man of
# ndeterminate
# Value

D0094111

# A Man of ndeterminate Value

## RON FELBER

BARRICADE
BOOKS

Published by Barricade Books Inc.
2037 Lemoine Ave., Suite 362
Fort Lee, NJ 07024

www.barricadebooks.com

Library of Congress Cataloging-in-Publication Data

Felber, Ron.
  A man of indeterminate value / By Ron Felber.
    pages cm.
    ISBN: 978-1-56980-490-2 (alk. paper)
  1. Abandoned wives--Fiction. 2. Life change events--Fiction.
  3. Intellectual property infringement--Fiction. I. Title.
    PS3606.E3847M36   2013
    13'.6--dc23

                                                      2013008306

*There are mistakes too monstrous for remorse . . .*
—Edwin Arlington Robinson

# Dedication

*to Laurie and to Bill Blatty*

# Chapter 1

The Yellow cab slipped into a parking spot opposite St. Damian's monastery on Martin Luther King Boulevard in Newark's Central Ward. I felt remarkably well for a man who'd just been shot. "Hey, mister, you gonna be all right? You don't look too good," the Puerto Rican driver said. "Here," I answered slipping him two $100s for the $60 fare, "you stick to driving. You never saw me." "Sí, señor, no veo nada," he swore as I crossed the street holding my right hand over the crimson circle of blood expanding on my Tailored Image white shirt, from my left bicep, just above the heart. In my left hand, I clung to a leather briefcase filled with drugs, booze, even some papers.

I glanced over my shoulder to see if I was being followed—I wasn't—and climbed the five stone steps leading to the entrance of old St. Ann's Abbey. I rang the bell. My body threw off one enormous shiver as I waited thinking *'Come on, Father . . . Come on, for Christ's sake, I'm on the run and probably fucking dying!'* A monk answered. He poked his shaved head out beyond the door frame, looked to his left and right, and allowed me to enter.

"Jeremiah!" I gasped.

"Son, son . . ." uttered the priest, shocked at the sight of my ashen pallor and the edges of the blood stain I tried

1

to hide. Could he ever have imagined that John "Jack" Madson, his former student thirty years removed, would turn up like this?

"Did you get that room where I can write?"

"Yes, yes," the monk answered leading me down a darkened corridor before opening the heavy hinged door to a room that was empty save a chair, a hardwood desk and a lamp.

"Close the door."

Reluctantly, Fr. Jeremiah obliged.

I fell, exhausted, into the chair as I watched the door shut like the slab to a mausoleum behind him. I breathed a sigh of relief that caused me to grimace then pulled a laptop from my briefcase along with a half empty bottle of Chivas. I switched on the PC and took a long swig, washing down a handful of Adderall tabs.

Finally, tapping into the uncanny reserve of self-discipline the Brothers had ingrained in us since adolescence, I gathered myself and began typing:

I know I don't owe you anything, Phials, but I decided to write my confession, offer it on a silver platter, you might say. The reason is you deserve it. You worked hard to finally catch me and maybe you'll do it tonight if you did your homework. Fact is, I knew the first time I laid eyes on you that you'd be the one—my nemesis—the guy who's my exact opposite. You, so obsessed with every detail, so drilled full through with—what is it—OCD, isn't that what they call it? But you know and I know, it wasn't that simple. None of it. But now I'm going to tell you everything—about the murders, about my death, the women, and how this goddamned nightmare first came to happen. But it wasn't you who started all of this. It was—believe it or not—Tomi, who you know almost as well as me by now. I first met her in Ann Arbor, Michigan and fuck, it must have been the way Clyde Barrow felt when he first met Bonnie because, man, it was electric and I knew this girl was going to be crazy-wild.

I was there on business to shut down another plant in Detroit, and out to dinner to get the general manager, guy named Larry Bruner, on board with the program. So there we are sitting at the Black Pearl bar drinking when Tomi sits next to me. Funny, but the first thing I noticed wasn't those stunning black eyes of hers, or that dazzling 'let me melt into your universe' smile. No, it was a silver toe ring. She wore it on the second toe of her right foot and, Christ help me, I couldn't pull my eyes from it. So, she sits down, orders an apple martini just as Mr. GM and I down our third Glenlivet-rocks and the white guy who's playing the guitar and singing belts out Sam Cooke's "Bring It On Home To Me."

'What's that?' I asked, turning to her, the words tumbling out of my mouth before I knew it.

'You mean the drink?'

'No, I mean the jewelry.'

'It's a toe ring, baby,' she says, oh-so-soothing, 'it goes with the tattoo.'

'Can I see it?'

She giggled. It was sweet. Then she hikes up her skirt and shows me a red rose high up on her left thigh.

'They're a set. They go together.'

'If you say so, baby,' I say like the wise guy I am. Then my eyes creep up from that red rose, passed her midriff and the cleavage she offered as she bent toward me, up to her perfect white teeth, bared and smiling, to those eyes . . . eyes like your mother's eyes when you were a little kid and doing no more than what little boys do, so delighted at the simple fact that you were there, and you were *hers.* Those eyes said, 'You. You're the kind of man I could fall in love with.'

Now, I'm no Tom Cruise with Hollywood good looks and a $100 million smile, but I had qualities women responded to: thick black hair, fair complexion and high cheek bones, with a six-foot one-inch frame that carried my 178 pounds in a way most understood could spring to life against a bully as easily as laugh myself red-faced at a good bar joke. Still, it was that night, maybe even that instant, Tomi and I fell in love—or deep like, or lust—but, my god, whatever the chemistry was between us, it was fucking mystical. Half-hour later she was feeding me from her dinner plate while the singer wailed "Mystery Train" by Elvis and Bruner stared blankly at the image of himself in the large mirror opposite the bar when, ardent as a schoolboy, I look deep into those black dancing eyes, 'I *so* want to make love to you,' I tell her.

'Anything you want, baby,' she whispers in my ear slipping her long fingers between my legs. 'See you got the equipment for it.'

Well, once I ditched Bruner, Tomi Fabri and I drove back to the Detroit Hyatt and if it was fever started at the Black Pearl, it ignited to fire in the car, and was white heat by the time we entered my room. Tomi and me, we devoured one another, mouths, genitals, hands, tongues, ears, hair: totally, unconditionally, without limits. Until in the early morning we lay, drenched and exhausted, bodies intertwined like lattice work, black on white, white on black, when gazing into my eyes she tells me, 'The vibe is so strong, even at 7 a.m., I can't refuse you.'

'How about at 7:57 a.m.?' I asked, glancing at the digital.

'No, not even now,' she pledged spreading her body wide and long on the white sheets for me to do with her as I might.

Of course, I cancelled my morning meeting (couldn't just leave her after a night like that) and we batted the fat in the room over coffee. Tomi worked for Head2Toe, an escort service in town. She was twenty-six. Her mother taught mathematics at a black college nearby but retired and was now a nondenominational minister tending to a congregation of five hundred souls.

'My father was a good man,' she told me, 'like to think of him that way, anyhow. Fact is, he was a heroin addict, couldn't leave me alone once I developed breasts. Mom let him go on account of that. He went off to prison on a drug charge, died there.'

'Sounds tragic.'

'No, just real.'

'Yeah,' I answered. 'And working for the escort service, is that also real?'

'I don't do much with that, not really. See guys for money. Sometimes ladies. Hang out with 'em. Let 'em have some fun with themselves while I watch. If I like them a lot, we have sex. I do the guys, they do me. Women, too, mostly after couple of martinis.'

'So you're bisexual?'

'I like people. I like sex. I also like martinis. Say, I'll bet you're a man lives with a lot of rules, ain't you?'

I didn't answer immediately, just nodded. 'Yeah, that's it. I am a guy lives with rules. Too many goddamned rules!' I finally answered, laughing as Tomi Fabri pulled me down on the bed on top of her and, yeah, we started all over.

# Chapter 2

T he full impact of meeting Tomi didn't really hit me
until much later. Exactly when I can't say. But what
struck me was her lack of, what was it? Inhibitions?
No, it was fear. She had no fear, sexually, financially,
emotionally. Despite her lack of social status, financial
stability, house in an upscale neighborhood, Ivy League
education, or even a steady job, Tomi had something that
I wanted more than any of those things. So totally unlike
me, Tomi was free. In fact, she was as proportionately free
as I was living with the kind of deep-in-your-gut dread
people with something to lose carry inside them, real as
a lung. And in a way, it seemed to me, her freedom wasn't
so different from outlaws in the Wild West or gangsters
in the 1920s. Jesse James, John Dillinger, even some of
the Mafia-types I met growing up in Jersey, rooming at
Georgetown freshman year with Congressman Rinaldi's
son and the son of Gambino Family capo Anthony "Tony
Boy" Bontempo. These were men outside society. Outlaws.
And once someone figured out they had nothing to lose
but dread, the realization came that there was a way out,
there was a kind of freedom. You just never looked at life
that way before.

Near as I can figure it was three, maybe four months
after I'd met Tomi, alone one night, sitting in a hotel

room, smoking a cigarette in the dark, that it occurred to me. You see, it was my life, Phials. Not one thing about it. Every thing about it. Fetid and stale as the taste of tobacco, booze, and amphetamines on your tongue in the morning. Truth be told, I couldn't stand the sight of myself in the mirror anymore, and that was long before I'd ever laid eyes on Tomi Fabri. In the late evening or early morning back from a foray of booze at The Palm in Manhattan and marathon negotiations on the next acquisition NuGeneration Holdings could pillage and plunder, I'd stare into my bathroom mirror, disheveled as a Bowery derelict, reeking of scotch, exhausted to my soul while Jennifer, my wife, and Tiffany, our eight-year-old, lay together sleeping, and whisper to myself, '*Who the fuck are you?*' The answers were never very encouraging.

Fact is, I was a guy with two years of university education at Georgetown by way of an inner city prep school who'd gamed himself from being a DC cop, to sales, to a VP position at a mid-sized Wall Street take-over shop and marriage into a family he had no business even socializing with. 'Jennifer Lawrence Crowley, daughter of New Jersey Supreme Court Judge Barton Crowley,' I'd say to myself during those early morning self-examinations, 'and what had it gotten me?' Arguably my position at NuGen but, more to the point, a wife who still thought she was a debutante living off her daddy's dole (which of course she wasn't), a daughter who really was living off her daddy's dole (mine), and personal debt ranging somewhere between three and five hundred thousand bucks depending how you chose to look at it. Fancy that! A life that if I wrote a book would be called *How To Move From Lower Middle Class Status Into Intractable Depression Without Really Trying.*

Despite swimming underwater as I was, and my father-in-law's stature, I was pretty good at what I did for a living. Ours was a slam-bam-thank-you-Ma'am kind of operation. 'Jack the Magician' our boss Rion McCorkle called me but there was nothing very magical about it: identify an undervalued target, usually family-owned or held by a socialistic European entity, get rid of the senior management (anyone over fifty), cut staff by 30 percent, cheapen health care and go 50-50 employee participation, replace pensions with 401K retirement programs, and put a team of overly aggressive thirty-year-old NYU MBAs to run the place with obscenely generous bonus programs based on short term profit incentives. Then, *voila!* There it was! Move over, Criss Angel! With profits soaring—but training, R&D, and any long-term programs eliminated—there were fortunes to be made "flipping them" to larger competitors (owned by investment bankers) based on EBITDA (profits) multiples of seven to ten. "No Time to Wait!" that was NuGen's motto with the logo of a Remington cowboy on a charging horse. No time to wait for bonus. No time to wait for stock options. No time to wait to hollow out the guts of another moderately successful company like a game of musical chairs always wondering, who would be stuck with no chair. Who'd be holding the bag when the place went under like a scuttled ship at sea so China and India could pick up the expertise and market share, throwing millions of Americans out on the street.

But you, Phials, even from the first day I met you investigating an insurance claim for that poor bastard who committed suicide over at Granger Equipment ten, twelve years ago, it was like you were thinking 'this guy's dogging it, he's not *really* one of us, he's not *really* what he appears to be.' And guess what, Martin, I heard you—some inner part of me, and I said to myself, 'This guy right here. He will be my executioner.' But still, it was Tomi Fabri; she set the chain of events off in me and like a string of dominoes, one after another, they came tumbling down, *way down*. It was maybe three months after I met her that things kind of coalesced, came into a unique perspective, you might say. I began to see how futile my life really had become and one night—before I'd gotten to the mirror—I sat in a garden chair on the back deck of our home in Summit, New Jersey watching the canopy of tall treetops that shrouded our place wafting back and forth in the fall wind when the thought popped into my head: my life, our life, the life of the Madson family, was unsustainable. Worse, booze and a steady diet of prescription amphetamines aside, I knew I was only months, maybe weeks, away from being unmasked as a fraud and embezzler. *Fraud. Embezzler.* Just words, each of them, true. And, even if, I didn't see myself that way, the police would. The newspapers and media would and, God help me, my 'friends' at NuGeneration Holding, LLC—once the shock subsided—most definitely would. So firm was this conviction in my mind I'd anticipated how the *New York Times* or *Journal* would report it.

## WALL STREET EXEC FALLS IN SEC PROBE

*John Madson, partner in NuGeneration Holdings, was indicted yesterday for improprieties involving the illegal sale of chemical formulations to foreign interests. The Security and Exchange Commission, working in conjunction with the Federal Bureau of Investigation, announced the indictments at a press conference.*

*Rion "Corky" McCorkle, Chairman and CEO for the firm, denied reports that Madson had sold military technology to the Chinese. "The information Jack Madson had access to was nothing 'top secret' or directly related to the U.S. military in any way. These were, at best, old school patents, most of them available on the internet." Madson was indicted for insider trading as well as patent theft and embezzlement.*

*Neither the government nor McCorkle commented on allegations by AvaTech Industries that Madson had sold breakthrough research studies in the area of self-generating cell replacement. Lisa Ellison, senior partner in charge of NuGen's Bio-Tech Division, also refused comment.*

Of course, that would be their version, Phials, not mine. As you'll find out reading this—if you read it—my gambit into the world of journalism wouldn't be so simple and a lot darker. Still, one way or the other, my version or theirs, I knew that night the walls were closing in on me.

That's when I decided Jack Madson had to die.

# Chapter 3

Beaucoup questions swirled through my brain that night but really there was only one: how was I going to kill the man I was, bury him forever, and start a new life? Truth be told, I'd been selling chemical formulations from NuGen acquisitions on the black market for years. Before new managers took over I made it my business, as interim CEO, to check the value of their intellectual property. In industrial markets it comes down to three things: patents and technology (formulations), cheap production (manufacturing) and channel to market (sales force). If those could be kept intact post-acquisition, a chimpanzee could usually run the place while we went to town stripping out overhead and people. But technology—that's what I looked for because, once I got access, I could negotiate its value to Asian markets with Johnnie Eng, my intermediary in Hong Kong, and sell the download to him. I never asked where they went. Likely everywhere they shouldn't: China, India, Thailand, Singapore. Countries where patent law wasn't worth dog piss, places that had been eating away at U.S. manufacturing like termites for decades. But the money was sensational and in less than five years I stashed a cool $2.5 million in a Nuevo Laredo, Mexico bank account under the name 'John Dempsey.' To me that was a kind of joke because growing up in Newark I boxed Golden Gloves so the made-up name 'John Dempsey' was to me 'Jack Dempsey,' a heavyweight mauler I admired back in the day, guaranteeing I'd never forget it.

Probably gets on your nerves big time when I digress like that, don't it Phials? But remember the last meal I had was a fist full of amphetamines and that I got a .32 slug put a hole in me the size of a quarter courtesy of Tomi Fabri. Don't forget that. Anyhow, that's how I managed my end financially, but being raised Catholic with guilt piled up to the rafters since birth, having cash enough to keep me in whores and tequila for ten years didn't cut it. See, despite the lousy opinion you must hold for me, I'm not the loser you think because I wouldn't take off south of the border without tending to the needs of Jen and Tiffany, whatever my feelings about the two of them. True, Jen and her would burn through the four and a half million without breaking a sweat but that's the number I wanted to leave if only for conscience's sake while maybe stirring a little sympathy (and guilt) up for me in them at the same time. And, sitting on my back deck that night, I figured a way to get it. Better than that, it was you who gave me the idea!

You remember six years ago, you and one of your brokers from Surety Insurance put on a seminar for a company we owned named Century Chemicals. You didn't see me but I was listening when one of the hotshot execs asked about his policy.

'Mr. Ledford, I have a question,' a guy named Mike Watson asked the broker. 'What if I was involved in, say, a plane or automobile accident and died, what kind of benefit would your company pay?'

'Fine question, Mike, but when it comes to accidental

death, well, that's Martin Phials' area. Martin, you want to take that one?'

'Sure,' you answered as officious as I'd ever seen you. 'If a Century executive was a fatality in an accident on his way to a vacation in the Bahamas, let's say, Surety would pay the face value of the policy times two because there's a double indemnity clause in your policy. For those of you in the room today that would be $2,000,000, the face value of the policy, doubled. If, on the other hand, a Century executive was a fatality in a work related accident, on your way to a sales meeting on the West Coast, let's hypothesize, well, sir, this policy has a clause — a 'work related indemnity clause' — that would pay four and one half times its face value for a total value of $4,500,000. Enough, hopefully, to afford your loved ones the lifestyle they're accustomed to for quite some time.'

Of course, what you didn't tell them, Phials, is that the odds of a white male living in suburban Cincinnati, age 47, income of $250K plus, dying in a plane crash is something like one in twenty million. And the odds of that same white male dying in a plane crash on his way to work less than one in a hundred million. But it wasn't then that I first saw it, that gleam in your eye when you talked about death and actuarial tables and people's lives. It was later in a smaller group when Watson met you and asked about your job as Director of Claims Investigation. Swear to Christ, Phials, it sent a chill down my spine, the words you said and the way you said them. 'To me a claims investigator is like a watch smith. The kind they don't have in this country anymore. I take the face off the watch and I study the inner workings of every cog and every spring and how they interact with one another; what makes a man tick, so to speak. And, you know, it's amazing what you see inside a claimant's head when you study it like that. You get to know him better than his own mother. Every dream, every nightmare, every twisted ambition and where it will lead. A claims man is like a watch smith who takes people apart, Watson, except they don't always put them back together again.'

Well, that day I checked and found the policy NuGen took out on its VPs had a clause like that, a 'work related indemnity clause.' And that's when the dominoes started tumbling, one after another. Maybe it was the notion of screwing with your head, Martin, but when I considered faking my own death so Jen and Tiffany could collect four-and-one half times one million, I thought about you, too. You, so by-the-book, with your ponderous heavyweight frame, horn-rimmed glasses and three-piece suits. And that's when I decided to do it. Four and a half million buckeroos and a chance to have some fun with you and Surety Insurance Company of America's data-stuffed computer banks, brimming with statistics: facts about the lives and deaths of men and women, blacks and whites, Hispanics, gays and lesbians, acrobats, and ice cream vendors. People, Phials. Flesh and blood human beings. But to you it's all about money and actuarial tables. You're in the statistics and death business, in case you don't know it, and worse even than me.

See, I had one idea, only one, this one. But what you do — investigating dead people, crushing a widow's last hope for some kind of future on a technicality or debunking her husband's accidental death claim by proving suicide like the day I first caught sight of you, well, that sure don't make you better than me. In fact, after I read about what you guys did to those widows of soldiers who died in

Afghanistan and Iraq? Holding their death claim money, collecting five percent in interest while giving the widows one? Good business until the media catches hold of it, eh Phials?

So maybe you figured this out and maybe you didn't, but deciding to fake my own death was my one big idea. The one I prayed would break me loose from feeling like I'd been buried alive, choking in bills and loans and credit card debt, not to mention the hypocrisy of my work at NuGen—destroying healthy companies, leaving only enough juice in them to sell to the next investor group who'd take whatever we'd left behind, dress it up and pass it along to the next taker. Christ Almighty, it was like participating in a gang rape! And then there was Jennifer and our marriage of eight years. Of course we hadn't slept together for the last three (which I suppose was what made my lovemaking with Tomi so ferocious) but it was worse than that. Somewhere, I can't identify exactly when, I stopped hating her. Despising someone you once loved can be like flipping a switch: 'I loved you once but now we are in hate.' But what Jennifer and her Mafia-connected Judge father had left once they'd gotten through with me was nothing. Like a catheter had pulled out whatever life force a man has inside him, until there wasn't a morning I woke that didn't start with vomiting my guts out, then breaking down bawling. But to actually do it, to kill the man who I was and start completely over, I knew I needed something more than an idea. I needed a plan and it was NuGen's Chairman and CEO, Rion McCorkle, who gave it to me.

McCorkle was always talking about team spirit and corporate culture (yeah, we had one all right!) and all kinds of military crap—you know Sun Tzu's *The Art of War*, Patton, Von Clausewitz—the works. So what better way to cover the 'work related' part of your policy's indemnity clause than to organize a team-building exercise for my Industrial Division at NuGen. From executive admin to VP in charge, I was going to pay homage to Corky's colossal ego by doing exactly what he claimed to believe in—rah, rah, rah!—only it wouldn't be Outward Bound or some rip off of it. It would be a program of 'our own design,' working together as a seven person crew on former Supreme Court Judge Barton Crowley's 34-foot Bristol Channel Cutter, setting out on a two day sail from his Long Beach Island compound, through the Barnegat channel into the ocean, then on to New York Harbor and back. Only that sail would never happen because prior to it while performing a dry run on *Scammelot*, my own Tanzer 22, I was going to take a tumble overboard in the channel, my body swept out to sea never to be seen again.

It was a simple plan and the more I studied it, the more I became convinced it was one that had a real chance to get me what I craved so desperately—a chance to start over.

# Chapter 4

Business gurus like Tom Peters (*In Search of Excellence*) and Jim Collins (*Good to Great*) talk about the importance, not just of analysis and planning, but of execution. By rule of thumb that generally means if you believe a strategy has a 70 percent chance to succeed, *do it.* And as late summer began to usher in early fall, I became convinced that the chances of my plan succeeding were better than that, and this was why: first, I already had my piece of the pie taken care of with $2.5 million comfortably deposited in the Nuevo Laredo bank Johnnie Eng had recommended. Flush with South American cartel drug money, Banco Nacional de Mexico was a no questions asked operation where large deposits and sudden withdrawals of huge sums was a common practice that went under both the U.S. and Mexican government's radar screen.

Eng had been my contact to the Chin Chou triad, an Asian syndicate that distributed the formulas I stole for nearly five years now. Over time, I realized he was nothing special—gold fillings in his teeth, diamond pinky ring—Hong Kong-flamboyant. A bottom feeder who, like me, worked the traditional business sectors that Ivy Leaguers and high echelon crooks turned their noses up at. Just three weeks before I did my dive off the side of my boat, his boss—guy named Wei Li—contacted me by phone to undercut him.

'Johnnie's a lightweight, Jack,' he tried to convince me. 'He don't have juice to sell nothing but old shit—industry formulas from twenty year ago. Come with me and make some money.'

Well, it didn't take a genius to figure out what Li wanted. He wanted the high tech stuff. Bio Tech. The kind of R&D studies Lisa Ellison had and, if I wanted, probably could get hold of. But Johnnie had been good to me and, let's face it, he was the one who started me out in the business and, I guess you could say, I was loyal to him.

'You ever hear the myth about Icarus, Mr. Li?' I asked him.

'I don't know myth, Jack.'

'Well, long story short, he dies.'

Li chuckled, "Okay, okay, so you like Johnnie Eng, but in case you change mind, here's number you can call if you need anything. I man with lots of friends, Jack.'

'Everyone knows that, Mr. Li,' I said very humbly, and he laughed again before he passed the number along.

I took down Wei Li's cell number, then pretty much forgot about it because Johnnie was okay by me. Aside from the electronic bank deposits he'd arranged, through him I'd also hooked up with a husband-wife team from Texas that specialized in passports and border crossings, taking an individual in or out for between five and ten thousand bucks, depending on how hot a ticket their customer happened to be. For me, already presumed dead by then and making like shark food at the bottom of the Atlantic, well, it didn't get much colder than that. So I figured my half of the equation was pretty well taken care of thanks to Johnnie. Sure, after I crossed the border I'd have to settle in somewhere but I'd thought of that, too. About two hours north of Mexico City I'd found the greatest little place in the world—Queretaro. Spanish architecture, beautiful women, upper middle-class, all of it supported by an enormous stretch of state of the art German, French, and Japanese manufacturing companies, it was located in the middle of nowhere and had a history I liked. It seemed that a hundred fifty years ago Pancho Villa began his revolution against Spanish tyranny in Queretaro. Revolution against tyranny, I liked that just fine.

Then there was part two of the equation: faking my death by drowning and making it to Nuevo Laredo without getting picked up by the cops once I made my escape. Funny—though I guess you know me as well as I know myself by now—but I used to be a cop, and when I had to, knew how they thought, how they did things. Bottom line, cops are criminals turned inside out. I learned that being one. See, when I dropped out of Georgetown University it wasn't because my grades were lousy. It was because I ran out of money. My father drove a beer truck in Newark for Ballantine, Rheingold and, finally, Pabst Blue Ribbon as they went under, one after another. So in addition to an academic scholarship I received for straight 'A' grades at St. Damian's, I borrowed $40,000 from the Teamster's union (a lot of money back then) when Dad got caught between companies. But even working two jobs—one at The Tombs parking cars, the other at Clyde's washing dishes—wouldn't make a dent in the tuition I needed. So, to prevent the union from going after Dad who'd co-signed the papers, I took whatever work would pull down enough cash to pay off the debt and still keep me afloat. As it turned out, working as a Deputy Sheriff in the District of Columbia transporting federal prisoners filled the bill, you might say. And, yeah, I met them all: hit men, serial rapists and killers, con artists who preyed on the elderly, even a terrorist or two. Bad men, nearly all. "A mutant sent from hell," one judge called a Hell's Angel I'd transported who raped a twelve year old girl, chained her to a tree, and tortured her to death with a blow torch. But no worse than the seven hit men sent by Elijah Muhammad from Philadelphia to wipe out the entire family of Sunni Muslim cleric Abdul Khallis in Washington, D.C. Thirteen in all. Shot the men and women in the head. Took four babies seven months, two and three years old, drowned them in a kitchen sink. Like the man said, *mutants sent from hell.*

Anyway, it wasn't the cops that worried me, Martin. I knew how overworked and lazy they were. So I talked up the team building exercise at the office, mentioned it a time or two to Jen and Tiff, and to Tomi Fabri, who I understood would be identified through telephone records, located and questioned. But my story was air tight. I studied the tides and currents that swept through Barnegat Channel from Coast Guard maps and researched newspaper accounts where bodies of drowning victims from surrounding beaches were discovered sucked into the channel high tide by those currents (two in 2012 alone!) just like a body would be sucked out to open sea by currents that swept from out of the channel come low tide.

In the latter case, it could happen like it did to Miguel Marquez, a vacationer from New York, piloting a skiff by himself in '03. Man decides to stand up and start his outboard just outside the channel where the water is white capped and—bam!—he takes the plunge. Body isn't found for four days. And when it is? You ever seen what a corpse looks like after it's been tossed around in salt water after for a week, devoured by every kind of scavenger fish you can think of? Ain't much left, Phials. And what is left don't make pleasant viewing.

But there were other cases, ones that go back decades, like the one in 1984 where eight college kids go out from Port Harbor in their parents' sailboat, drinking beer, smoking weed, and—*cah-bang!*—three of them get knocked overboard when the sail's full-up and a twenty foot boom slams into the back of their heads. Two are former lifeguards. Kid named Dougherty. Other, name of Eilbacher. But the third, a freshman at Holy Cross by the name of Joseph Caruso, he can't swim at all. The others catch up with the boat just before it flies out the channel like it had wings. But the third kid, Caruso, some see him go down but no one sees him come up, ever. Two weeks later, he's declared 'missing and presumed dead' by virtue of accident at sea.

That was going to be me, Phials. I just needed a way for the cops and Coast Guard to somehow verify it. A witness, or something like it. But before it was all over, I'd have that too.

# Chapter 5

Around that time, to support my story, I began to live and breathe sailing. Most knew I loved it, and in happier times, Jen and I sailed the Greek Isles together. During those days I became a voracious reader of books about the sea—Bill Buckley's trilogy starting with *Atlantic High* to Robert Stone's *Outer Bridge Reach* and a half-dozen advanced instructional manuals. I spent the summer, leading to my presumed death, practice sailing *Scammelot* and studying the intricacies of Judge Barton Crowley's 34-foot Channel Cutter, to give authenticity to my team exercise alibi.

Most importantl, I applied myself to my day to day work at NuGen like never before. At the time, I was working two acquisition deals, both in the Midwest, and managing an industrial ceramics business in Ohio on a temporary basis while Korn Ferry was headlong into a job search for a new CEO. Still, busy as I was, I made time to have drinks with Corky over at the Oak Room in the Plaza Hotel, careful to talk up my 'teambuilding' sail and all the benefits the LLC would get from it. Better communication, friendships outside the office, the elimination of silos—accounting versus sales, sales versus marketing—TEAMWORK! And, man, did it work, feeding back to him every speech he'd ever given on the subject of NuGen's corporate culture and the charging cowboy that was its logo.

Maybe it was Wei Li's offer to fence bio-tech studies still percolating in my brain, but I even forced myself to have lunch with Lisa Ellison around that time. Now, don't get me wrong, there was nothing wrong with Lisa physically. Matter of fact, to the right guy, she was probably pretty sexy in that clean and scrubbed brainy older sister kind of way. She had great legs, a body to kill for, and a pleasant looking face, tight and in control, I guessed, until you broke past the façade when maybe there was maybe a 30-40 percent chance she'd turn into a jungle sex beast. And that was the problem. I didn't want to invest the energy to get there and it seemed like no other guy wanted to either.

Anyhow, we had our lunch at a little place on E. 57th called Les Sans Culottes. I even paid. And it was interesting if not altogether worth it because it was there she told me about a company called AvaTech Industries and a breakthrough in self-generating cell replacement that got even my attention.

'Animals like newts and zebra fish can regenerate limbs, fins, some can even regenerate parts of their heart,' she tells me, leaning across the table, her face all flush with color. 'If only people could do the same, amputees might grow new limbs and stricken hearts catalyzed to repair themselves.'

'Yeah, if it could happen.'

'But it *does* happen, Jack. It *did* happen at AvaTech's laboratories six months ago. They've passed through animal experiments—you know, mice and chimps—and have done control studies with elderly volunteers suffering from Alzheimer's. Seven out of ten patients experienced a remission of symptoms in those clinical studies, Jack. Seventy percent.'

'And?'

'And we're moving to an IPO. No later than the first of the year. It's a formality, but there's an FDA approval we need before going forward.' 'Congratulations! Jesus, I'm jealous!' I told her and, swear to god, she smiled at me like the proudest daughter at the Baptist revival.

But none of that did anything for me! As a partner in NuGen, I was forbidden by law to invest in it. So was she. But the idea lingered. See, NuGen was divided into four divisions: Industrial (old school and fading fast to Asia), Electronics (computer information storage already relocated to Asia), Pharma (commercial drug intermediates), and Lisa's Bio-Tech division (cutting edge R&D for the ever-expanding life sciences sector).

Of course Wei Li's offer was interesting but Lisa's was high visibility technology, watched by financial analysts world wide, even the military establishment, with billions of dollars in play, not the chicken shit intellectual property I had access to and was selling. But that chicken shit IP had made me my $2.5 million without all the risk that was part and parcel of what Li wanted. True, I'd left, maybe $5 million more on the table, but I wasn't in jail, and still on my way to a new life south of the border.

As for the plan itself, after my research I'd decided it was, at this point, mostly a matter of timing. By that I mean, it was clear in my mind what needed to be done—like a black and white film playing out the future. It was just a question now of what day filled the criteria. Coast Guard maps confirmed what I already knew about the shoals and shallows of the bay, but gave me real insight into how everything needed to play together if I was going to convince the cops I'd drowned and my body taken out to sea. You see, just one-quarter mile out from Barton Crowley's compound was the international waterway. The Barnegat channel was fifty feet deep and choppy but the waterway leading there was one hundred fifty. The channel had a reputation for turbulence and powerful riptides but the waterway, so near my father-in-law's place, was like the gulfstream operating mid-bay like a magnet pulling everything and everybody out to sea. So, for starters, Phials, the international waterway could not have given me a better entree into the 'twisted ambition' that was my plan.

In terms of weather, the best time, I concluded, was about twenty-four hours after a storm at sea. I studied the drowning of Miguel Marquez and Joseph Caruso and came to the conclusion that storms at sea exaggerated the incoming and outgoing current's effect on where the body was discovered (Marquez), or never found (Caruso). Both drownings happened within twenty-four hours of a significant storm and five to ten miles off Long Beach Island, but in Marquez's case the storm was moving west toward the island while in Caruso's case it was moving east and away. *Important for me.* The day I chose needed to duplicate the Caruso, not the Marquez, scenario. Another interesting piece of information came from a local fisherman I talked to over at Callahan's bar in Surf City. 'Sounds ridica-lis,' he drawled over a half dozen beers, 'but way most guys drown on a boat is takin' a piss off the stern. No life vest, no shoes, a speedboat goes past 'im and they fall overboard 'n drown. Imagine dyin' while takin' a piss!' he lamented. 'Son of a bitch,' I agreed, but now I had another piece of the puzzle that was going to confirm my drowning and disappearance to police and maybe you.

I knew Surety would balk at the idea of me being drunk, but drinking—say, two, three cans of beer—verified by a couple of Ballantine Ale empties in the hold, well, that just seemed like good drama to me.

But there was more, Phials. I knew that there had to be. The police never worried me *but you did.* You did because, for you, it was more than a job. Tracking down guys like me was an obsession. I understood that and tried to take it into account. Sure, I figured out the parameters of what would make my drowning seem plausible but afterwards how did I make my escape? Like Jesse James or Dillinger, Phials, I needed to make my getaway, so I arranged to buy a gray 2010 Ford Escape (gray as a mouse!) from a neighborhood buddy named Danny Brennan who owned a used car lot in Bayonne. Danny, we all called him 'Dooney' back then, was one of the few Newark guys still around. Most had bought the farm with heroin overdoses three decades before as teenagers, courtesy of mob families like the Bontempos who distributed the stuff and guys like Judge Barton Crowley, Esq., who were paid to see the wise guys never got sidelined for long.

If anyone proved himself a stand-up guy, it was Danny. A year before we married, living together in a Montclair studio, Jennifer—fascinated with me as a kid with a frog and brand new dissecting kit—insisted on seeing the place where her "nasty boy" cut his teeth. Just prior to a customer visit in Hartford (I was a salesman then), she came along to Catena's, a local dive where my old school pals still hung out. So, me and Jen, dubbed "The Tourists" after about a minute and a half, chugged our beer, drank our whiskey and were off—me to Hartford, her back to Montclair. But next time I stopped by the place everything and everybody went dead quiet. Danny had a cast on his arm and that night he confided that four guys decided to follow Jen back to our apartment and rape her once I left for Connecticut. The only person who tried to stop them was Danny. He got into a shoving match outside the bar, when one of them broke an empty Boone's Farm bottle and slashed his forearm wide open. With blood spurting all over the place and cops on the way, I guess the romantic spell cast over them by my future bride was shattered. No jaunt to the burbs. No gang rape.

Danny never regained full use of his arm and never escaped the neighborhood. But he did okay for himself with his used car business. Never too involved, never too far removed from the good guys or the bad. So after I bought the Escape from him under the name John Dempsey, I knew I could count on him to drop it off at my father-in-law's place in Loveladies and suffer a bad case of amnesia once it got there ('Hey! I get it: Jack Dempsey, you bein' a boxer 'n all!')

For me, then, everything became a matter of twos. Two cars: Car #1, to drive from my house in Summit to the island, drown, and leave it for the cops to discover. Car #2, to be waiting when I got there, drown, and used to take me from New Jersey to Laredo, Texas, where I'd meet the Blunts who'd take me over the Mexican border and on to my new life in Queretaro. As important, were two life vests to take with me onto *Scammelot* for my trial run from Long Beach Island to New York Harbor. The first vest, I'd wear. Hell, the plan called for me to swim mid-channel to shore. But vest #2? This one they'd find, along with a brand new pair of Dockers, leading them to create a hypothetical scenario that went something like this: Jack Madson, liked to drink, so he did, though he was something short of drunk (three beer cans). Madson stocked up his sail boat with supplies for an overnight sail to New York, took his Tanzer into the international waterway not realizing a storm had churned up deceptively dangerous currents. Madson takes his craft beyond the international waterway and into the channel when, just beyond it, he decides, shoeless and without life jacket, to take a piss off the stern. A large wave or passing motor boat jars his boat, he slips, hits his head, and falls into the ocean whose currents—churned up by storms—sweep his body miles out to sea where it gets snagged underwater by debris, is devoured by sharks, or simply vanishes like so many other fisherman and sailors before him.

That was my world of twos. Two cars. Two life vests. Two scenarios because what they wouldn't know was there'd be two Jack Madsons. Jack #1, presumed dead with corpse missing and Jack #2, who instead of falling off his sailboat and dying, would dive off the Tanzer as it exited the channel, life vest secured, and swim to the channel's shoreline just 250 feet away. Once on shore, I'd change to dry clothes in Car #2 and as Jack Dempsey, make the three day trek to Laredo where Johnnie Eng's friends, Bobby and Twila Blunt, would supply me a new passport and safe passage over the border to Mexico and the $2.5 million that waited for me there.

# Chapter 6

That was my plan. A good one, I thought, but I couldn't just *do it*, like the Nike people tell you. I had to wait, living a double life each day, working ever harder to convince those around me I'd never been more serious about my career while secretly holding my breath until the right conditions materialized. It was hard work. Hard work at NuGen, but near impossible at home.

I remember a night, just days before I did the deed, coming home after a long day's work at 9 West and a nightcap or two at Alfie's. I turned the key, heard Jennifer's dog, Regal, yap once or twice, and pushed open the door to find—oh, god!—Jennifer waiting for me standing like a Queen (or executioner) above me on the staircase landing.

'Welcome home, Darling,' she drawled.

'Jen, didn't think you'd be awake.'

'At 3 a.m., why, of course, love, isn't this the best time to be awake? Isn't that when all the excitement around here happens and you finally come home? From your little nigger girl?'

It was then that I noticed she'd been drinking, standing on the landing vodka tonic in hand.

'You're drunk, Jennifer. I don't know what you're talking about.'

'Oh? Care to take a trip down Memory Lane with me? Like to see the video tapes and photos Daddy's investigators have come up with?'

'You're drunk,' I repeated, head down like a fullback on the march, throwing off my suit jacket on the banister, and making my way up the staircase. And I suppose it was fine until our bodies confronted one another, on the landing. I tried to pass and she shoved me back into the wall. '*Go easy*,' I warned her.

Then, as she put her weight back on her hind foot and I made a second effort to pass, a low rumble and then a long piercing howl made its way to her lungs, then expanded like a fog horn from her mouth. '*Oh, no, you don't!*' she screeched, shoving her right hand between my legs, and clenching my testicles.

'*Get out of my way, you cunt*,' I growled as she squeezed my balls with all her might but such was my rage—at her, at McCorkle, at Barton Crowley, at myself—that no amount of pain could dull it. '*I'm going to kill you*,' I swore, raising my fist about to hit her with a blow that I knew without any sense of calculation would smash the life out of her, when our daughter Tiffany seemed to materialize before us at the top of the stairs.

'You two are keeping me awake!' she pouted with the entitlement of a kid from a British debating team. 'You're drunk, both of you, and I think it's terrible, *terrible*,' she added, suddenly emotional as Jennifer stood there, my testicles firmly in her grasp, and me with my right clenched fist milliseconds from thumping her skull, ready—literally—to beat the life out of her with my bare hands. Like the man said, 'Ain't life grand!'

Later, with Tiffany back in bed, in the privacy of our

bedroom the decibels lowered but our animus intensified. Sitting on the edge of our oversized bed as she covered her face with moisturizer ($150 per ounce), I said, 'You loved me once. I know that because you told me, but also because of the things we did together — sexually.'

Jennifer was nothing if not theatrical, 'If you're referring to oral sex, the thought of it now sends me running for the bathroom, desperate to gargle a bottle of peroxide. If it's anal sex you're talking about, it's true, every time I defecate, it's you that I think about.'

Even I had to snigger at that one but as hard as she tried she couldn't get my cock up enough to go *mano a mano* with her. 'You're talking that way to hurt me, Jennifer, but I'm way beyond it. I'm immune. I don't care about you enough to hate you.'

'Oh, I know all about it, that's true enough . . . All about what? Your little nigger girl. The one in, where was it, Newark? Watts? No, I remember. It was Detroit. It must make an underachiever like you feel so powerful having your way with a minority high school graduate. Does she tell you have a big cock? Does she '*ooh*' and '*ahhh*' when you stick your little ornament inside her because you know, Jack, she does that for any man with $300 in his wallet.'

'She's got her charms, Jennifer, kindness would be one of them.'

'Oh, yeah. I forgot "poor Jack," isn't that one of your many personas,' she went on, walking into the bedroom. 'Jack, the inner city ruffian. Jack, the sexual Prometheus. Jack, the serious business person. Jack, the rough at the edges hoodlum-intellectual. Seems like it's all about you, Jack. You and your little nigger girl, but just in case you'd ever considered it, I would never give you a divorce. I'd fight it, legally. Abandonment, oh yeah, there's a possibility, but my God, the things Daddy and I'd take from you, including your career. No divorce for you — too easy. Let's just let you have your nigger. And me?' She held her nightie up to reveal her bare genitalia, 'I may fuck, suck and go anal for the mailman. Maybe even an up tempo gang bang by those swarthy little spics that pick up the garbage each morning. But you? I wouldn't have sex with you now unless there was a disease involved. Something fatal that created long suffering pain. That's how much I hate you now. Night, Jack,' she said turning off the bedside lamp.

And it was then I wondered if I could make it. Meaning, could I stand living my life enough minutes and hours and days to make it to the moment when Jack Madson would just fucking cease to exist.

# Chapter 7

When I woke the next morning it was in the guest room bed where I'd spent three years of mornings just like it. There was no mistaking my relationship with Jennifer had jumped the rails. From quiet loathing we'd traveled to this terminal stage fueled by the need to destroy one another. To attack, literally, with an abandon I never knew even as a boxer in the ring pumped with adrenalin, or street fighter trading punches outside Catena's bar. No, Jennifer had a specialty all right. She had mastered the art of fucking with me — the shell-less, clueless soul inside — pushing all the right buttons, playing on her supposed superiority against the not very subtle veins of inferiority that ran through me: deep-seated fears, angst, complexes that hung onto my bones like flesh and sinew, as much a part of me as a heart, an eyeball, a tongue.

These were the dark, miserable thoughts running through my mind that morning as I stood barefoot in front of the bathroom mirror splashing cold water on my face, staring into bloodshot eyes rimmed with black circles and an expression hopeless as a hound dog. Then, like a line cast to a drowning man, the realization surfaced. Soon this would all be over. The gnawing pain that tore at me every minute of every day would soon vanish. And that single thought carried with it a jolt of hope that sent me bounding down the staircase, past the landing where the rancid fury of my battle with Jennifer lingered, and into the study.

I logged onto my laptop, furious with expectation. I hit the Coast Guard 'ocean conditions' icon. The website posting the seven day tidal movements, weather forecast, wave heights and water temperatures flashed onto the monitor. There was a storm all right. A drizzly, mid-September weather system that hung like a shroud over Long Beach Island and much of southern New Jersey, stubborn, gray, and windless. *Okay, I thought grimly, it won't be today and it probably won't be tomorrow.* But even that simple prediction wasn't written in stone. Not on the Island where beach weather and violent storms famously played with the lives of weekend renters and sailors alike. One moment it would be sunny, the next storm clouds would appear from nowhere bringing with them monsoon-like rains, thunder and lightning, or they'd just hang overhead, heavy and damp enveloping the island for days at a time.

I left the house that morning—Brooks Brothers suit, red and white striped power tie, Johnston Murphy shoes—with a sense of purpose more powerful than ever before. I took the 9:10 into the city, stopping by NuGen headquarters just long enough to show my face before heading out to our latest target, a bowling ball manufacturer named Etonics located in the university town of Ann Arbor, Michigan where Tomi Fabri waited for me.

It was during that short stop at 9 West that I ran into Lisa, who waved me into her office as I passed through the corridor.

'Close the door,' she whispered urgently. I did but she waved me still closer in that brainy older sister way of hers,

'I shouldn't be telling you this, but I know the way you do things, Jack. With expense accounts and travel.'

'What way is that?' I beamed, giving her the heat.

As expected, she got flustered, 'I'm trying to tell you, Jack,' she pled. 'I want to warn you that Corky's got Deloitte and Touche here week after next to audit the executive staff. With the AvaTech IPO gaining steam they're looking for anything—big or small—that could muck it up with the SEC.'

'So?'

'So I wanted to give you a heads up to fix anything that might raise an eyebrow, 'cause if you don't and they find something—any little thing—Corky will go apoplectic.'

'Fair enough, but Lisa? My personal and corporate accounts are up-to-date and beyond reproach. Frankly, I'm stunned, shocked, that you could imagine otherwise.'

'Whatever you say, Jack. Just remember I warned you,' she groaned.

Of course everything I told Lisa Ellison was bullshit. Over the past five years functioning in the surreal hyperspace of non stop drinking and amphetamines, I'd been financing assorted sexual liaisons with Tomi and anything else I could get receipts for through my personal expense account and those of former CEOs I'd replaced at companies along the way. But Lisa's warning left me unconcerned, even jovial, as I said 'So long' to Kevin Dugan (Pharma), Marci (secretary), Corky (CEO) and, significantly, Bobby Connell, NuGen's CFO, who'd signed off on every one of those reports. First, since Sarbane's Oxley, the banking meltdown, and Washington's new financial regs, we were used to outside audits and had learned to cover our tracks as a way of life. Second,

I reasoned, hopping into a limo headed for Newark airport, it wasn't my problem to fix whatever balance sheets or expense accounts needed fixing. As CFO, those inconvenient truths were Bob Connell's to handle, after all it was his signature that followed mine as the legal sign off. Besides in a matter of days, I told myself, none of that would have anything to do with me and by the time Deloitte and Touche did their damage, I'd be long gone.

After I checked into the Westin, a passable hotel set smack in the middle of Delta's terminal, I got a call from Tomi on my cell to say she was on her way. Of course, like always I'd pick up the cab fare and the cost of everything from Surf 'n Turf to pitchers of martinis and Magnum "hot rod" lubricated condoms. But it seemed like the bill was going up 33.3 percent this time (not that I minded) because Tomi was bringing along Ericka, one of the girls from Head2Toe she'd been seeing when Ol' Jackie Boy wasn't around, and today, when I was around.

'You said she's a sender, did I hear right?'

'To heaven and back. You're going to find God tonight, Jack.'

'How fast can you get here?'

'Pullin' up now, lover. Fare's eighty dollars.'

'Eighty or eight hundred. I got a friend, too. He don't care about money.'

# Chapter 8

When the knock came at my door I was wearing a pair of work out shorts and a T-shirt that read, 'Wrigley Field—Chicago.' Tomi entered first looking better than I'd ever seen her with hair up and a long Asian-type dress wrapped like a satin, emerald colored sheet around her, tight and revealing. And still those eyes! Large, bright and ever-inviting as she smiled a smile that could launch ships, or me anyway. 'This is Ericka, Jack. The friend I told you about.' Ericka stepped forward and, swear to Christ, for that instant I felt like a Sultan, one beauty pulling a half step back while the second presented herself to me.

Ericka was a star spangled knock out: nice face, fair complexion, blue eyes, short blonde hair, and a sensational body, accentuated by jeans that must have been painted on, and a set of large firm breasts that filled the black blouse she wore—first three buttons undone. Ericka was drop-dead sexy in a dykey kind of way, meaning she seemed formal, maybe even cold toward me (was I competition?), though studying her for even that split second convinced me that whatever detachment there may have been wouldn't last long.

'Pleased to meet you, Jack,' she said extending her right hand to me. 'Tomi's told me a lot about you.'

I bent low and kissed her hand lightly, genuinely. 'Glad

you could make it. How 'bout a martini?' And with that simple question, we were off to the races.

No brag, but I've always thought of myself as sexually experienced. I'd done two Russian hookers in a Frankfurt, Germany brothel once, but as it usually turns out with paid-for sex, whatever we did—one on one, two on one, or all out free for all—it was clinical. No kissing. No caressing. Mechanical. And later, when I went for something anal while one had her way with the other, ass arched up and out like a bull's eye, there came a loud yelp and indignant cry '*Verboten!*' Anyway, Phials, just so you know for your records, what happened with Tomi and Ericka that night? It was nothing like that.

It turned out Ericka was a lesbo of grand proportion. After three martinis and a glass of champagne she was hanging all over Tomi who sat slung low on a couch topless as she caressed her neck, the sides of her face, and breasts. But Tomi, though burning with desire, wasn't buying, not totally. 'Come here, Jack, 'n take me, baby,' she sighed, breathless as her lesbian buddy started in on her lower regions. So, like a good Joe, I did what she asked, standing over Ericka who, to my surprise, turned her attention to my needs, before I turned my attention to Tomi's, and Ericka repositioned herself above Tomi's wriggling asp of a tongue, pink and swollen, suddenly come to life with encouragement from above.

It went on like that for hours. Three hours, more or less, lost in the ecstasy of configurations sensible and unlikely, performed at fever pitch and fueled by passions so profound in their building, explosive release, and building again, I wondered if men and women could die this way, having literally fucked their way to extinction.

Then, with nothing left, delirious and exhausted, our session ended with the master stroke I was denied the last time I courted two women together. But, lo and behold, it was Ericka who offered the prize to me, ass arched up and frothy with anticipation, which I took lustily over and over until the three of us, spent, lay in various positions of repose, passed out on the hotel floor.

Was it thirty minutes gone by or sixty when I groggily stood up to find Tomi sitting on a cushioned chair, naked? She sat there quietly studying the movements of airline passengers on their way in and out of the Delta terminal through the plate glass window. She held a half full glass of champagne in her right hand and seemed locked in deep thought as I poured myself a Glenlivet-rocks and sat down across from her.

'We're not in love, are we, Jack?'

I thought for a moment, 'No, I don't think so.'

'Only with yourself?'

I took a gulp of scotch knowing it was tricky water I was about to navigate, 'Maybe. A priest friend of mine, a monk, said I was a hedonist. May have been right. And you? Do you love me?'

'No. Heavy like. Though, Jesus knows, you make me so awfully hot, baby,' she added fanning herself with her free hand.

'Thanks,' I offered a toast. 'Fact is, I had sex the first time when I was fifteen. It was Newark. It was a ghetto. Black girl, twenty-four or twenty-five. A prostitute, I suppose, at a place called Jackson's Lounge. My God, I was hell bent to get laid. Senior from high school drove me. I had seven dollars and a phony draft card and just kept asking every woman there, 'Hey, wanna ball?' until a woman at the bar said, 'Sure, I'll fuck you. Come with me.' And I did. Walked three doors down to the wooden stairs of a tenement where she took her panties down, pulled up her dress and said, 'Well, go 'head.' It wasn't a few seconds after I pulled out of her that a gang of black guys, one of them her boyfriend, walked in, surprised to find us at first, then mad. 'Look! Look! I got money!' she showed them, pulling my seven bucks from her brassiere. And I left, just kind of drifted away. But she wasn't so lucky. They raped her. Later that night, back at Jackson's, I saw her. She was in a fight with another woman, had smashed a beer bottle on the bar top, and was holding it out in front of her like a weapon.' I looked across to Tomi, who had tears in her eyes, 'Guess it doesn't qualify as a great way to lose your virginity.'

'No. But it's better than the way I lost mine. Every night for five years,' she said looking suddenly like the loneliest woman on the planet.

After my trip to Etonics (strictly for show) I decided to head down to the Jersey shore. Of course, I took care of preliminaries. Our team building sail was ten days away so I touched all the bases with Corky, my staff at NuGen, Jennifer, and even Tomi, who I knew you'd eventually uncover if the cops didn't. My story was like this: I was headed to Crowley's compound to be there for a trial run on my boat the moment the weather broke since I was skipper and wanted our sail to go smoothly when we later set out on the Judge's much larger Channel Cutter. And at least some of that was true. Mainly, I knew I needed a day close to optimal conditions and was running out of time. More, I needed to move on. The tedium of my day-to-day life, even after my escapade with Tomi was getting to me. I wanted out and I wanted out now.

# Chapter 9

I had to laugh when I pulled my Jaguar into the Judge's $9 million bayfront compound, remembering Danny Brennan's reaction when he first saw the place. All ten thousand square feet of it, with attached two-bedroom guest apartment, caretaker quarters, private tennis court, heated pool.

'Holy shit, Jackie! How many people live in this freakin' place?'

'None,' I answered once he parked the Escape at an out-of-the-way spot near the guesthouse and we strolled into the main living quarters. 'My father-in-law got bored with it just after he bought the yacht. Don't know why, maybe age. He's eighty-two and I suppose it's a lot easier hangin' out with old legal buddies at Short Hills Country Club or playing nine at Baltusrol.'

I handed him a cold bottle of Grolsch from the fridge. He stared at it like I just put a five hundred dollar bill in his hand.

'Well, you sure stepped in it, Jackie,' he said half raising the bottle with his bum arm before chugging most of what was in it. 'If I knew you was gonna marry Crowley's daughter, I woulda been nicer to you in grammar school.'

'You were always good to me, Danny. And I know what a pain in the ass you can be about taking money,' I said pulling $5,000 in large bills from my pants pocket, 'but I want you to have this—no, no,' I interrupted before he could reject it. 'I know I can trust you—with my life—which is what I'm doing, got that?' I had his attention. 'I'm going away for a long time. In fact, probably forever.' His eyes narrowed as he held the money in his open palm. 'You remember Jay Murphy?'

'Insurance guy, North Ward.'

'Remember when we ran errands for him that summer? He'd be in the back drinkin' with Woody, the detective, and Gianotti, from the grocery?'

'Yeah, so?'

'You never saw Murph after that summer, know why?'

'He owed the Carbone brothers twenty thou, is the way I heard it. Disappeared. Never seen again. I figured they killed 'im.'

I closed his gnarled fingers over the $5,000 in his palm, 'He started a new life, Danny. A new life in another state. New identity. New work. New family. I know because I heard them talking, drinkin' whiskey and beer like always, when Murph came up with an idea. Kill a bum that looked like him. Dress the guy in his clothes. Plant his wallet on him, even his wedding ring. Put the body in the family car and push it off a cliff so it'd burn to ashes. Everyone would think Murphy had met his demise. But Woody told him it wouldn't work. Postmortem lividity, he said. Forensics would know the guy was dead before the accident, and even if they didn't, between fingerprints and dental records, he was better off getting out of Jersey for good. Somewhere the Carbone brothers didn't know how to spell—Mississippi or Tennessee. And so he did.'

'Yeah, and what's that got to do with you, Jackie?'

'I'm going the first route, Danny. For what I'm doing I don't need a bum because they're never going to find a body. But to the cops, and everyone else, I'll be just as dead.'

I smiled at Danny. He nodded his understanding, then took the five grand and stuffed it into his back pocket.

'I want to tell you somethin', Jackie,' he said then. 'I don't know how you got into this mess, maybe tryin' to score some quick money on the Street, maybe just tryin' to earn people's respect by marrying a Crowley. But I do know this much. Whoever's chasin' you, for whatever reason, I known you for thirty years, and you're worth the whole lot of 'em put together.'

That was one week ago but the irony of my situation, and Danny's, and Jay Murphy's, still made me grin. What did it all mean, this life of ours, scrapping for nickels and dimes while trying to convince the world we were Boone Pickens, or Brad Pitt, or David Beckham? Big house. Beautiful wife. Fancy car. And debt up to our asses with creditors closing in like Mexicans on the Alamo, I mused, entering the foyer of the Judge's bayside estate and switching on the light above. The place was damp and musty, vacant—aside from my recent visits—for months, if not years. I walked from the foyer into the kitchen, then the dining room, living room, and finally the den, switching on lights along the way.

The Judge's study was like a church's sanctuary, I noticed, so quiet, so set, untouched and untouchable. At the far end of the room was a large desk, an oil portrait of the Judge in full regalia hung on the wall behind it. Off to the left side was a file cabinet, and to the right a wet bar fully stocked, which I'd become fond of over the past

few weekends. Bourbon. Vodka. Brandy. Every liqueur you
could think of.

I poured a glass of Talisker's 25 straight, no ice. I savored
the single malt as I took it down, admiring the collection
of photos hung like icons in a shrine so strategically along
both sides of the walls. On one side was *Judge* Barton
Crowley, public servant, patriot, standing alongside Rudy
Giuliani, Mayor of New York City, Chris Christie, Governor
of New Jersey, President George W. Bush, White House
Deputy Chief of Staff Karl Rove and, going back in time,
Secretary of State Henry Kissinger and his boss President
Richard M. Nixon. On the other side was *Citizen* Barton
Crowley, third richest man in the state, host of gala parties,
purveyor of spring, summer, winter, and fall events, posing
alongside singer Frankie Valli and the cast of *Jersey Boys*,
baseball star Derek Jeter, New York Yankees owner, George
Steinbrenner, legendary entertainer Frank Sinatra,
Mafia godfather Paul Castellano, his former boss, Carlo
Gambino, and murderous Teflon Don, John "Johnnie
Boy" Gotti.

'Oh yeah,' I was thinking as I poured a second glass
of scotch, 'A real piece of work Jennifer's daddy was,'
wondering whether Giuliani, Bush, Kissinger, or Nixon
knew how Crowley had climbed the ladder from son of a
Brooklyn bartender-bookie to New Jersey Supreme Court
Justice. Maybe. Maybe not. But I did. Back in the sixties and
seventies, the mob owned New Jersey and if a mayor like
Hugh Desiderio was "Pope" of a major city like Newark, a
sitting judge was Deity. And his blessings? The favors he
handed down at the right moment to the right people?
There were fortunes to be made in that kind of ol' time
religion, Phials. Kickbacks from city and state construction

contracts, a piece of the action from gambling and prostitution rings in Jersey, New York, and Vegas, and let's not forget drugs. Literally tons pouring in from Southeast Asia funneled through the distribution networks of the Gambino, Genovese, Luchese, and Bontempo families ending up in neighborhood pizza parlors and the veins of kids I played ball with in grammar school, dead from heroin overdoses thirty years now.

But more than money, once a man like the Judge broke loose from the wise guy circuit to the political power brokers who ran crime along the Eastern Seaboard came, POWER. Now retired, untouched by FBI takedowns that marked the two decades that followed, Crowley successfully graduated into establishment politics. Philanthropist. Socialite. Staunch Republican. Stock market guru. Societal icon. It made me laugh out loud as I ambled out of the main compound to the bulkhead where his yacht, *Mi'Lady*, was anchored. But two years ago when Fortune magazine did a feature on "The East Coast's Wealthiest," the Judge was furious, *beside himself*, that Bloomberg and Morton Zuckerman were there with him. 'Jews! Two liberal Jews on the same cover with me,' he stormed. 'As if I'm anything like them simply because I have money!'

I chuckled, blurry eyed, taking in the beauty of Crowley's 34-foot Bristol Channel Cutter. Even with sails wrapped and still in the water it looked regal, like a lady-in-waiting. Waiting, yeah, for a sail that would never happen, I reminded myself, before taking a look at my Tanzer, moored nearby, bobbing and clanking dockside in the bay. Carted down in late June, it was 22 feet with modest sail, jib, puny 40 hp Yamaha motor, cabin for two, and ready as it would ever be: ready for its trek into the intercoastal waterway, on to the Barnegat Channel with 150 foot-high red and white lighthouse towering above, then out—sans captain or crew—off to its lonely cruise into the unpredictability of the open sea.

From yacht to Tanzer my eyes went to the horizon wondering if it was possible the blanket of clouds that hung over the island for two days was finally lifting. I was on my fourth scotch by the time I recognized the chance this could mean and it was already three o'clock but I ran in from the bulkhead to the kitchen where my grip was on the floor along with the briefcase that held my laptop. Again (it must have been thirty times in the past forty-eight hours) I checked in with the Coast Guard website and, son of a bitch, it was true. The forecast had changed! Almost immediately I tore through my grip to get my meds, tapped out four pills from the plastic container, and downed them with my drink, understanding I would need to be plenty alert for what came next.

I scrolled down to the twenty-four hour forecast and with the 40 mgs of benzedrine, the first snake or two of thought began winding through my brain. This was it. The moment I was waiting for. Weather. Tide. Currents. The storm was receding north and away swiftly, tugging millions of gallons of water from the bay into the channel like a funnel and out into the Atlantic.

# Chapter 10

As dusk settled over Barnegat bay, with Car #2 relocated just beyond the channel and *Scammelot* stocked for the overnight, I took a final look back at the Judge's compound understanding that it wasn't a house I was leaving behind that day: it was my family, my possessions, my life. 'Had I ever in my life contemplated anything so bold as this?' I wondered, turning my attention back to the Tanzer. My eyes raised to the churning clouds on the horizon and for a split second I considered turning back, waiting for better, more predictable conditions. 'No fucking way!' the interior part of me argued. 'This is it! Today is the day! If your heart turns to shit now, will you ever really do it?' I must have been nodding as I undid the painter line and hopped into the boat starboard side. 'He's right,' I admonished my more cautious exterior self. 'You didn't get where you are today playing it safe! Let's do this thing!' And I did, releasing the sail tie, cranking up the main sail, taking *Scammelot* boldly into the wind toward the international waterway, death, and freedom.

From the outset there were signs that even a half-assed sailor like me could read. Bad ones. The wind was gusting. The main sail and jib were full so I was moving north and away from the island at a steady clip. But as the dock and Webster lagoon faded into the distance a low, heavy feeling washed over me (was it the booze?) and it was then that I realized: that window. The one I jumped through just sixty minutes before? It was closing—fast. And the waterway? As roiling storm clouds snuffed the sun, day became night, and the bay was slashed in two by the deep black river that carried me forward toward the channel, it occurred to me—as I clutched the tiller—that I was not nearly so in control as 'it' was. 'And what was "it"?' I asked myself. "It" was fate,' I answered. The other current that propelled me, grabbed me by the lapels and dragged me to this exact moment in time.

I snatched a can of Ballantine ale from the cooler, popped the flip-top and took a long swig. I savored it, face craned up toward the sky, as the chill of beery froth stormed down my throat and into my stomach, co-mingled suddenly with a less welcome sensation. Raindrops. Just one or two at first. Like the bully at the bar who gently nudges you, 'Hey, friendo, you're sitting in my seat,' while still you know in that interior part everyone has and usually tries to forget about, 'Hmm, this could mean trouble.' And it was right—that interior part—because by the time I tossed my empty beer can to the opposite side of the boat, it was raining big time. Torrents of rain. Sheets of water and wind so sudden and so violent, I raced toward the bow desperate to take the main sail down so I could start up the outboard even as the waterway's current pulled me nearer the channel.

It felt like seconds but must have been much longer when I spotted Ol' Barney, the hundred-year-old lighthouse that towered stoic as a sentinel over that part of the island. They put it up because of the scores of shipwrecks that occurred over the centuries and here I was looking up at it bleak as any doomed sailor, halyard tangled, mainsail stuck at half-mast, panicked as I struggled to regain control of my vessel. 'Outboard' was the word that shot through my head just then. With wind and rain beating down on me and no time to consider throwing on a life vest or shedding my jeans and sweatshirt, I plodded toward the stern handling the tiller good as possible while turning half crouched over the SAIL 4-Stroke to start it. Already the Tanzer was swept like a plaything from one end of the channel to the other when something I never considered possible happened. The channel was choppy but the point between its fifty foot depth and the Atlantic's three hundred created a cauldron of competing currents. That was the last thought that crossed my mind before *Scammelot's* bow hit a white cap and my body lurched forward over the stern and into the drink.

The fisherman at Callahan's bar told me that drowning or near-drowning was 'unearthly' (that was the word he used) and of course I nodded, rolling my eyes as I took another pull from my scotch-rocks. But at that moment, when I found myself looking ten feet below the surface with thunder roaring, lightning splitting the sky wide open, and torrents of rain pounding, I understood exactly what he meant. With each lightning bolt I watched, mesmerized, as pearls of light darted down from above, my body twisting and turning like a spastic as I raced instinctively back up toward—AIR. I could see the boat's bottom floating like an eerie shadow above me as my body was drawn by the current along with it further from the channel and deeper into the Atlantic. Then, finally, frantic with fear, I lunged with all the power in me at the outboard's propeller, latching onto it long enough to poke

my head above the surface and take a gulp of air before the
Tanzer's half drawn sail caught a burst of wind and darted
away. Then, down again I plunged. Again the jewels so
graceful, so pure, floating ever downward as thunderclaps
loud as cannon blasts sent tremors through the briny water
and bolts of lightning slammed into the ocean, shattering
that light until it looked to me like thousands of luminous
plankton falling all around me.

But it was air I needed. I understood that, disoriented
as I was. And that was the word my brain held onto as if
it had to do with something physical like the metal of a
swimming pool ladder or the propeller—that fucking
propeller—edging further by the moment away from me.
But that was not the only word. Or should I say, phrase,
because as I battled with all my strength and will to make
it to the surface and the dimming prospect of taking hold
of the propeller, a voice came into my head—very clear,
very present. 'The organism is dying,' it was saying. 'The
organism is dying,' as I scrambled upward to gain hold of
the propeller a second time, took in a lung full of oxygen,
and spiraled down again. 'The organism is dying . . . The
organism is dying,' over and over like a kind of mantra.
Only this time when I gazed up from ten feet under and
through those millions of gallons of water I didn't care if I
made it up or not and like a weepy nutcase on *Oprah,* I swear
to Christ, Phials, I knew what that voice was saying. My body
and my mind were separate. Like they had nothing to do,
one with the other. Me? I was still alive and kicking. But
it? My body? It was dying, dead as a pulled tooth, while my
mind, or soul, or whatever the fuck you want to call it, began
to gravitate up and over—everything—watching like a
kid from a tree house as all the human beings, everyone

else, everywhere, my old man and Mom, my brother, Jennifer, Tiffany, Tomi, and even the Judge continued on doing the things they did. And I could see it all, everything at once, Phials, so that truth be told, I had no interest in going back. To the real world, I mean, and the nightmare going on all around me, until I hear this voice screaming at me, 'Take my hand! Grab my hand for Christ's sake!!' So I look up, feel the rain on my face, and realize my right hand is clutching the shaft of the outboard and I'm between two boats, mine and another—a dinghy—with an old fisherman outfitted in raingear who's got his hand reaching out to me before I take my final plunge. 'Take it! Take it!!' he's screaming. And so with the rain pounding, lightning flashing so you could see Ol' Barney clear as day and thunder echoing through the channel like it was the Grand Fucking Canyon, I reached out toward him and he pulls me on board his dingy just as *Scammelot's* main sail catches a burst of wind and suddenly sets to racing away from us like a banshee out of hell.

Now, do I expect you to believe what happened next? I mean, believe it the way I say? Probably not, but you know how they tell you big events—like, say, the Kennedy assassination—are filled with coincidence? How Oswald kills JFK, Ruby kills Oswald but that don't necessarily make it a conspiracy? Sure, for all I know it may have been CIA, Mafia, FBI, Castro, or all four. On the other hand it may have been coincidence because what happened next seemed unbelievable even to me, but once the old man gets me on board and I collapse onto the deck, he bends over to check me out when the dinghy gets rocked and he tumbles overboard. *'Help! Help me!!'* he's screamin', reaching out to me as I crawl toward the bow on my hands and knees portside still numb from what happened. *'Help me! Please!! Pull me in!!* 'he's yellin' over the sound of waves, and rain, and thunder. So I reach out to him and lock his outstretched hand into mine, but I swear to Christ, Phials, it's frightfully cold and my fingers are numb, raw, from the freezing sea water. Then a huge wave sweeps over him, and he lets go, and I watch him like in a dream, get ripped away from me. Dressed in raingear, he looked like an inflatable doll, just his face exposed as he floats away, the current pulling him, and him still screaming for me and then at me, spreading his arms wide in a final sweeping motion that reminded me of a convocation, or a gypsy's curse, until I couldn't see him anymore and he vanished into the waves and into the darkness.

I keep thinking about that night, Phials. You know, maybe I could have saved him. Could have pulled him in if I tried harder. But back of my mind, way deep somewhere in that interior self, a part of me was thinking: 'Could be this old man drowning helps your alibi. Could be cops—and you—think it happened about how like it happened. Madson falls overboard, old man tries to rescue him and falls overboard himself. Both drown. Both boats discovered five, ten miles out to sea. One body gets recovered. Other one don't.' It could be that's what I was thinking but I really don't know. I really can't say. Though one thing I knew sure: I had to get off that piece of shit dingy and swim. Swim like my goddamn life depended on it because guess what, Old Buddy, it did.

If I told you I wasn't scared shitless, I'd be lying. The dinghy's Mercury 25 hp Sea Pro, set in idle, was losing ground by the second. No more than a wooden flatboat with reinforced steel bracing, every wave that hit, from every angle that hit it, threw the dinghy sky high into the air until it came crashing back down into the trough and the waiting riptide with the force of a head-on. By then I figured a way to position myself low to the deck, arms and legs bolstered against its port and starboard sides like a man crucified, to stay stable while the wind and rain whipped down on me. But even then I knew riding it out was a no-go and once the storm ended I'd be left stranded, proud owner of the old geezer's corpse, stuck on one of two boats left adrift miles from shore by daybreak.

No, if it was going to be lights out for me, I decided, it'd be with a bang, not a whimper. So, shivering, drenched to the bone, desperate to find a way out, I scoured the dinghy's deck for any edge I could find on the growing odds against me surviving when my eyes locked onto it. A life jacket. One of those 1950s-type, orange ones with white canvas straps, the old man stashed underneath a wooden slat set across the width of the boat to sit on. At the sight of it, I jumped to my feet and let loose a cry of rage that shocked even me. '*Fuck it*!!' I screamed, defiant, into the night and the storm, battling my way from stern to bow to get my hands on that vest like an infantry man slogging through enemy fire to take a hill.

And I did. Twisting my arms through its straps, clamping the black metal stays that ran down its front, I struggled to hold my balance, the terror of falling overboard without it near-paralyzing, as I alternated between standing and sitting before finally securing it. Even from a distance of a hundred yards or more, with torrents of rain obscuring my vision, I could make out Ol' Barney standing dark and tall above the rocky coastline beyond the channel where the Ford Escape and salvation waited.

Call me brave, stupid, or just indifferent to whether I lived or died, you decide, Phials, but I leapt out of that goddamned boat without any thought besides making it to that lighthouse. The water was cold. Freezing when I first dove in. And I panicked, arms and legs flailing, until I felt the overwhelming force of the current, realized I had the life jacket to keep me afloat, and experienced a sense of relief so strong I started bawling. But the riptide had me and I was helpless as it dragged me further from shore until I decided to stop fighting and ride along with it twenty, maybe thirty yards further and at that point my patience was rewarded. The pattern suddenly altered! It was as if someone or something monumentally powerful had held me in its grip and now decided to let go. I could sense that, very noticeably, very suddenly, as it began to arch in on itself, looping back—me with it—toward Ol' Barney though a mile, I guessed, or maybe two, further east back toward the towns of Loveladies, Harvey Cedars, and North Beach.

The swim back once the current released me may have been the only break I got during that night of catastrophes. My body was so pumped full of adrenalin I thought I'd explode out of the life vest to become something like the Incredible Hulk, so fast was my mind racing, so powerful my arms, legs, and chest. The pulse from my heart was more like surging electricity than blood. My fingertips and toes ached from the speed as it coursed through my veins, and I swam and swam with abandon, using Ol' Barney as my only landmark just like sailors of old, but not like murderers of old which I had become.

When I reached shore, I washed up on the boulder-studded coastline lying like a dead man as the Atlantic washed enormous waves over me. Gradually, I pulled myself up like some 'thing' emerging from the shallows, scared I'd be torn to shreds by the jagged rock formations. But I survived to find the lighthouse standing no more than a hundred yards away.

The rain had settled into a misty drizzle. A dense fog came in with the storm and hung at the outer reaches of the island, thick and smarmy. My first impression was that it was much darker than I thought here at the tip of the island. My body shook like a leaf soon as the thought came to me—as much from physical and mental strain as the cold—and it occurred to me I better check to see if I was still all there: arms, legs, fingers, toes. I was. But more battered than I figured. My forehead, above the right eye, had a gash over it I could feel with my fingers, though it was no longer bleeding. Both legs were cut and bruised badly but I felt nothing, no pain at all anywhere. Just this intense feeling, strong, physically powerful, with my mind operating at levels way beyond normal as were my senses—smell, touch, sight.

And that was the way it was as I made my way up through the palisade to the northwest edge of the state park where Ol' Barney towered on my way to the empty lot where I'd parked the Escape.

# Chapter 11

The sharp rap on the door came like a wake-up call from another dimension. It jarred me in the chair where I sat, interrupting the dark rivers of thought passing through my mind so that I wondered for a fraction of a second, '*Where the hell am I?*'

I took a pull from the bottle of Chivas to the left of my laptop, 'Yeah, what is it?' The bulky door—probably a hundred years old—creaked open.

"It's me, Jeremiah. I brought you a sandwich."

"I don't want it."

The monk seemed to float rather than walk to me, tray in hand. He nudged the laptop over ten inches and put the plate in front of me.

"You need to eat something. You don't look well." He reached for my shirt just below the left shoulder where the circle of red had turned a crusty brown color. I pushed his hand away. "Let me look at your wound, son."

"Can't you see I'm working, Father?" I protested without conviction as the priest bent over me.

He peeled back the shirt. "*Jesus, Jeremiah!*" I winced but the priest continued his inspection pulling the shirt stiff with dried blood away to expose the spot on my arm where Tomi Fabri's .32 had penetrated.

"It's hot, Jack," Jeremiah observed removing his palm

from the wound, purulent but no longer bleeding. He
put his hand on my forehead where another wound—a
gash—was nearly healed and scabby. "You have a fever, son.
Won't you let me call a doctor? He's a contributor to the
school. I know he'd come in secret if that's what you want."

"I need to do what I'm doing, Father," I told him.
"Remember you promised you wouldn't turn me over.
Swore on your sacred vows! Look here," I said taking a
bite of the sandwich. "See, I'm eating like you want!" I
swallowed and took another gulp of scotch.

Jeremiah shook his head miserably, "Son, son . . . " he
lamented. "Scotch whiskey! Pills! A gunshot wound! Here,
this is for you," he told me his voice dropping both in pitch
and volume as he handed me a Bible. "You need food. You
need medicine. And you need treatment from a doctor.
But more than any of those things you need this, Jack,"
he said moving toward the door. "Please read it, son, and
make your confession. Not to the police or whoever you're
confessing to, but to Jesus Christ, your Lord and Savior."

These were the priest's last words before he walked
through the doorway and shut it again. Shut it so that
more than a room, it felt like he was shutting the door to
the outside world leaving me lost and alone, a man on a
freighter on a dark sea.

I stared at the heavy wood door for a full minute
gathering my thoughts and my strength to continue, then
reached into my briefcase to retrieve the plastic container
where a rainbow combination of amphetamines—Adderall,
Benzedrine, Focalin, and Metadate—stared back at me, and
took a handful washing them down with a slug of scotch.

My eyes fell on the Bible. I took it into my hands and
paged through it, stopping at a passage from the prophet,

Ezekiel: *And when they ask, 'Why has the Lord done all these things to us?' say to them, 'As you have forsaken me to serve strange gods in your own land so shall you serve strange gods in a land not your own.* I shook my head at the notion of Jeremiah and the life that he led at the monastery. 'Like a fortune teller's riddles anybody could make anything they wanted out of these words. Here was a man who'd devoted his entire life, *every breath of every day,* to a book of riddles!' And maybe it was the jolt of amphetamines coursing through my veins, or the white heat of the liquor pulsing in my brain, but I continued on to a passage from Mark: *Jesus rose from the dead early on the first day of the first week. He first appeared to Mary Magdalene out of whom he cast seven demons.* Again, I had to laugh. 'Not three demons, not four demons, but *seven bad-ass demons.* Move over William Peter Blatty! Tinseltown, here we come!' I chortled, stopping finally at a passage from Acts: *the natives showed us kindness by lighting a fire, for it was growing cold. Paul had just fed the fire when a poisonous snake fastened its fangs into his hand, and the natives said to one another, 'This man must really be a murderer if, after his escape from the sea Justice will not let him live.' But Paul shook the serpent off into the fire and seeing him unaffected they changed their minds and began to say he was a god.*

I closed the book, shoving it back and out of the way then re-booted the laptop. 'A god!' was the phrase stuck like a steel hook in my brain. In the minds of religious fanatics, it was that simple. A man was either a 'murderer' or a 'god,' but in reality it wasn't like that at all. Most individuals were not murderers or gods. It wasn't like there were magnets, one 'evil' and one 'divine' that pulled a person to one pole or the other. Rather, it was like the magnets were inverted—like-pole facing like-pole—so that they repelled each other, with the average person in the middle gravitating toward one and the other, but never embracing either, their life and fate, indeterminate. True, for every Hitler there was a Gandhi and for every Bin Laden a Mother Theresa. But most were neither, ergo, bottom fucking line: they were nonentities. I mused momentarily over my foray into the realm of the philosophical, taking a nip from my bottle and savoring it.

Still, there was no denying that when I was driving those days and nights—Long Beach Island to Laredo—a fair percentage of the thinking I did was about St. Damian's and the guys I grew up with, I remembered, as the computer screen brightened and my attention bore down on the growing text of my confession. Not my real confession to God for the three deaths I'd been involved with, but the one to you, Martin Phials, Director of Claims Investigation, Surety Insurance Company of America.

# Chapter 12

So where do we take it from here, Phials? I know you want to know everything about everything because that's your nature. You not only want to know what I was thinking back then when I was headed off the Island, you want to know what I was feeling. What did I do once I got back to the Ford Escape? Did I change to dry clothes in that car or go back to Crowley's place? What road did I follow off the Island? Which highways once I left Jersey? Did I feel remorse about the old man that drowned in Barnegat? Was I always the cold-blooded killer you think I am?

Know how I know so much about you? I know because of the way you handled that suicide at Granger Industries, Lima, Ohio. What was his name—Tom Slezack, was it? I was acting president for those five days immediately following his car accident and, of course, you were there with your hired guns from Secur-Tek, the agency made up of ex-CIA guys you brought along to 'get to the bottom of the imbroglio.' Imbroglio? Who else would use a word like that? But there you were drilling everybody and everything this guy had ever been in contact with including his poor wife, who had MS, and their three kids. Even the kids, right Phials?

Maybe you remember saying these things and maybe you don't but I recall standing on the sidelines in awe of your colossal ego, your coldness.

'First we interview co-workers, "Was he depressed, did he take any medication you're aware of, prescription or otherwise? Did he ever talk about suicide? Was he a heavy drinker?" Then, boys, we go to the phone records—landlines at work, same with e-mails, text messages, and internet sites he visited, especially on his laptop, those are all property of Granger Industries, Inc., and open to us. So far as the rest—the ones effectuated on personal devices—I think you fellows know who to talk to and what to say,' you told them, eyes leveling with theirs to guarantee understanding. 'Regarding family members I'll meet with them as there's more to discuss than Mr. Slezack's background—legal formalities, funeral arrangements—the personal touch. So far as police and coroner reports, Surety would prefer to leave the procurement of state and local records up to you boys since your relationships run deeper than ours. Any questions?'

'No, sir,' the three of them all buttoned down as J. Edgar Hoover's replicants answered.

'Very well,' you told them, 'we meet to compare notes tomorrow at three, Surety Headquarters, Newark, New Jersey.'

And that was it, at least with them. But then you spoke to a younger man, black guy named Stanley Wilson, who was your assistant, 'They'll see,' you told him. 'I've handled too many cases, Wilson. When you've handled hundreds of them like me, you know, and you don't even know how you know. This is suicide, Wilson, plain and simple, wheelchair or not, young kids or not, I'm not going to make a $100,000 donation to Slezack's widow on behalf of Surety for a bogus fatal car accident. Suicide, as you know, Wilson, is not covered by this, or any other, policy.'

'Is it worth it, Mr. Phials?' Wilson asked you then. "The cost of Secur-Tek, our time, the company's, and the adverse publicity over a number like that?'

'Yes, it is worth it. To me it's worth every penny of expense and do you know why, Wilson? It's because the little fish encourage the big ones. It's the cheaters I go for, Wilson. It's all I go for, ever.'

So now that we agree on what a cold-hearted bastard you are and how your OCD-soaked brain operates, I'm going to give you the satisfaction of knowing. Not because I want you to feel good because I don't but, truth is, I'm still trying to figure some of this out myself, so I'll tell you how I was feeling after I got back to the Escape that night—very, very tense. Fact is, soon as I got to it and opened the driver's side door, everything cracked. I fell down on my knees and was sicker than I ever was in my life. Afterward, sitting in the dark, engine running, I got a chill ran from my toes up to the roots of my hair and started to tremble like a wet dog on a cold winter's night. Stupid, I know, but then I started to think. I tried not to but it would creep up on me. I knew what I had done. I'd watched a man drown. That old fisherman. Just let him die. Watched him float away like in a dream. And then I began to feel like I was in that dream, locked in it, in a kind of perverse Fun House like they have down at Seaside Park. With mirrors that make you big and long. Others that make you squat and wide. But, thing is, you're not you anymore once you step into that Fun House. And that was how I felt, Phials. You like words, big ones. Well, here's a word for you: I felt 'estranged'. Like I was a stranger to myself.

Must have been a full thirty minutes I sat there in a sandy lot near Ol' Barney and I knew I had to pull myself together or I'd never make it out of Jersey. To call what I was feeling "paranoia" as I drove down Ocean Avenue toward Rt. 72 and the parkway would not nearly cover the base. I was saturated with dread. Every passing car. Every pedestrian. Every cop car parked by the side of the road. I studied them all, praying to Christ I could hold it together long enough to at least make it out of state before the boats were discovered, I was called in missing, or some tourist out deep sea fishing to catch blues early that morning pulled up the old man's body attached to his hook.

Then, just before I make the turn from Ocean Avenue to Rt. 72—at that intersection by *Ron Jon's*—I stop for a red light and a cop pulls up alongside me. Cop looks at me, takes a sip from a cup of Starbuck's. I look at him. We both smile. That's right, smile. Me, to mask the sheer terror I was feeling. Him? Well, to me his smile was saying, 'Hey, fucker, I know you're out at this hour for a reason. So what is it? Screwing your girlfriend and trying to make it home before the old lady wakes up? Night out with the boys—poker, NFL—six pack and a few shooters and you're really tanked right now? Or maybe you're one of those work-a-day types, wife and kids on vacation down in Lavalette while you schlep back and forth to the office every morning and night?'

But whatever he was thinking—good, bad, or ugly—with the muscles in my neck tight as piano wires, I was thinking, 'You know, Cop, I'm off to Mexico, two and a half million bucks, and a life of leisure. I don't know why you're smiling, but that's what got me feeling so peachy this fine morning.' Then the light turned. We gave each other a confidant nod and off we went, him up toward Beach Haven and me off to . . . well, I thought, even in the condition I was in, I could at least make it to a state like Maryland or Virginia before calling it a day.

I set out beyond the Parkway to the Turnpike headed south, my brain racing as the Escape trundled nearer the state line, me ever-cautious of local cops, state troopers and anyone else wearing a uniform. Like bad men of old, I was headed over the border beyond the reach of U.S. law. Over the border, too, waited my winnings, $2.5 million of it. No small number to a dead man traveling with ten grand in his pocket and a new identity.

I crossed into Delaware like a swimmer breaking water, so intense were my emotions: from cowering dread to my first taste of freedom. For five years I'd been treading water in a sea of filth and moral decay that left me washed up on the malignant shore that had been my life. But at that moment, looking over the Delaware Bridge into the early morning sky with rising sun and river winding like a long black ribbon below, I don't believe I ever felt more—joy—like I was weightless. Fact is my body was beat to hell from the surf and rocks after fighting my way back to shore, but despite the cuts and bruises I didn't feel anything in the way of pain. Just happiness for the first time in a very long time. Mostly I attributed it to adrenalin and the shock. See, from the adrenalin side (and I don't discount the benzedrine) my mind had gravitated into a kind of hyperspace above anything I was doing or thinking. And so here was this bridge that separates my shit life from a chance to start over and I'm crossing it. Get it? That was my deal, this crossover, beyond the state line and river into a new life! Well, it seemed profound at the time but this much was true: desperate to get out and blowing out of Jersey at 70 mph, I was leaving behind every

ghost that ever haunted my existence from distant past to
that very morning: the boat, the old man, the compound,
the lighthouse, my hate-filled marriage, the half-mil of
debt, the stench of NuGen's hypocrisy, all exorcised like
demons from an horrific dream. So by the time I crossed
that bridge I was euphoric, popping a stick of Trident in
my mouth, cranking up Springsteen's *Bad Lands* loud as
the car speakers could handle.

'Lights out tonight, trouble in the heartland.

Got a head-on collision, smashin' in my guts man.

I'm caught in a crossfire that I don't understand,'

I wailed like I was nineteen again.

And it was like that for a long while. Springsteen,
CCR's *Fortunate Son*, the Stones' *Shattered*, the Ramones'
*I Want to be Sedated* from their first album! The energy
injected into that hour and a half carried me deep into my
escape south and as I left Delaware for Maryland I rebel-
yelled '*Ye-eee Ha-aah!*' at the top of my lungs remembering
that real outlaws—guys like William Bonnie, Jesse James,
and Dillinger—would never stop. They'd keep the music
pounding until it popped eardrums pushing themselves
wounded, tired, cold, and hungry toward that border.
And so would I. That's how rip-roaring I was feeling. At
least, at first when I decided to ride the Escape straight
into Dodge, or in my case, circa 21$^{st}$ century, Georgetown,
Washington, D.C.

# Chapter 13

B y the time I neared Baltimore, the elation of the first three hours had evaporated like the adrenalin-liquor-amphetamine high that it was and like a tide receding it left me feeling stranded—lonely, worried, and slightly depressed. The Escape, plunging ahead onto new horizons, now surrounded by commuter traffic and littered with MapQuest printouts, empty soda cans, even the old-fashioned life vest that saved my life, left me feeling alone as a man sitting to dinner in an empty castle and it creeped me out.

Stopped dead on the highway, buttoned-up government workers glanced my way, curious, then disapproving and, Sweet Jesus, I must have looked a wreck! Moms in Chevy SUVs stared at me wondering 'Who is this guy? Where's he headed? And what's with that gash on his forehead?' while five and six-year-olds made faces from the backseat, me responding with an uninspired wave of the hand. And if my mood had switched from 'let's have a party' to a 'stale pretzels and warm beer' morning-after mode, yet another frame was creeping into the grainy black-and-white film that began playing in my brain. It was the life vest, I concluded, looking over at it across from me in the passenger seat, stark as the old man's corpse itself. To me the bright orange vest might as well have been a neon sign flashing the words 'Clue #1! Clue #1!!' to the Coast Guard and cops that were sure to follow.

What would they make of the pieces to the sprawling crime scene I'd left behind? The boats they'd certainly find early along. If it was now 7:15 a.m., a good guess would have the captain of a deep sea fishing vessel stumbling upon one or the other of them drifting and unmanned on his way out of the channel, depending on how far the current had pulled them. Maybe they'd gone aground, spun back to shore, and were at rest on a rocky shore or sandy beach still visited by postseason tourists. Could be the Tanzer had gone deep out to sea—five, even ten miles—while the dingy wouldn't go half so far. I considered all these possibilities with equal weight which is to say no weight at all given the unpredictability of the tide-current-storm combination. Still, taking any or all of these outcomes into account, those craft would be found no later than late afternoon when both commercial and private boats made their way back to dock for the night.

And what about the old man's body and the missing life vest? The old boy was buoyant as a rubber ducky bobbing in bath water so far as I could see as he drifted from the dingy that morning. But that would not have lasted long. It was the raingear that held him up that way and with the ocean stirred up as it was, and him flailing like a bug turned on its back, the old man would go down just like I did and, by the fourth time, wouldn't surface until he was long dead and bloated, body gases floating him up again. That much I knew from my research. And a lot more. Like, for instance, the body would surface sometime between fifteen and twenty hours. By my calculation that launched him early evening which meant he probably wouldn't be found until the next morning after his wife discovered him missing and a search got underway.

Now the life vest. Yeah, it had me drumming my fingers on the steering wheel all right, wondering how that would go down with the cops. And for that piece of detective work I had to think with your brain, Phials, not theirs, given the degree of paranoia that life vest had planted like a stake in my brain. The Coast Guard? Well, they speculate—vaguely—because that is their mindset. You know, 'Freaks of Nature,' 'Wonders of the Outdoors,' all that Discovery Channel bullshit. Two boats. No bodies. Violent storm at sea. Let's say they're found near one another. Could be they're two separate incidents. But odds are against it. The last double drowning where two skippers fell overboard on their own vessels in separate instances? Well, there was no 'last time.' However, just six years before—not far from Barnegat, in Belmar—something like that *did* happen, a Coast Guard veteran would definitely remember. A fourteen-year-old black kid out on a day trip with pals from an inner-city YMCA wades into the water and gets sucked out with the undertow in over his head. His older brother and three other kids see he's drowning and try to save him, only they get sucked out with the undertow and they start drowning. Father and mother of the kid and his brother, see all of this happening from shore but can only stand there screaming for help watching because they can't swim as their two sons buy the farm right in front of them. That's the story he would tell. And that's what would get the Coast Guard believing that old Otis Lugnut (or whatever his name might be) came out to rescue me and met the same tragic fate. The cops? They'd buy it right off, and fifteen minutes later put out an APB for divers and nets to search for two bodies, Otis Lugnut's and yours truly.

You, Phials, on the other hand, would listen to Coast Guard folk lore for all of about twenty seconds but then begin thinking about mathematics and the $4.5 million your company would be paying if it turned out to be 'accidental death.' Then you'd start calculating the odds of 'suicide,' 'fraud,' maybe even 'murder.' Then you'd ask to see both craft. You'd notice the beer cans, two life vests, and Dockers in mine and think *clever boy.* You'd notice no life jacket in Otis Lugnut's dingy and think *How could this be? A professional fisherman with no life vest on his boat? No, no this doesn't add up!* And that's what got me thinking, Phials. Not about the Coast Guard. Or the cops. Long and short of it, it came down to you. Always just you, Martin. These ideas, by themselves? Just speculations, I realized, hanging like a wet blanket on top of my morale from the time I finally got beyond the Beltway to the time I decided to park my ass in D.C. for the night. So what to do? *Put as much distance between me, you, and the cops as you know how,* I was thinking. Of course there *could* have been no life vest in the dingy. The storm *could* have blown it from the boat, into the Atlantic and left it as unrecoverable — presumably — as my bloated, half-eaten corpse. But still those demons of doubt tormented me until a second film began playing in my head. And that was the one about Jennifer and Tiffany once they heard I was missing and about my possible demise.

Jennifer and I first met at a fundraiser to battle AIDS that she held at her apartment overlooking the East River Drive. And there was a fight that night, I remembered, leaving the Baltimore Beltway for I95, but it had more to do with me, her, and an up-and-coming New York Yankee named Johnnie Savitch than fundraising. Jen was crazy-rich back then, dating all kinds of men—politicians, race car drivers, tycoons, and at that time Johnnie Savitch, a ballplayer who actually lived up to his hype once he made it from Triple A to the majors.

'Jack Madson!' I remember her calling, champagne glass in hand, as she set a course toward me.

I'd started early and was already drunk but what I saw was a tall, lean woman with a mass of brownish-red hair, full lips, and green eyes that sparkled with the amused arrogance of a queen collecting anecdotes for her next dinner party. She had an aristocratic nose—bobbed with plastic surgery, I guessed—a wide sensuous mouth and cream white complexion that looked to me like great sex, vitality, and *trouble*. But it was her voice that seduced men, I thought, more than even her appearance. Playful. Commanding. It was a voice that let you know she was in control and whatever intimate moment you may be sharing could end as swiftly as a matador sinking his sword into the front lobe of the bull's brain.

'Mr. Madson, I'm so pleased you could make it. Corky said you'd be coming and I could hardly wait to meet you,' she gushed, extending a firm hand my way. 'Such a bore, this party—until now,' she added, green eyes blazing.

'Corky never told me you were so beautiful.'

'Or you so intriguing,' she uttered, her stare suddenly fixed on—of all things—my hair. 'Why just look at your eyes, and your hair, thick and black as the mane of an animal! May I touch it?'

'Help yourself.' And she did. A touch at first followed by a stroke and then another stroke of her long fingers through my hair. 'I read in the *Post* you're dating Johnnie Savitch. They say he's the next A-Rod.'

'Oh, yeah, I'm seeing him and if it's baseball you want to know about he's your man. Every batting average, RBI record, and home run percentage Babe Ruth to present.'

'I'm guessing the shimmer is off the apple.'

'Don't guess, I'll tell you. He isn't man enough for me, Mr. Madson,' she said plain as that, downing her champagne in a gulp. 'Do you smoke marijuana, Jack? Acapulco Gold, Thai sticks, Jamaican Prime, I've got it all.'

'Maybe I'm not man enough for you, either.'

'I don't believe that. Not for a minute. Corky's told me about you. He says you like to live dangerously. That you were a boxer and a D.C. cop.'

'That was a long time ago.'

She took me by the hand, 'A man never loses those kinds of qualities. They soak in through the skin and stay with men like you forever.'

I don't remember if I was about to agree or disagree but what I do recall was Johnnie Savitch, all six foot and four inches of him juiced-up and ready to pounce.

'Say, what's your name, pal?' he asked making a point to step between us.

I gave him a stiff shove — both hands to the chest — to get his attention, 'Back off, Ball Boy, I don't think I like your attitude.'

'You know who I am?'

'Ball Boy, that's what I'm going to call you.'

He reared up at that, 'You know I could fuck you up good, pal . . . '

I was smiling broad and taunting when Jennifer stepped in on us, 'Johnnie, why don't you get yourself a

Coors Light while Jack and I do some blow in the master bedroom. You remember that room? It's the one you will never see again.'

And that was it. Johnnie Savitch, the "Twenty Million Dollar Man" the *N.Y. Post* and *Daily News* had been vaunting for months, murmured something, then ambled to the bar while Jen and I made a beeline for the bedroom.

Of course we didn't have sex that night, not in the master bedroom anyway, I remembered, turning the Escape onto Constitution Avenue bound for our nation's capitol. See, once Jen had her hooks into you, those hooks gave birth to other hooks, with sex dangled like a prize she offered only after her criteria was met. 'I like my men to *earn* it,' she used to say. And earn it we did—each of us in our way. So, no, it wasn't in the bedroom that night that she went down on me. It was later, once the party ended, with us lighting Thai sticks and sniffing lines of cocaine in the master bedroom as her guests wandered into the hallways and eventually home. Then, and only then, while in her daddy's limousine—after she'd seen me drunk, spaced-out and sick—on the way back to Hoboken where I was living, did she allow me entrance beyond those lush red lips where she worked her magic up, down, and around again.

'*Where did you learn to do that?*' I gasped after she'd finished licking her fingers clean, beaming up from my lap like something as beautiful as it was alien.

'You like that, Jack, do you?'

I nodded.

'Then you can be my husband,' she said resting her head on my thighs and falling asleep as her daddy's driver entered the Lincoln Tunnel headed for Jersey.

# Chapter 14

I couldn't know then how right she was that first night
we met, I recalled, staring out the Ford's windshield
at D.C.'s burnt-out motel buildings and tenements. We
got married a month later with a reception that hosted
better than five hundred, all of it over the objections of the
Judge who I'd met just twice beforehand and who hated
my guts thirty seconds into the first.

'Your boyfriend has the look of a peddler from the
Lower East Side!' I heard him raving once alone with her
in his study, me no more than twenty feet away in the next
room.

'His father was a truck driver, Barton,' she told him.

'Don't I know it!' he shouted back at her. 'And don't
think for a minute I buy his Catholic Church bullshit. He's
a Jew, sure as I'm a capitalist. I can hear it in the way he
whines!'

'Well, his family never hurt anyone, particularly,'
she spat back. This, a reference to his dealings with the
Bontempo clan.

And with those words came a crack I could hear
through the walls. He must have hit her with a tremendous
backhand because when she left the study, the side of her
face was purple and swollen and her upper lip bleeding.

'*Let's go,*' was all she said, and we did.

Now I'm sure you're wondering after that display of
loyalty, how things could have gone so wrong between
Jennifer and me. Well, let's start with the premise. It wasn't
loyalty to me. It was rebellion against her father. And what
I saw then as my entry into the Big League was her sidling
up to the guy who would disgust the Judge more than any
other, a 'peddler,' but one with balls enough to give him
some of his own and then some. It was a marriage made in
hell but she was not alone in her motives. You could say I
loved her but not with my heart. I loved Jennifer with the
kind of post- September 11$^{th}$ American rage that showed
through in our love making, intense as it was violent. See,
I had a secret ambition to parlay my success at NuGen
into politics and maybe run for Congress someday or even
the Senate, an impossible campaign without the Judge's
connections. But that never happened. In fact, the old
bastard never gave us a cent. We lived on the money I made
and that was his revenge because Jennifer never gave up
the taste and habits of the money he made, leaving me
marooned on an island of never-ending debt.

Strangely, the Judge had something else right.
Something about me that I never knew, Jen had
suspected, and he had calculated all along. The 'peddler'
thing? One night Jennifer came to me carrying two vials
and a double-tipped swab. 'Rub this end on the inside of
your cheek and the other under your tongue. Tonight,
we're going to get to the root of your DNA,' she told
me. It was a kit supplied by *National Geographic* magazine
that promised to identify a person's ethnicity with 99.9
percent accuracy. 'Sure thing,' I laughed then. Only what
came back from the testing lab turned out to be not so
funny. Seems my Dad had it wrong. All of it. We were

not just Irish (his side) or Russian (my mother's). I was also, the lab certified, *one-half Jewish*. All of those Sunday masses, for what? Each of those Catholic schools, to what purpose? Immaculate Conception grammar school with its nuns, St. Damian's with its Brothers, Georgetown University with its Jesuits. Catechism enough to teach the Pope Catholic doctrine!

From that moment, things between us started heading south. Not that it wouldn't have happened anyway. Jennifer was a man eater. Like Johnnie Savitch, she'd have had her fill of me sooner or later. But it was the DNA that started my unraveling, one prick at a time. 'My god, you smell awful,' she would say. 'You really reek, honestly, of hovels and Jewish ghettos in Minsk.' Well, you could multiply a comment like that by a thousand, one skin prick at a time, because Jennifer was an artist with the needle. But never did those tiny punctures add up to so much as when I took to heavy drinking and she took to the white stuff.

Like a pattern that keeps repeating until there's no meaning to anything you say or do, I'd been out drinking with Corky who also saw some political mileage in the Madson-Crowley connection. For Jennifer's part, with Tiffany spending the day with her granddaddy, she'd been sniffing coke since her morning workout at Canoe Brook. And with that, the chess pieces were on the board and ready for action.

'I bought a new car this afternoon,' she started in. 'A Mercedes convertible. It rides like the wind.'

'And how much will that be costing?'

She dipped her head back down to the coffee table where three white lines ran parallel to one another, 'Who cares? It's only you who thinks about money, *perpetually*.'

'That's because it's only me that has any,' I answered.

'Well, it doesn't matter. I've decided to leave you. You have no relationship with Tiffany. You, with all your ambitions, political and otherwise.'

'Who told you that?'

'Corky and anyone else you have more than two drinks with.'

'I love Tiffany and I love you,' I swore.

'No, my darling. You love you. And if you tolerate me at all, it's for Daddy's political connections which he won't let you near, and my body which I'd give to ten others before you.'

'Truth be told, you're not as good as you think.'

'Not one of them complains. Most say I give better oral sex than the professionals. Number 7's taught me the cleverest technique . . . '

'Shut your fucking mouth!' I threatened.

She took another sniff, dabbed away a clot of white powder from above her lip with her middle finger, then sucked it, 'Come to think of it, I may stay after all. It's entertaining watching the deterioration of a Golden Gloves boxer from Newark. Like watching meat tenderize.'

'You're your father's daughter,' I growled. 'All that corruption. A Judge. Pillar of society. How many hit men did he let walk to whack some poor stiff who owed them money? How many drug dealers?'

'Holier than thou, is it? You and Corky and NuGeneration Holdings. It makes me physically ill how you actually believe trashing American companies and shipping jobs to the Chinks for money is, what, moral? At least we know what we are.'

'And what about Tiffany?'

'You don't have to worry about Tiffany, Jack. I've been meaning to tell you, she's not yours.'

'Not mine?'

'You are not her father. I married you knowing I was pregnant, my love.'

'Was it Savitch?'

'No, a man far more interesting. A *real* politician who some day may be president.'

'You're lying!'

'It's true.'

'Do I know him?'

'Of him, my ear. Only *of* him.'

'Are you seeing him now?'

'Quietly. Very quietly and in secret because, unlike you, he's a powerful man whose privacy must be protected from the public and for me you're the perfect cover. You see, Jack, in case it's never occurred to you, we have a marriage of convenience. Mine.'

There were times prior to that night when we shared something like happiness. One of them was the birth of our daughter but even that Jennifer had stolen from me. And that night I came to the end of a very long street and confronted the fact that I was finally a failure in marriage, in business, and in life.

So you see, Phials, I wasn't expecting much in the way of hysteria from either my wife or daughter when they got word of my ill-fated sail. But after a phone call from the Judge—or without one—it wasn't hard to imagine the questions directed to your office by my distraught spouse with daughter in tow, 'And how does that clause, the "accidental death while working" one, apply? What I mean to ask is, when will my missing husband be officially "dead"?' Of course, the official answer would be 'After seven years. However,' one of your staff, impressed with power as you, would add, 'given the discovery of the two boats and second victim, and the police report (along with strings the Judge would pull!), Surety's investigation summary filing should be all that we need.' 'And, I hesitate to ask, the money? When would the $4.5 million be available to the survivors?' You get the picture, Phials. And I bet five-to-one odds it didn't go a hell of a lot different from what I'm saying, *did it?*

Anyhow, as I made my way into my old stomping grounds as a university student, taking the Escape down M Street and onto Wisconsin toward the Georgetown Inn, a crawly feeling dark as a dead man's shadow overtook me. For the first time I really had become John Harrison Dempsey. My driver's license gotten through Johnnie Eng, my car registration gotten through Danny Brennan, even the name I would sign into the hotel registry that night was no longer my own, but the name of John "Jack" Dempsey, the "Manassas Mauler," heavyweight champion of the world, 1919–1926.

# Chapter 15

Come daybreak, after a cup of black coffee, half a dozen white pills, and a scotch chaser, I was on the road again feeling fresher. Out of D.C. and back onto I-95 headed toward Richmond, then Raleigh, with good prospects for a stopover in Tallahassee before making it, Day 3, into Laredo.

But I've got to tell you, Phials, once I hit the highway, the chain of memories set in motion while driving the day before—and weird dreams that followed about the ocean, the Judge, and the old man—kept floating up from my subconscious like ghosts from the nether regions. Now you'd think they'd be about college. You know, 'young men well met, hale and hardy' and all that crap, since I was in Georgetown, for Christ's sake. But they weren't. That day, as I made my way south, mostly I was thinking about my high school, not college, days and I had the ring on my finger to prove it: *scientiam, fiden, humilitatem*. The three virtues of St. Damian, the three "legs of the stool," . . . *knowledge, faith, humility* . . . set in each corner of a pyramid that if followed would keep a young man on the path to a moral life.

I remembered how they called me Jack "The Madman" Madson and how two or three guys crazy enough to hang with me back then ran around Newark drinking, picking up go-go girls, listening to James Brown, Junior Walker and the All-Stars, and Wilson Pickett at nightclubs. I recalled training after school each day at Market Street gym set up above a penny arcade, the race riots and the savagery that followed.

One day, I marched up the flight of creaky wooden stairs through the musty hallway leading up to the gym where my trainer, guy we called Buddy Gee, waved me off. 'You cain't come here ta'day,' he yelled down at me from above. See, race relations—aside from me and the go-gos—were raw at the time. With Mafia exploitation, corrupt politicians, and infrastructure deteriorating by the day, cities like Newark, Philly, Detroit, even Watts and Oakland on the West Coast, had turned into powder kegs. 'I paid good money ($2.50/month) to be here!' I hollered back up the staircase. But Buddy would hear nothing of it. 'You get outcha here, hear me? Get outcha here and git back home, Jack. You listen to what I say!' And, reluctantly, I did. Just in time to watch the *Six O'clock News* where reports of rioting had already started. A cop in Plainfield castrated, stomped to death and dismembered with a meat cleaver by a mob of angry blacks, St. Damian's firebombed, my dad driving a truck on Springfield Avenue shot at by snipers from tenement rooftops, an eleven-year-old murdered in cold blood by police, Mafia capo Anthony "Tony" Imperiali patrolling North Ward streets in an army tank complete with machine guns and a cannon and, ultimately, entire sections of the city set ablaze.

If there was violence and mayhem then, there was also the peculiar humor that could only be mustered at an all-boys Catholic prep school made up of the sons of blue collar workers, mafia middle management, and ghetto families trying to escape the dead end future of the inner city. A group of wise guys in Sophomore F (classes ran A through F) who removed the hinges from the heavy wooden door Fr. Lawrence used to swing open with such enthusiasm each morning; a dead frog from biology class someone put in the lunch box of our eighty-year-old Latin teacher, Fr. Ignacious; and Fr. Mark, the sex education instructor, who began class each year by raising a large jar bearing a woman's vagina and uterus floating in alcohol like the squid-like parasite from the movie *Alien* before announcing, 'Well, guys, this is what it's all about!'

Given the variety of backgrounds each of us brought to the school, who could imagine where life's path might lead? Some became doctors, lawyers, and engineers. Others chose the lives of their fathers to become bartenders, cops and detectives. But as many went on to become criminals: petty embezzlers, middle-rung Mafia types, drug dealers—one became leader of The Crypts street gang! See, there really was a kind of precedent for all of this, meaning the monks at St. Ann's Abbey who ran the place were holy, but not naïve. In days gone by, tough guys like Watergate villain G. Gordon Liddy attended St. Damian's. So did Ritchie Bontempo (whose grandfather, Rugerio, practically invented the Jersey mob) who I roomed with freshman year at Georgetown, and Robert E. Gallagher who ran East Jersey Securities whose "pump and dump" penny stocks scheme netted him $150 million and St. Damian's the $20 million under-the-table donation that rebuilt what was left of it after the riots.

So I was not particularly surprised when for our class reunion I was selected along with three others to receive the "Most Distinguished Alumni" award because—truth be told—the barriers to entry were not so great and the number of guys physically available to accept it was limited. Still, the three other recipients *were* 'distinguished:' Two-time Pulitzer Prize winner Gil Flanagan, who wrote for the *Washington Post*; Brigadier General Stan Yankovitch, serving his second tour of duty in Afghanistan; Fr. Dan Filipski, a Brother, who'd spent the past decade working as a missionary in Uganda—and me, a quasi-successful Manhattan take-over artist whose best friend happened to head up the Awards Committee, and whose philanthropic wife happened to donate $25,000 to the school on the family's behalf!

But mostly what occupied my mind as I blew past Richmond and into Raleigh, North Carolina was not the guys I knew who *were* there but the ones I knew who *were not*. Frankly, Phials—and you would know this better than me—life is a motherfucker! Take Chucky Diebold. Here was the most intelligent guy in the class. He graduates, goes on to Johns Hopkins and becomes an M.D. Ten years into a distinguished career, he gets addicted to talwin, starts injecting it between his fingers and toes so no one's the wiser, and ODs. Dead! Lights out! Can you imagine? Or Lemar Williams. Guy graduates valedictorian, makes the speech at our graduation along with the local congressman. Only student in the school's history to get accepted at Princeton. We're all so proud of him! He starts dealing smack sophomore year, winds up shot through the head by a pair of Cubans during spring break in Miami! Another was Bob Lanier. Class cut-up. Okay, expectations are not too high. He gets big into real estate, right time, right place, and becomes a multi-millionaire. At least until the Feds catch up with him and he's sent up the river for ten years!

But the one who abso-fucking-lutely blew my mind was Jay Duncan, a close friend who went from Damian's to Georgetown and like me, dropped out in sophomore year. Me, you know about. Jay? He drops out of college because he's a compulsive gambler, plain and simple: cards, horses, football, you name it. Duncan was a guy who'd bet $20,000 on two cockroaches put on top of the bar at Clyde's to race! Well, that's what had me stopping for the night at the Georgetown Inn. What drew me was the fact that on a lonely winter's night in a room in that hotel, Jay Duncan hung himself. That's right, Phials, one of those suicides you're so hot to uncover! And who knows why he did it? Gambling debt? Could be. Women problems? Possible. Or maybe he just woke up one morning 45 years young with no wife, no kids, no house, no money, and no friends, and said, *Fuck it! I'm outta here!'* Who's to say? Certainly not me.

So bothered was I about these four guys, these friends of mine who were now dead, that I thought about writing a biography or some kind of story about them. I ran the idea by another classmate, guy named Mark Shields, a lawyer who also graduated with us.

'I know it sounds stupid,' I told him over dinner out one night with our wives, 'but I'm thinking about writing a story about those four guys, about their lives, I mean.'

'Jack, no one cares about four losers from St. Damian's Prep in Newark.'

'Losers? How do you know that, Mark? How do you know they were losers? How do you or anyone know what they were really like? What they were thinking? What they were going through in the moments before they died? Maybe they were sick? Maybe depressed or worried about money or someone they loved but couldn't be with anymore? How do we know? How does anyone know that they weren't good guys who somehow lost their way? And that's what I want to write about. A kind of defense of them that I'd call, "Men of Indeterminate Value." Or something like that. Some title to try to capture the fact that no one knows what went on inside their heads and so no one can really judge them, except maybe God, if there is one.'

'Jack,' Shields said, leaning toward me so his wife would not hear what he was about to say, 'I met Bob Lanier after he got out of prison. He asked me to defend him on a real estate fraud charge at Newark courthouse. The night after he was acquitted I took him to dinner in Iron Bound and going home I'm greeted by three black guys who surround me and put a knife to my throat. While Bob stands there watching, they rob me of everything I have—about $3,000 cash—money that only Lanier knew I'd be carrying that night. He set me up, Jack. Can you fucking imagine? I almost got my throat cut because of that asshole. No Bob, and all of those fuckers, they are not 'men of indeterminate value!'"

# Chapter 16

Those were the kind of quirky things running through my brain from Richmond through Raleigh all the way to Tallahassee, Phials, where I finally stopped at a Motel Six for a few hours shut-eye. There was no internet access but I managed to scrounge up a copy of *USA TODAY*, ready to tear it apart for news, even a line or two, about what happened at Barnegat two days earlier. I didn't have to look very far. As I sat on the side of my bed that night, right there in front of me, page one, in that side bar column, "Headlines in Brief," was the story I was looking for:

### N.J. EXEC MISSING IN BOATING MISHAP

*The twenty-two foot sailboat owned by Manhattan executive John Madson, husband of Jennifer Madson and son-in-law of former N.J. Supreme Court Justice Barton Crowly, was found unmanned in the Atlantic Ocean yesterday. The Coast Guard speculates that Madson, a novice sailor, may have fallen victim to a sudden storm at sea. A second deserted craft was found three miles north of Madson's boat along with the body of Salvatore Soto, a local fisherman, who apparently drowned in the storm.*

*Yes!* I was thinking as I dropped into one of the soundest sleeps I can ever remember. *The Coast Guard went for it which meant the local police probably did too!* But when I woke up the next morning 5 a.m., as planned, I wasn't thinking about the Coast Guard or the police. I was thinking about you, Phials. And you know what? It motivated me. That's right, *you* motivated me. Better than benzedrine. Better than Adderall. Better than ten cups of black coffee. And yeah, man, I wanted to put the pedal to the metal and move my ass down Rt. 10 west from Tallahassee to San Antonio and on to the Blunts' front door in Laredo.

It was then I turned my tunes back on with volume cranked and cruising again, only this time it wasn't the Stones or Springsteen, it was Merle Haggard singing "Working Man Blues" and Willie Nelson wailing "Whiskey River," thinking now about livelier days, better ones, that focused not on my failures but on things like the guts it took for me to break away from the football and baseball everyone else did to fight Golden Gloves. How when after getting clocked with an overhand right in the first round of the finals, I had the courage to get up off my ass, embarrassed and angry, to march across that ring and knock Kareem Brown, middle weight state champ, on his ass in the very next round. But, I never turned pro. Never had any intention to, that wasn't the point. I wanted to prove myself. Show myself and everyone else that I had the balls to do it without anyone's help, and I sure as shit accomplished that. There were other times, too, in this winding path to hell and back I called my life. Like how I got into Georgetown was one. Guys like Bontempo and Rinaldi used their old man's connections but I got in on my own—no old man, no 'I'm black' or 'I got a pussy' affirmative action bullshit. And yeah, I dropped out like Duncan. But he dropped out and hung himself because he couldn't stop gambling. For me it was money, or lack of it, had me leaving to become—of all goddamned things—a cop. Hell, I never even liked cops let alone wanted to be one! But the money was decent. It paid my loans once Dad got laid off and, truth be told, kept him in his house until the day he passed.

Even as a cop transporting prisoners, people around me sensed, what should I call it? 'An imminent sense of danger,' let's say. Broke, frustrated at my shit luck, filled with a kind of menacing rage, it was me, now tagged with the nickname "Mad Dog" Madson, who volunteered to get hostile prisoners out of their cells for transfer from city jail to the state penitentiary in Richmond when they refused to go. It was me and another guy, Mike Berrey, and we'd enter those cells like primitives entering a dark cave never knowing what to expect, only that it would be bad, and *violent.* If ever either of us doubted that, we had only to take a gander at Sergeant Cook, reassigned to Booking, after a weight lifter high on Ecstasy bit off half his face in a scuffle. One just like the battle royals we got into when it was decided two of us needed to walk into those cells holding our breath to keep from choking on the stench that pushed out like smothering waves of madness. Ever see a guy been bit? Human bites, I mean. Never heals, Phials, even after surgery. Infection—planted so deep from the saliva and crap guys like that got thriving in their mouths—never gets completely out of the tissue so that side of the face, chewed up in chunks like Cook's was, just festers, deep down, then flares up suddenly like all raging hell. Berrey and me knew that when we went in to extract those kinds of prisoners, we had one chance to take them down, subdue them, and get them the fuck out and into chains or a straight jacket fucking-ay-pronto.

Well, maybe you get the point and maybe you don't, but in the end these crazy bastards—hit men, rapists, terrorists—I won their respect! Like the students at Georgetown and the cops who hated college kids. I proved myself, Phials, and did the same at NuGeneration Holdings. 'Tell me something about yourself, your background and education,' Corky asked during my interview. 'Tell me three qualities you possess,' 'Tell me three shortcomings,' 'What has been the greatest accomplishment in your life so far?' 'Why should I hire you?' To those questions, I had answers. Good ones. And, Christ, I needed that job! Until finally he said, 'Kid, you look like a guy who could use a break and NuGen's going to give it to you. You're a fighter and in this financial jungle, we need fighters.' That was it. Getting the job was my first accomplishment, but I followed that with one business success after another. Business triumphs, driven by something Corky taught me better than anybody could—ruthlessness. The art of dehumanizing everybody and everything in a targeted company, buying it cheap, stripping it of anyone who could not abide the same level of ruthlessness. Triumphs! One after another. It reminded me of a story Ritchie Bontempo's father, "Tony Boy," once told two of us over dinner at The Tombs.

'I knew the Kennedys,' he bragged after some wine and a Grappa or two. 'I ever tell you boys that? Bootlegging back in the day. My father, your grandfather,' he told Ritchie, 'worked with Joe Kennedy for a coupla years. Scotch, and plenty of it. Come in by ship to Cuba. Cuba to international waters off the Florida coast. We'd take speedboats. You know, like PT 109, Jack Kennedy's Navy boat? Anyhow, Rugerio, God bless his soul, used Cubans for labor with instructions to the captains that if the Coast Guard gave chase, you throw the booze off the boat to make it lighter and faster while you make a run for it. Not so with Kennedy. His instructions? Throw the Cubans off the boat. 'Let 'em drown,' he told those captains, 'I want the fucking booze!' That's the difference between men like your grandfather, Ritchie, and the Kennedys. People from our world? We put a full stop to doing business with Joe Kennedy. He was immoral!'

If you can believe it, Phials, Corky was like Joe Kennedy. And Jennifer's father, Judge Barton Crowley, well, he was like the devil incarnate. Too much hypocrisy for me, all of it, and finally I just had to leave. See, the criminals, them, I always understood. They did it for money, occasionally a woman, or because they were crazy. Cops, and so-called bearers of society's torch, them, near as I could tell, they just fucked everyone over because they could.

So now I'm on the last leg of my escape with all these thoughts tumbling around in my head when I glance to my left and again I see it. And, I swear, a chill passed through me. It was the life jacket, Phials. To me, that thing was cursed, sitting there in the passenger's seat, bright orange, staring at me like the ghost of Hamlet's father. Christ, I could almost hear it talking to me, whispering, as if it was a living, breathing entity. And this is what it was saying. It was saying (and I know this sounds crazy) *telling me*, 'You're not Jack Madson no more. You're not John Dempsey, either. You are a fraud. You're not Jesse James. You're not William Bonnie. And you ain't John Dillinger. You, you are nobody. You are a lost soul who is feeling his way through the corridors of Hell.' 'Fuck you!' I shouted, trying my damnedest to ignore it, but that life jacket, it was like a magnetic field that kept pulling me back and it wouldn't leave me alone! 'What are you looking at?' I demanded, glancing back at it again, propped up on the seat, prim and proper, like it had come alive and was invading my brain. 'Nothing,' it answered. 'Nothing because you are nothing. Ambition is what you are. But you don't even have that no more!' Finally, I took that life vest and threw it like some 'thing' half-alive, half-inanimate to the back of the SUV so that it hits the side window then slides down to the floor of the car and out of sight.

Then, disgusted because of how that collection of stuffed rags took me out of a good mood and reminded me of the boat and the old man and the drowning, I switched on the radio, pushed the scanner and listened as it sailed through half a dozen Baptist preachers, radio talk shows, and born-again faith healers, until I heard Marty Robbins singing "Streets of Laredo." Finally, I stopped, breathed a sigh of relief, and listened, calm now, to Robbins' honey-laced voice catching exactly the right emotion from every single lyric.

I listened intently, more intently than I ever listened to a song, remembering the words from when I was a little kid dressed up with a six-shooter and cowboy hat, and I started singing along in a low voice. And after it ended, I sat there in the car, tears streaming down the sides of my face as I drove. The song had been like a superhighway to some isolated part of my brain far removed that I'd never encountered, I realized, wiping the wet away with the side of my hand and pulling the Escape next to a neon sign that read, GRACELAND TRAILER PARK.

The place Bobby and Twila Blunt called home.

# Chapter 17

I got out of the Escape. It was already evening and I knew I looked like a wonk, unshaved, rumpled shirt with jeans, and that wasn't even getting into the scabby mess the gash on the side of my head turned into. But it was a trailer park, not a Jersey McMansion I was walking up to, right? So I rapped on the aluminum screen door and a tall guy, balding, with round red face and cowboy boots and toothpick in his mouth answers. 'Who are you?' he asks.

'My name is John Dempsey. If you're Bobby Blunt, I think you're expecting me.'

He smiled and rolled the toothpick around in his mouth like he was proving he could do it, 'Well, come on in, Mr. Dempsey.'

'Jack, you can call me Jack,' I said, stepping into the trailer which was really like three small trailers put together so it had the look of, well, an aluminum house, at least in dimension.

Bobby walked ten steps to the fridge, 'Wanna beer, Jack?' I shook my head. 'Well, I might just hep myself anyway.' It was a line that he must have believed was clever because a horse laugh erupted from him as he lifted the pop-top.

'Robert Earl!' a woman's voice called out. 'Who's that just entered our abode?'

I glanced into one of the adjoining trailers but all I could make out was a dart board hanging on a wall with the photo of a woman's face glued on it. I watched for a short while as one dart followed another, right eye, left eye, mouth, and nose.

'It's Johnnie's pal,' Bobby hollered back. 'Guy he told us about, Jack Dempsey.'

'Well, are you or are you not going to introduce him to me?'

'Oh, yeah, Peach. Straight along.' Then turning to me he whispered, 'Ya gotta watch yourself with Twila. You been warned.'

*Warned?* I thought to ask but didn't because from out of the other room bolted Twila Blunt, long blonde hair, dressed in fringed leather cowgirl blouse, skirt, and boots, standing—I had to guess—no more than three feet and eight inches in height.

'Pleased to meet ya, Jack,' she said shooting a miniature hand in my direction. But I wasn't so quick on the draw, extending with a lot less enthusiasm, caught off guard by the fact that she was . . . a midget. 'I know what you're thinkin',' Twila spat-out suddenly, looking at me, then over to Bobby.

'No, I wasn't thinking anything.'

'Liar!' she roared taking a step forward. 'Look where I come up on you.' She leveled her hand with her mouth and moved it forward to my crotch. 'You're thinkin' little women must give great blow jobs, wadn't ya?'

'No, Ma'm.'

'Never crossed your mind?'

'Never, Ma'm.'

'Robert Earl?'

He took a swallow of beer, 'Now, Twila, if the man says he wadn't thinkin' that, you gotta take him at his word.'

She nodded and took a step back or two. Her face—actually very pretty for a 'little woman'—softened, so that her blue eyes seemed more understanding, even sweet.

'All right, then. You ate any supper?'

'Not yet, Ma'm.'

'Call me Twila,' she countered. 'Robert Earl, cook up a steak on the grill for this man.'

'Sure thing, Twila,' he said hustling to it.

She motioned to a metal chair in the kitchen, 'So what are you wanted for. Everybody Johnnie sends our way's wanted for somethin', some worse than others.'

'Guess you could say, I'm running away,' I answered, sitting.

'Bad marriage?'

'You could say that.'

'Don't I know what that's like,' she said, taking two Lone Stars out of the fridge and handing me one. 'You ain't killed no kids nor had your way with 'em?' she checked.

'No, nothing like that.'

'Okay, then. I got a United States passport in my top dresser drawer for ya. But just to be safe we'll drive ya over the border tomorrow mornin'. Nothin' to it, gettin' into Mexico. Other way, not so easy.'

'That would be fine. Thank you.'

She grunted, if only a little begrudgingly, 'Robert Earl'll have you a steak ready. You eat it. Hep yourself to the beer. Room's over there,' she said pointing, ''cause tonight my old man and me, we'se goin' out on the town dancin'.' She stared at me deadpan, 'Not recommended for wanted men.'

I nodded as she left for the dart room, 'Twila?'

'Yeah, Sugar Bun.'

'Who is the woman whose picture you throw darts at?'

'Most evil bitch in the world,' she growled, suddenly snake-mean again as Bobby laid down a steak in front of me.

'Amen to that,' he affirmed.

'That is Mrs. Tim McGraw, also known as Faith Hill, you know her, Jack?'

'She's a singer, isn't she?'

'Some think so, but I don't 'cause I know her for what she is,' Twila said closing the distance between us, 'the foulest, lowest, stinkin' cunt in all of these fifty states. And my beau, Tim McGraw, handsomest, noblest, best singin' man God ever turned the dirt beneath our feet into, married that daughter of a whore!'

'So you throw darts at her?'

'Every day since the Soul2Soul tour in '09. Now, ain't that a crock a shit!' she said as she turned and walked out of the room, slamming the door to the dart room behind her.

I stared at my steak wondering how this situation was going to turn out before hunger took over and I put my fork and knife to it.

'My Twila, she's a special lady,' Bobby ventured by way of an explanation. 'Seems a little ornery when ya first meet up but believe me that woman's got a heart of gold. Just when it comes to Faith Hill she got no patience. Used to be Twila was a singer. Ever hear the song "I Can't Do That With You No More!"?'

I shook my head.

'Twila recorded it with Curb Records, Tim McGraw's label. She thought they had somethin' special goin', but

Ol' Tim, well, he just went off and married Faith Hill. Left a bad taste in Twila's mouth, if ya know what I mean.'

'Oh, I do, really. I hate Faith Hill, too.'

I was so spent I barely got through dinner that night. The stress of the accident and all that followed, driving all that way wondering moment-to-moment if the cops were after me, state police, local police, FBI, or someone like you. It all caught up with me there at the dinner table so that once I entered that tiny closet of a room and stretched out on the cot the Blunts had made up for me, I crashed and burned. Simple as that. No dreams. No dark rivers of thought. No recriminations. Nothing. Just black, *lights out* until morning.

# Chapter 18

That is what I thought, but it is not what happened because around about two a.m., the sound of a woman's voice woke me, 'It's him, Robert Earl. It's him! That man is *our* John Dempsey!' Then my one eye pried open in time to see Twila, barefoot and dressed now in a floor-length cotton nightgown, drift into my room like a one-woman carnival, iPad in hand.

'You're a celebrity, Jack! Why didn't you tell us?' she asked as she slid herself down alongside me on the bed. '*New York Daily News,* Jack! And the *Post!*' she told Bobby who came in behind her as she read from the screen. 'And look at this, the *Star Ledger,* a tribute. A kind of tribute to our Jack and his beautiful, rich family!'

I took the iPad from her, sitting up in the cot, laying it on my lap. It was true, articles. Several of them written from different perspectives about me, the accident at Barnegat, my work at NuGen, even the Judge who spoke to *Page Six's* Robert Johnson about "the tragic loss" of his son-in-law who he was "all but certain" had drowned, body never to be recovered.

'Oh, yes. Very flattering,' I muttered amiably until Twila tried to take the iPad from me just as my eyes caught sight of a less prominent article titled "The Man Who Investigates the 'Dead,'" and I snatched it back from her.

'Wait. Wait just a minute.' Then I read solemnly as Twila
looked on, horrified.

### THE MAN WHO INVESTIGATES THE 'DEAD'

*You can see that Martin Phials is a forceful man if not
from the clear staccato cadence of his voice, then from his
heavyset, dug-in appearance, conscientious demeanor and
the three-piece suits that he wears, "I've been in insurance
claims for twenty-eight years,' Phials is not shy to tell
you. "First with the U.S. military investigating MIAs for
death claim verification. For the past twenty, verifying
and sometimes debunking, individuals' death claims, for
Surety Insurance."*

*Phials' most recent investigation centers around the
disappearance of New York-based executive John Madson.
Madson's twenty-two foot sailboat was found adrift ten
miles out to sea after a storm with its skipper missing
and presumably drowned. These and other intriguing
facts make Madson's disappearance precisely claims
investigator Martin Phial's "cup of tea," but when asked
for his assessment, the normally outspoken death detective
becomes reticent, "Too early to say exactly what happened,"
he opines standing on a dock overlooking Barnegat Bay
with its famous lighthouse in the background. "As you
can see, the police are dragging the Bay theorizing that
the body, if there is one, may have washed back with the
tides, but they haven't found anything. Not Madson's body
anyway."*

*Though the Manhattan executive, who made his home
in the upscale New Jersey town of Summit, is still listed*

*as missing, Coast Guard officials familiar with Barnegat Channel mishaps speculate that Madson fell from his craft during the storm and probably drowned. "We've seen this before," Captain Rick Dawson of the U.S. Coast Guard stated earlier this week. "People underestimate the dangers of boating and swimming in the waters around here. The currents and riptides, particularly immediately following a storm, well, it's something you have to respect or there's always that danger."*

*While Captain Dawson has his point of view, Phials does not allow himself the luxury of speculation. "It's facts I get paid to care about. I don't like mysteries, except in books and Hollywood films," he adds with a tight smile, "but in my business, we need to know exactly what happened and why. That's my job. That's my life," he states emphatically. Asked whether he believes the Madson mystery will eventually be solved, he is quick to respond, "Absolutely. We're like the Canadian Mounted Police," he quips, serious and determined. "We always get our man."*

*Adding to the mystery of the disappearance of John Madson, son-in-law of former New Jersey Supreme Court Judge Barton Crowley, is the fact that the body of local fisherman Salvatore Soto was found just three miles from Madson's unmanned craft. For police and Coast Guard officials, Soto's death has already been ruled an accidental drowning, a victim who, like Madson, may have fallen from his boat during the storm.*

*For claims investigator Martin Phials, the man who investigates the 'dead,' easy conclusions are anathema. "The two may be related in ways that are obvious or not so obvious. Talk to me again in six months," the death-*

*detective promises.* "*By then I assure you, John Madson's disappearance won't be a mystery any longer.*"

The tone of the article and Phials steely approach to the investigation left a vibration in the air—ominous and chilling—that even Twila could feel.

'They're after you, Jack. That man, Phials and the insurance company! He said, "If there *is* a body." That means he don't believe there is one, which means he thinks you're still alive, which means he's comin' for ya!' Twila pulled me toward her, smothering my face in her cotton nightgown between two perky, little breasts. 'Oh, my poor, Jack. Hunted down like a common criminal despite all a his efforts. Pursued by The Law like the Jesse James of his times!'

My wide-opened eyes narrowed. Could there *actually be* some kind of ESP operating between Bobby's wife Twila and me? I wondered.

'Know somethin', Jack Dempsey?' Bobby chimed in, pulling a Nikon camcorder and a Smith & Wesson .45 pistol from a wooden dresser. 'Twila likes you. And she don't take to just any swingin' dick passes through here on they way to Mexico.'

'Thanks,' I could hear the muffled sound of my voice try to say, but as I lifted my head from Twila's chest, she seized it between the flat of her two hands.

'No need to thank anyone!' she laughed, tiny heart pounding. 'Why look at you. You're hurt,' she noticed, stroking the partially healed gash on the side of my head. 'Let Momma make it better,' she soothed planting tiny kisses around it and lifting my face up to hers. 'You know, Jack, what I said about "little women" and blow jobs?'

I nodded.

'You were correct in those naughty thoughts went through that sacred head of yours. Little women, well, we're just anatomically constructed to give the best head in God's holy universe!'

'Amen to that!' Bobby affirmed, focusing the camera with one hand as he trained the .45 on me with the other.

'Now I'd like to prove that to you while Bobby films a memento for the two of us to share for all eternity. See, Jack, we don't see too many celebrity-types 'round here. Mostly just druggies runnin' from the Texas Rangers. But you, you're so smart and handsome!' Twila's face slid from my chest to my abdomen to between my thighs. 'And Jack?'

'Yes?'

'If this is what my mouth feels like,' she asked, delivering cat-like licks to the head of my cock, 'just imagine how my little woman pussy's gonna feel.'

I contemplated that question for what seemed like seconds, but may have been longer.

'Wait,' I objected, finally breaking loose from the spell that Phial's interview and Twila's tongue had cast, signaling Bobby to stop recording. 'I don't think I . . . '

But then she took it, just the head, into her tiny mouth and my sentence, my train of thought, and all of my qualms seemed to vanish as my penis, ardent as a soldier, snapped to attention.

'Umm, yummy,' Twila lolled playfully running her little asp of a pink tongue up and down its shaft. 'I think I'm going to call him "Pincus," Jack,' she uttered, breathless. 'Name of a elephant my daddy took me to see at the circus as a chile. Didn't know nothin' 'bout it then, but I believe I got Pincus' cock in my mouth right now,' she growled, taking me from bottom to top and back again, 'and it's big, and it's long, and it's wonderful tasty!'

I agreed as best I could, everything considered. Something that probably played out in their sex tape like one sustained 'AHHH!' as Twila took Pincus full bore beyond her mouth, deep down into the exotic depths of her 'little woman' throat.

# Chapter 19

I woke the next morning to the smell of Folgers brewing and sound of Twila singing "I Can't Do That With You No More!" occasional interrupted by Bobby. 'I say we take him over this morning, set him up in his motel, an' that's that. He don't need more'n that, and probably don't need that, neither.'

Twila was cooking bacon and eggs in a frying pan, '"What you done to me, cain't be matched, Your love drove me crazy but there's just this one catch,"' she continued singing before she stopped to answer and I rolled from my cot, threw on a pair of jeans and moved toward the bathroom.

'Well, Bobby, as you have no doubt discerned I like Jack and want to make sure to a certainty that those Mexican drug dealers don't get they hands on him . . . Jack? Oh, Jack,' she beamed as I crossed the narrow passage that separated bathroom from facilities. 'And how are you this fine mornin'?'

I smiled weakly, 'A little tired, but . . . good, thank you.'

She smiled and winked, crossing the tiny kitchen toward me. '"I loved with my heart and I loved with my body,"' she began crooning again. '"If I cain't have you total, then I don't want nobody!" Like that, Jack?'

'Oh sure, that's your song "I Can't Do That No More!"'

'Hah-huh,' she corrected, kissing her pointing finger with pursed lips and touching it to mine. 'The song is "I Can't Do That *With You* No More!" See what I'm tryin' to tell you, Jack? I was a naughty little woman last night and it can't happen ever again. Jesus wouldn't like it.'

'You don't think so?'

'No, though it may tear our hearts asunder, I fear he wouldn't,' she confessed, clasping my hand then gently releasing it as I went to the john.

Once I sat down to breakfast, Bobby who'd been laughing and making small talk became more serious, 'You know, I wouldna shot you last evenin'.'

'No hard feelings,' I said taking a sip from my coffee cup.

'That's good 'cause Twila, she likes you some and let's face it, Jack, you got to trust me, given the business situation we struck up 'tween us.'

Twila joined us at the table, 'What Bobby's tryin' to say is we'se worried about you crossin' the border down here in Laredo. Johnnie Eng's been good to us. Always pays the money he owes and never done nothin' crossways. But these Mexicans,' she shook her head, 'they's some nasty hombres 'cross that border, Jack, so Bobby and me, well, we want to cross with you, get ya set up in your motel. Help you along with whatever business you got there.'

Bobby pulled his .45 out from the waistband of his jeans. 'I got weapons, Jack, plenty of 'em. Why you think those little fuckers don't come 'round here? They know I'd blow they goddamned heads off, is why!'

I downed my coffee and pushed my plate forward, 'I appreciate that, really I do, but I won't be in Nuevo Laredo more than a day then I'm headed south to a place where it's beautiful and safe.'

'From the Mexican police and Federales?'

'From everyone, Bobby. All of them.'

'Fair 'nough then, Jack. Here's yer passport,' Twila said handing it over. 'That'll be $5,000 you owe us, cash.'

I paged through the document:

| | |
|---|---|
| **Name:** | Dempsey, John Harrison |
| **Place of Birth:** | New Jersey, USA |
| **Place of Deliverance:** | Pennsylvania, USA |
| **Date of Expiration:** | 17 Feb 2016 |
| **Authority:** | Philadelphia Passport Agency |

The photo was a bad one taken three years before for my real passport.

'Look close at that signature, Jack,' Bobby instructed. ''cause from this day on it's yours. You need to practice that signature, you hear?'

'Will do,' I told him reaching into the front pocket of my jeans and pulling out ten five hundreds. 'Thanks,' I told them handing it over as I got up to leave.

'Jack?' Twila asked. 'You sure there ain't nothin' we can do for ya 'fore you leave?'

'There is one thing,' I thought to tell her. 'A life vest in my car needs gotten rid of.'

'Is it evidence, Jack?' she asked.

'Yeah, it is.'

'Ain't no problem,' Bobby offered. 'We're fryin' up a turkey tomorrow. I guess a life vest burns as well as any other thing.'

I left the trailer that morning agreeing it was best to

follow them to International Bridge #2 which I'd take across the Rio Grande River into Tamaulipas. Driving the Ford Escape that had taken me halfway across the U.S. and out of danger was almost nostalgic as I followed their Dodge Ram pick-up down San Bernado Avenue. Once we hit the highway with signs a blind man could follow, they honked the truck's horn, waved and I was on my own.

What blew me away as I approached the border were the hundreds of trucks lined up to pass over the three bridges that connected the United States with Central and South America. Fact is, my choice could not have been better: Laredo was the principle port of entry into Mexico and least likely place to attract more than the wave of a hand from the cops at Customs/Immigration. And that's exactly what happened. The wave of a hand, simple as that, and I was in Mexico ready to collect the $2.5 million, escape my pursuers—real or imagined—and begin a new life in Queretaro!

Pulling off the bridge, I took the Escape south onto Carraza then down to Independencia and the Motel Paraiso just a half block from the bank where Johnnie had been wiring money into an account in the name of John H. Dempsey for better than four years. I can't say if it was excitement at having left the U.S. and its obsession with money and Wall Street, lawyers and credit cards, police and a tsunami of debt, or the sheer anticipation of collecting the millions I'd stashed away, but I was nervous. My tongue was thick, my hands sweating as I registered, paying the $35 USD, cash in advance. I used my passport for identification holding the driver's license for backup ID, but the man behind the desk, encased in bulletproof glass, never asked for it and I checked in without complication.

Can you imagine what it felt like turning the key to that motel room and laying down on that bed, Phials? Even though it was just a mattress for one in a cheap motel room reeking with the smell of tobacco, to me it felt like I was on an inflatable raft, frozen margarita in hand, floating in crystal clear waters outside a luxury villa in a place like, what, Monte Carlo? Well, that's what I was thinking and that's how I was feeling. Call it 'top o' the world' because given how smooth everything had gone from the time I left Jersey, with the Blunts, and my jaunt over the border, I didn't want to sleep, couldn't. I wanted to walk that half-block—Motel Paraiso to Banco Nacional de Mexico—get my money and fall asleep that night holding it in my arms until daybreak!

So, content as I was feeling, I willed myself up from that bed, washed my face with cold water, combed my hair, changed into a pair of khaki-colored slacks, Johnston Murphy loafers, black cotton short-sleeved shirt (just to look the part!) and left for the bank.

# Chapter 20

Banco Nacional de Mexico looked to have been constructed in the 1920s—heavy flat granite with the name of the place etched into it, thick glass windows fake gold-rimmed—more like a fort in the middle of a pioneer town on the edge of civilization than a financial institution. And in Nuevo Laredo, and much of Mexico, they needed a fort so prevalent were murders by the drug cartels these days! Of course, Johnnie Eng was into all of it: illegal drugs, counterfeit durable goods, stolen technology. All done for the Chin Chou triad out of Hong Kong, I was thinking as I entered through the bank's oversized doors, passed the island counters stacked with forms and pens chained to the desks, to the station marked "Intendente."

The teller looked up from the handful of cash he was counting and recorded the amount, *'Buen día, ¿en qué puedo ayudarle?'*

*'Hablo solo un poco de español. ¿Hay alguien aquí que hable inglés?'*

*'Yo, Señor,* I speak English.'

I opened my passport and handed it to him, driver's license with it. 'I want to make a withdrawal,' I said.

He studied the documents, nodding slowly as he matched the passport photo to my face, 'This would be a savings account, Señor?'

'Yes.'

'Please fill out this application,' he said sliding a form toward me.

I wrote it up, adding account numbers I can remember to this day, 0078-164-008.

'*Gracias, Señor.*'

I waited.

At first the teller seemed sure about what he was doing, fingers clicking like a master pianist on his keyboard, but then he paused, matching the numbers I'd written against the numbers on the computer screen and gave a disappointed look. Then he entered the account number a second time. Again no luck, I guessed from the expression on his face.

'*Un momento, Señor,*' he said looking at me through the bars of his station, 'Are you certain this is the number, Señor?'

'Yeah.'

'There is no second account?'

'No, that's it. Is there a problem?'

'Let me check with my supervisor.'

With that he walked to the desk behind him, talked with his manager, who glanced over to me, before the two of them marched to the closed door near the vault marked "Presidente," knocked and entered.

I don't mind telling you, there were about seventeen million thoughts bombarding my brain just then. Was it possible the FBI had gotten wind of the account and flagged it for the Mexican police? Had the teller seen something incriminating about the passport the Blunts had sold me? Had someone—Danny Brennan, though I'd hate to think it—ratted me out with the Feds to plea bargain some pending charge against him? Or was it nothing? Was it simply the amount, a $2.5 million withdrawal, had these guys so wound up? I didn't know and couldn't, but I can tell you this. What I didn't expect were the words Senor Luis Morales, broad and overweight, dressed in a white suit, with slicked-back hair, trundled over to tell me.

'I'm very sorry, Mr. Dempsey, but there is no money in this account,' he told me, so gentle it seemed like it was his $2.5 million missing.

'That's impossible!' I stammered. 'That is not fucking possible. Check again!'

He placed his hand on my shoulder, 'We have checked four times, Mr. Dempsey. Now please, come to my office, mi amigo, where we can talk about this most regrettable situation.'

The teller and his manager awaited my reaction which wasn't good, 'Regrettable situation? I showed you my passport. I gave you my ID. I am John Harrison Dempsey and I want my fucking money!' I shouted, my words bouncing off the high stone ceiling and echoing through the building's open lobby.

'*Señor Dempsey, por favor,*' he insisted trying to calm me before I took the hand he kept pawing at my shoulder with and threw it back at him,

'I want my money, Morales, and I want it now!' I raged until the cold, rigid feel of a Colt 9mm submachine gun barrel pointed at my back stopped me dead in my tracks.

'Señor Dempsey, I think it would be best if you came with me.'

Then I shuffled along behind him, the bank guard's machine gun barrel prodding me forward, all six feet and 178 pounds of me wound tight as a rattler ready to strike, 'Where's my money, Morales?' I asked.

'In due time, Senor, in due time' he answered as I repeated the same question over and over again, *'Where's my money, Morales?' 'Where's my money, Morales?'* until I found myself sitting in a leather chair in front of the oversized desk of the Banco Nacional de Mexico's president, flanked by two guards, each holding their Colt 9mm subs to my head. *'Where's my money? Where's my money?'*

'You Americans,' he said lighting up a Cuban cigar. 'Money is all you think about. It's all you live for. And it causes you to do crazy things, *cosas locas,* isn't that so, Señor Dempsey? You come here wanting to what, withdraw your profits from a drug deal? Cocaine? Marijuana? Methamphetamines? Oh, yes,' he said, exhaling a cloud of cigar smoke, 'and then you find that your partners—Mexican or Chinese or Americans—have taken your money and then you go even more crazy. If it's only money that you live for, what can be left when your money is taken? What do you have to lose then? *Nada.*' Enveloped in a cloud of smoke Morales looked like a kind of Indian guru, the Buddha, or maybe just a crooked Mexican banker holding the upper hand on me. *'Nada* is what you think you have and that is what you do have. But you? I think you are going to need to learn a lot of lessons during your stay here in Nuevo Laredo, *lecciones de la vida,*' he nodded, assessing me. 'So here is your first lesson, Senor Dempsey—though I doubt that is your real name—the $2.5 million from that account was withdrawn in a computer transaction last night. Your money, *the* money, was deposited at Asian Financial Trust in Hong Kong in the name of Mr. J. Eng at 11:58 pm. And so the first lesson, *la primera lección,*' "Never Trust Nobody With Your Stolen Money!"'

'You son of a bitch!' I swore about to go over the desktop at him, 'You were in on it!' but before I got to my feet the guard to my left clamped his right arm around my throat from behind, jerked me from my chair, and began dragging me toward a side exit.

'I don't think you are going to like it here, Senor Dempsey. Nuevo Laredo is not a very hospitable town for strangers,' he called out to me, cigar in hand as I twisted and kicked, trying to shove my hand beneath the guard's locked arms to break his hold, understanding that if I didn't these were men who'd kill me and leave my bones bleaching white in the Baja Sur. 'And now I will give you your second lesson, *la segunda lección*, Señor Dempsey.' "Never Come Unarmed Into A Room Full Of Strangers." It is very dangerous, mi amigo. Especially in a town like Nuevo Laredo. What were you thinking? What goes on in the heads of you Americans? *¿Crees que la vida en México es como una película de Clint Eastwood?*'

By the time they had me out the door I managed to compromise the guard's hold to the point where I knew I wouldn't pass out. Right hand twisted through his lock around my neck, I turned my fist sideways to get air as the two guards dragged me into an alley alongside the building where four men waited and threw me to the ground.

'*¡Ahora, él es cosa suya!*' the larger of the two told them, driving the heel of his military boot into my balls.

'Fuck!' I screamed as the two guards reentered the bank and the four men circled around me, taking turns kicking any spot of flesh they could make contact with.

'*¡Gringo hijo de puta!*' they cursed, spitting on me, the only thoughts pounding through my brain focused on simple fucking survival.

Then a strange thing happened. Ever been in a car accident, Phials? Where you're behind the wheel and in that split second before impact everything slows down? Like you can see everything coming together—the little kid chasing the ball, the telephone pole, the other car coming at you—only your body don't have time to react and you sit there watching? Well that's what it was like for me. Time seemed to stretch out before me so that as my mind raced the rest of the world seemed to be operating in slow motion. Knowing I'd be beaten to death lying helpless as I was and with flashing images suddenly rushing into my head of Tiffany, my eight year old; Dad with me as a kid at a ballgame; making love with Tomi; standing before classmates at St. Damian's receiving my Distinguished Alumni award, I summoned every ounce of will I had in me to catch a glimpse of a slow-motioned foot or leg as it kicked me, peeking from out of the ball I had rolled myself into.

Rather than see them as a pack, I focused on one man, not four, waited for my opportunity, and lunged like a jungle animal from my defensive shell at the blur of a boot coming at me. '*I want to live!*' my mind was bellowing, '*I want to live!*' it insisted, desperate, as my fingers and hands clutched at my attacker, knowing I couldn't afford to miss grabbing hold of that foot or ankle or leg and, if I did, understanding this was my one chance to escape and I couldn't afford to stop trying. Finally, I caught hold of one man's pant leg then hopping on my knees like an attack dog pursuing an intruder—*hop-hop, hop-hop*—I held his right thigh in my right hand as I looped my left around his other leg and seized it!

The sudden move caught the Mexicans off-guard with their kicking boots already in motion toward a target that was no longer there. Time stretched out during this briefest of windows like a tsunami rushing onto the shores of my consciousness: random images of prison inmates rioting; Golden Gloves fans crazy with excitement; Jeremiah granting absolution to a penitent during the sacrament of confession; a swimmer struggling against the currents to Barnegat Light collapsing, exhausted, on shore. *Yes!* my brain was screaming, *Yes! Yes! I want to live!!* And it was the confusion of my counter-attack that gave me the half-second I needed to get a firm grip on the man whose legs I held, toppling him to the ground in a heap—helpless now himself—as I threw my chest over his chest to hold him down while I smashed a right fist into his teeth which shattered, the pieces flying back into his mouth, causing him to start choking. 'You motherfucker!' I kept screaming as I continued to beat his face, and the three others, understanding the game had changed, stopped their kicking and tried to tear me off him.

Breaking loose from the blind rage that seized me and coming to my senses once I pummeled the first attacker, I could hear the others scurrying from behind, ready to knock me unconscious with an iron pipe or just shoot me in the back of the head as I fought on the ground. I knew I had to do something quickly. So I shook my torso loose from the clutching hands of at least two of them, rolling to my left to gain a better defensive position and as I did, noticed what felt like a gun pressed up against my hip from below. '*Yes! Yes, it is!!*' my racing brain confirmed in a rush of adrenalin and raw instinct that allowed me to snatch the gun from his belt strap from where I lay, and point it directly above me at the face of the fourth attacker who held a crowbar over his head about to bash my brains in.

Mid-motion the Mexican stopped, recognizing the gun — an old-fashioned Remington six-shooter — and the advantage I had on him as I scurried crab-like away from him and his battered friend who held his broken face in both hands moaning, '¡ *No puedo ver!* I think I am blind!'

The man with the crowbar grinned stupidly, '*Ya nos vamos, nos vamos tranquilos y sin problemas.* We go now. We go nice and easy,' he muttered, then dropped the steel rod into the dust, backed away slowly and ran down the alley into the street, the two others behind him.

'*Motherfucking!*' I blustered in an incomprehensible fury as I pounded the dirt in front of me. '*Fucking . . . fucking . . . motherfuckers!*' I shouted after them.

Then I crawled toward the bleating coward-bastard that tried to kill me, now holding bloody fingers over his smashed-in mouth, nose and eyes. I tore his hands away from the pulverized mess that was his face, pulled his head back by his greasy black hair and shoved the barrel of the .36 into the mush of lips and flesh and teeth that was his mouth.

'*So you want to kill me?*' I screamed at him. '*So you want to steal my fucking money?*'

Muffled sounds, not words, Spanish or English came from him, black eyes bulging like blood-filled balloons, tears streaming down his temples, mixing with the blood like red streams of terror and fear. I could feel his heart pounding like a drum in a death march, smell the stench of fear exuding from his body, the heat of his reeking blood-drenched breath, the sweat like tar oozing out of his filthy carcass.

'*You like this? You like this, the way it feels?*'

Slowly I withdrew the gun barrel from his mouth and slid off him, exhausted.

'*¡Soy católico! ¡No soy un hombre malo!*' he started wailing as he reached beneath his shirt, red now and saturated, to pull out a religious medal. '*¿Ve? ¡Una medalla de la Virgen de Guadalupe! ¡Es de plata! ¡Soy católico!*' He tore it from his neck and handed it to me.

'*I don't want your goddamned medal!*' I said throwing it back at him. '*Get the fuck . . . just get the fuck out of here!*'

Then, more like an animal than a man, he gathered himself onto his haunches, picked up the medal of the Virgin, eyes glued on me, then got to his feet, started running, and never looked back.

# Chapter 21

I felt near to what Japs in WWII must have felt in the seconds before they died after having disemboweled themselves. Emptiness. Like my insides dropped from a gaping hole that once held the organs that enabled my body to function. The adrenalin and the remnants of speed I'd been taking receded like a tide withdrawing as I sat in the dirt of the alley alongside Banco Nacional de Mexico for a few seconds, I guessed, watching in a stupor as pedestrians who'd witnessed my death struggle stared from either side of the narrow passage leading to the street. No shots had been fired and that was a plus, my shattered brain tried to process. Still, Morales and his guards were probably being told the outcome as I sat there and police couldn't be too far behind. *'Have to get up! Have to go now'* the parts of my brain still functioning alerted me like a knock on my front door, *'Hello? Anybody there? Think you were lucky this time? Just hang around and see what happens!' I got it. Message received,* I was thinking as I pulled my seemingly unconnected body parts together to stand.

I positioned my feet and legs under the upper half of my body and straightened them. I could detect blood, salty and dull as the taste of water run through rusted iron pipes in my mouth. I coughed, choked on it, and immediately vomited mouthfuls—a belly full of blood—some fluid, much of it already coagulated. My head throbbed as I stood unsteadily and ambled forward the way a bad impersonator might mimic John Wayne's walk, "All right, Pilgrim, it's about time we took this wagon train west!" I may as well have been saying as I staggered from the alley back to Independencia toward the motel.

Every step along the way, I expected one or more of the cops in patrol cars, whose sirens ripped through the city no more than a block or two from where I stood, to stop and arrest me but that did not happen. Instead, pedestrians, street corner vendors, and businessmen stared and clustered behind me while a solitary patrol car, silent as a shark, followed in the street alongside me, the uniforms inside joking between themselves. It's true, I must have been quite a spectacle, Phials, a gringo wending forward like a drunk on a mission, escorted by a patrol car and team of cops who clearly understood what had gone on and how this situation would be decided. John Dempsey was going to leave Nuevo Laredo the same way he got there that day. Over the bridge and back to the United States sans $2.5 million. He was going to like it, or he was going to die. There was no mistaking the message. I'd received it loud and clear.

By the time I got to the Paraiso, I realized I was lucky to have made it at all. Christ knew what Johnnie Eng's goons—from bank manager to president, hired thugs to local cops—would have done if I'd collapsed before that. Maybe called an ambulance and OD'd me along the way. Perhaps left me lying in the street, prey for a blood-thirsty gang who'd slit my throat after they'd picked me clean. No matter. Once I was back in my motel room, convinced those bastards had fractured three of my ribs, I swallowed four tabs of Percocet dry, then dug into my wallet and pulled out a scrap of paper with a phone number penciled on it. With more effort than you or anyone could imagine, I sat on the side of the bed, Phials, picked up the telephone receiver and dialed an international call.

'Yeah,' a voice answered.

'Li?'

'Who this?'

'Madson,' I uttered.

There was a pause.

'Ja-aa-ck! Nice to hear from you, but ain't you dead?'

'Only halfway,' I answered.

'Why you call me, Jack? Johnnie Eng double-cross you, eh?'

'Something like that.'

'I tell you he no good,' Wei Li laughed. 'Maybe we do business now?'

'I can get you bio-tech. Self-generating cell creation: Alzheimer's, heart attack, regeneration of certain internal organs. Company named AvaTech, but I need cash now—$250K up front, another five mil on delivery.'

'One hundred now, rest when you turn it over,' he snapped back. 'I send Fed Express.'

'Today?'

'Today.'

'I'm staying at . . . '

'We know where you staying, Jack,' Wei Li interrupted. 'Cops won't find you because they not looking. But *we* will, Jack. We give you money. You give us product. If not, we finish what motherfucker Eng start,' he vowed, then hung up the phone, leaving me sitting on the side of the bed, head aching with ribs hurting like they'd just been worked over by Sonny Liston.

I shoved the receiver back into its cradle. The dead man I was had been resurrected. Like it or not, I was headed back to the United States and all that went with it.

# Chapter 22

Some strange predicament I found myself locked into, I thought, burying my battered face into my hands as I sat on the side of the bed. Already my head was losing the outer wrappings of the morning's amphetamine fix as the first snake or two of sedation wound its way through my brain. The combination of drugs, exhaustion, and physical pain had me craving a drink even as I felt something like a drawstring pulling around my throat. I could feel my hands shaking around the purplish bruises around my eyes and knot the size of a lemon on the side of my head, but it was the pain in my ribs and diaphragm that had me sweating like a swamp rat. I tried to breathe thin and shallow but with each breath came the kind of mind-bending anguish that nothing short of morphine could relieve.

I picked up the phone wondering in thoughts flat as the desert terrain around me whether the son-of-a-bitch at the front desk spoke English. It was a woman answered.

'¿Habla inglés?'

'Sí, un poco.'

'Dos cosas,' I told her. 'Quiero tequila ahora.'

'Sí.'

'También, un paquete viene mañana Federal Express. Traiga a mi habitación pronto, ¿comprende?'

'*Muy bien, señor.* I send boy with tequila now.'

'*Gracias*,' I muttered, slapping the receiver into its cradle and rolling flat onto the bed, arms and legs spread out over the mattress like a man crucified.

I didn't regret calling Wei Li because I knew I'd come to a dead end. With less than three thousand dollars, a Remington six-gun, and a passport to my name, any plans I once had were smashed, run over by a steam roller! But now wasn't the time for self-pity. Shit, I could spend the next forty-eight hours going over all the crap that had gone wrong. My money stolen! My new life crushed! Left rolling in the dirt, beaten like a dog by those motherfuckers!

Again, I felt that drawstring tighten and a sob crept out of me. It was that same dread of old, oozing from the depths of my former life come knocking at my door, and if I let it take hold, I knew I was done for. I had to get myself under control. That was obvious. Come up with a plan. And maybe my first cut with Wei Li—driven by desperation, admittedly—was the right cut. Once the cash arrived I'd head back over the border. Depressing as that giant step into the past would be, at least I had a passport to take me over the border and the Blunts to heal me up and send me on my way, *but then what?*

Of course I was lying through my teeth when I promised Li the AvaTech studies but maybe, just maybe, there was a way to get back to the U.S., assess my situation with the cops and you, Phials, put a strategy together, and actually come out of the chasm I'd plunged into to collect the $5 million. It was an audacious notion that would take an audacious plan, but why couldn't I do it? When had anything ever been easy for me? In the boxing ring with Kareem Brown? At NuGeneration as the only VP without an MBA, law degree, or even a college diploma? No, I knew how to hang in there for the long haul—it was my MO. Hell, it took me twenty years to pay off the college and other loans that kept my father in his house until he passed! And even in business, wasn't I "Jack 'The Magician,'" the go-to guy when negotiations got rough?

Laying on the bed, head spinning as I stared at the ceiling, I remembered a paper I'd written for *CEO* magazine two years into my career at NuGen, back when I actually believed there was something 'noble' about what we were doing. It was called "Business Resourcefulness and the Criminal Mind." There was always something in me that loved taking chances and it was a risky premise even before the "Puritans," as Corky called them, were ushered in post-financial meltdown by the government Regulatory Commission. But I wrote it, NuGen supported it, and *CEO* magazine made it their cover story. I still remembered it or at least could paraphrase much of what I'd written.

'What is the quality that differentiates an average-performing middle manager from a superstar?' the article asked. 'Some would point to education, but there are thousands among the mediocre with degrees from the finest universities in America. Others would point to intelligence, but there are few CEOs unfamiliar with the "brilliant idiot" who knows all of the facts and statistics but is without the common sense to use any of his "bright" ideas effectively.

'No, it is not to our Ivy League colleges that CEOs must look to for those rare and gifted individuals capable of leading their business to the pinnacle of financial success. The reason is that the kind of success they are looking for cannot be ingrained by education, or even experience, from the *outside in*. Rather, it must come from the *inside out* with a basic survival skill—RESOURCEFULNESS, the most underrated characteristic of all!

'True, examples of this most rarefied skill can be found in the NFL quarterback who, with the clock ticking to its final moments, throws the game-winning pass; the slugger who, with the team down by three runs in the ninth inning and bases loaded, comes through with the grand slam home run; or the CEO, who pressed by his Board of Directors for a critical success, decides correctly to bet the farm on a new technology that saves the day!

'But these are games played for entertainment or the civilized business environment we all work in today,' the article argued. 'If the pass is dropped, no one is arrested. If the slugger strikes out, he is not deprived of an arm or a leg. If the CEO's decision is the wrong one, he is not executed. And so, we will examine the most poignant examples of RESOURCEFULNESS by studying men outside both the law and society. We will examine the inner workings of the minds of America's most notorious outlaws—Jesse James to John Dillinger—to better understand how they survived for decades against all odds using the ultimate form of resourcefulness, "criminal intelligence," their apparent ability to see a way out of situations that for the average human being would be impossible!'

That was the gist of the article, I remembered looking back almost fondly on those days of piss and vinegar and hope, as a knock sounded on my door. I forced myself up from the bed like a man in his nineties and took the bottle of tequila from the Mexican kid that stood there tipping him with money I'd probably be needing sometime soon, then opened the bottle and took a long gulp.

In my article I analyzed John Dillinger's most daring exploits, I remembered, focusing not so much on his crimes as his escapes from capture against all odds: from a jail in Lima, Ohio guarded 24/7; from the Little Bohemia Lodge in Wisconsin surrounded by G-Man Melvin Purvis and his crack Dillinger Squad; and Public Enemy #1's most ingenious break-out: using a wooden pistol to cow guards, steal two Thompson sub-machine guns, then drive past scores of National Guardsmen in the Sheriff's brand new Briggs and Stratton Flyer as he made his escape.

Jesse James in making his getaway from his failed robbery at The First National Bank in Northfield, Minnesota, and Billy the Kid's escape from the Lincoln County jail, manacled hand and foot, were other examples. Like Dillinger, each—when confronted with insurmountable odds that most would have never taken or been checkmated by—called upon that rarest of qualities that only the boldest men possess. *Fubria* is what Mafia Boss of Bosses Carlo Gambino called it, 'the natural criminal intelligence that permeates a man's being: the way he walks, he talks, his charm, his cunning, the depth of the resourcefulness he taps into in times of challenge.'

Of course, I took great pains to explain that my argument was no attempt to glorify these criminals—the Kid, Jesse, or Dillinger—or to advocate anything but the highest ethical standards for American business. But with a nod and a wink Corky, and senior execs all across Wall Street, wondered over martinis at Alfie's, The Palm, and Delmonico's, 'Wasn't it interesting to speculate that via background, life experience, or simple genetics, the instinct for survival and therefore business success somehow resided deep in the inner recesses of the mind, spirit, or DNA of certain individuals. More, wouldn't it be really cool if CEOs could *somehow identify them!*'

Well, that was the article I wrote, my weary, thumping brain recollected as I downed the last of the pint bottle of tequila, meandering like Dorothy through the cottony opium fields on my way back north to find the Wizard of Oz . . . Or was it Tomi and the five million bucks Li had pledged for the AvaTech formulations I was looking for?

I wondered.

# Chapter 23

That night I slept black velvet deep. Like somebody had pulled the fucking plug. My body was out but my mind prowled landscapes I never imagined possible. I wasn't scared. No, I was in control, standing on a beach watching, and seeing what others could not. Those around me—tanning on beach blankets, playing net games, building sand castles at the water's edge—were doing what you'd expect them to do on a summer beach day. But my eyes were not on them. Instead, they were riveted on the ocean and a series of waves flocked together like gulls set deep out at sea and building on the horizon.

I tried to make light of what I was seeing to a group of teens horsing around next to me but realized they couldn't see or hear me. I was a ghost, backing up steadily from the shoreline, careful to notice that each time I moved away the waves crept up along with me. Bigger waves, until I left the beach entirely. But when I turned back, instead of seeing the wooden planks of the boardwalk, there were arches. High, tall, stone arches like from Roman times. Like from the ruins of a coliseum or giant arena. And the waves, huge now (one hundred-fifty feet high!) came towering over those arches, running that freezing cold ocean water over my feet and ankles.

And then I ran . . . fast as I could . . . finally looking back

to see how much larger the tsunami-like waves had grown
and if I had a chance of escaping. But then I wasn't in the
street running anymore. I was on an esplanade leading
to a large government building made of stone with Doric
columns from what I guessed was ancient Rome, or maybe
Greece. Stolid, upright, in disuse for what I imagined to
be centuries, it stood with the awe-inspiring stillness of a
pyramid. And the oncoming waves ran up that esplanade.
Over my feet and ankles, way up to the huge entranceway
of the building.

The rushing water was white and foamy as I shifted
my feet struggling to stay upright. And that's when to my
horror, I noticed what washed up with each one of them.
*Alligators!* I know it sounds crazy but that's what they were.
Not long and serpentine. No, they were something like two
feet in length. And know what else, Phials? *They were white.*
Albino alligators! I could feel them nipping at me. At my
legs and thighs, my ankles, toes and arms. And with every
wave—roaring up and pulling me back again—there
were more of them stranded on that train of stone stairs
beneath the building's columns and entranceway, until I
had to start pulling them off me! Relentlessly attacking
with their razor-sharp teeth. Biting, ripping! Ripping,
biting! And that's when I woke up breathless, a cold sweat
matting my face and chest. Flailing at the gray U-shaped
mattress as if it was alive and those creatures were all
around me!

I wouldn't be lying if I told you it took me several
minutes to get a grip on myself. Sitting on the edge of
the bed, bare feet pressing flat against the cold tile floor.
But what did it all mean? What would a fortune telling
gypsy or Madison Avenue shrink have to say about the

Twilight Zone rollercoaster ride I'd just taken? The fall of Western civilization? A grim reminder of the '09 financial meltdown? Or simple Freudian blowback from the manic frustration of the past four days and nights?

Whatever the cause I knew it was time to do some hard thinking. I took a handful of Metadate caps casting a woeful glance at last night's empty tequila bottle, then washed them down with a gulp of water. *Think! Think!!* I told myself, a shock of pain reminding me of my three cracked ribs, battered face and legs. My last thoughts before passing out ten hours earlier were of what? Jesse James, wasn't it? Dillinger, William Bonnie, and my *CEO* article on 'criminal intelligence . . . And what else? What was it came out of those Percocet-booze induced mental ramblings? Then, like the six-shooter bulging from the Mexican's belt for me to pull and save myself, the underpinnings of my exit strategy out of this border town shithole and into the arms of my $5 million were there for me to discover!

It was Tomi Fabri I had on my mind before taking that jaunt through Crazyville and with goddamned good reason. Who else could I trust once my package from Wei Li showed up? Sure Twila and Bobby might do as a jumping-off point but both were crazy as loons. And how did I know they weren't part of Johnnie Eng's plan to smoke me all along? Eng! Now there was a star spangled scumbag! Set me up. Stole my money. Then tried to have me killed! *Who was going to miss a guy already missing?* he must have reasoned. *Who was going to solve the murder of a man already thought to be dead?*

No, it was Tomi I needed. At least in the short run, I concluded, getting up off the side of the bed—sweat soaked T-shirt still sticking to my skin—and pacing like a caged panther up and down the motel room floor. Yeah, I'd use the Blunts for a stopover, but for no more than a day. There, I had access to Twila's iPad and the internet to book my flight to Detroit, then rent a car to make my way to Ann Arbor. The gun? I wondered, eyes shifting to the Remington resting on the night table next to the phone. That I'd take with me. After all, a six-shooter was a collector's antique and if anyone knew how to get it onboard a plane it was sure as hell Bobby.

So there I was in Ann Arbor, I tried to visualize still pacing the room, with $100K in cash, a working weapon, and a black mistress half my age who is—let me get this right: *Confused*, 'Jack, what are *you* doing here?' *Happy*, 'My God, you're still alive!' *Pensive*, 'So, what really *did* happen?' *Pissed-off*, 'Why the hell didn't you tell me you were doing this?! Do you know how much I worried!? How depressed thinking you were dead made me??'

All of this to be expected, I conceded, but, clever boy that I am, there was an explanation. 'Tomi, baby, I knew the cops'd be here asking questions. I knew they'd find us out—detectives, insurance investigators, maybe even the FBI—and I figured if you didn't know, no one would suspect you were in on it. That it was you I intended to come back for, so we could start a new life together!' Hmmm, I thought, stopping to take a swig of bottled water, visualizing like in a movie how I would look talking and how she would look hearing it. 'Of course, I kept it all to myself, buried deep inside, and it wasn't easy: the mental anguish, the danger, risking my life like I did! See, I never wanted to put you through any of that, follow? Not until that was behind me and this . . . new opportunity came up. *Tomi, I did it for you!*'

Guess that took care of Tomi, I concluded, but Tomi Fabri wasn't all I had to sort through to figure out how what I was thinking could fit together. How The Eagle might land, so to speak, safe and intact back on U.S. soil to exploit the new opportunity Wei Li came up with.

Up front I realized I couldn't flash-drive AvaTech's research files from Michigan so I'd have to leave for New York once I got Tomi on board with the idea. Once there, I'd have to find a way to gain access to Lisa Ellison's office in 9 West and her computer where the formulas resided. True, I was no high-tech computer geek like many at NuGen, but I knew my way around the company's firewalls and security blocks. More importantly, I knew Lisa: the way she lived, how she thought, what steps she'd have taken to secure the documents. Passwords? No need for those, I reasoned, over the past five years I'd mastered the art of glomming onto new identities wholesale to tap into the expense accounts of NuGen execs and 'casualties of war' from the dozens of other companies we'd acquired then gutted. No, none of it would be easy, but it wasn't impossible, either. So says, 'Jack the Magician,' I pondered, nodding slowly, a smile suddenly passing over my lips.

With the Metadate kicking in big time, I felt like writing it all down, my plan to snatch 'victory from the jaws of defeat,' like Corky used to say, but before I could do it I heard a knock at the door. It was the little boy who'd fetched me my booze the night before.

I smiled. He was already smiling, '*Aquí está su paquete, señor.*'

'*Gracias,*' I told him taking hold of the Fed Ex mailer, but the kid just stood there smiling. '*Para usted,*' I apologized reaching into my pocket for a five peso note.

'*Gracias, señor Enigma,*' he blurted running off as I closed the door behind me, then sat down at the tiny desk with a mirror before it and ripped open its wrappings.

The size of, say, a coffee table book, inside was the cash—all $100 and $500 dollar bills bound in stacks 3 inches high—with a white jewelry box tucked off to the side. I let out a long shriek at the sight of it and then a high pitched laugh that must have rumbled the rafters of hell (my fucking salvation!), flicking through the stacks with my fingers the way a Vegas dealer would play with decks of cards, smelling the money, rubbing the crisp new bills over my face and eyes and hair, kissing it in something not far from sexual ecstasy. *Money . . . Money . . . Money!!*

Then, with the orgy waning but—swear to Christ, Phials, with a hard-on like the Empire State Building—I took the long, white jewelry box into my hands, curious now to see what other pleasures came courtesy of Mr. Li. Unlike the larger box, bound up as it was, the lid to this one opened easy. And like a little kid opening a present on Christmas morning I removed it only to recoil at the smell, and then gag at the sight of what lay atop the white cotton packing.

It was Johnnie Eng's diamond-studded pinky ring. Problem was his finger—black and swarming with maggots—was still in it.

# Chapter 24

It didn't take long before I was out of the Paraiso and in the Escape on my way back north. There wasn't much for me to pack, just the money. I sure as hell wasn't taking Eng's rotted finger along, though I did—with great pains—take the ring off and put it in my pocket before flushing the pinky down the toilet.

There was no question in my mind that Johnnie was iced by Wei Li. That was how the Triads operate. Zero tolerance for exposure. Meaning Li hated Johnnie's guts anyway and with me still alive, killing Eng not only took out one of his competitors but showed good faith for our AvaTech arrangement by disposing of one of my enemies. All of this loaded with symbolism for the higher-ups in the Chink syndicate. They thrive on crap like that. The more complex the better!

Still, I knew I shouldn't feel too bad about what happened to Johnnie, though somehow I did. Eng had fucked me big time (did his best to have me murdered!) but I'd known him for five years and actually took a liking to his Chinese hipster image, wild gambling sprees, and the fast women who hung around him. It was Johnnie who first came to me about selling technology through the Chin Chou at a bar in Macau. I was there on a gambling junket. He said he'd gotten hold of my name from a mutual acquaintance (though he wouldn't say who), checked me out on Linked-In, and later through a private detective. I'd be amazed to know who was already involved with the Chin Chou, he told me, 'government think tanks, corporate CEOs. Hell, five or six members of Congress!' So, desperate as I was for money and figuring everybody these days was fucking everyone else whether on Wall Street, Main Street or in Government, I started farming out files, some by overnight courier, others on flash drives over e-mail accounts I set up under phony names.

Johnnie and I only met in person three or four times after that. There was really no need for face-to-face meetings once things got underway. And, man, did they! He sent me cash at first. More than I knew what to do with! Chinks like cash because most of it comes from their interests in the heroin trade, so bribes and pay-offs were an easy way to get rid of it. Millions, if not billions, of dollars, Johnnie told me. It was only later—after I'd gained his trust—that he came up with the idea of money transfers into the account of John H. Dempsey and a Mexican bank. Well, I got to hand it to you, got me on that one, Johnnie! But know what? You're dead now and I'm still living, though—Christ knows—something deep inside me wishes you hadn't crossed me and you weren't dead.

I'm not going to bore you with the details of my trip back into the U.S. except for a couple of items that might be of interest. First, I passed through Customs and Immigration over Bridge #2 and the Rio Grande River like the natural-born American I am. This time, however, they took a peek at my passport and I'm pleased to report Twila and Bobby put out a quality product. The agent ran it through his screening device and it passed with flying colors!

From there I headed straight for the Blunts' place, still feeling less than perfect, and wondering if they were in on Johnnie's plan to kill me. They didn't seem unduly surprised at my visit, patched me up, and sent me on my way. But not before I booked my flight to Detroit on Southwest Airlines and Bobby gave me a hard box case for the Remington so I could transport it on board. While there I also searched the internet for follow-up reports on how the cops, Coast Guard, and Surety Insurance were handling the riddle of my disappearance/drowning. And I wasn't disappointed.

One thing about guys like the Judge is while they're about the biggest assholes you're ever going to come across in life, they got where they are by grabbing hold of something and never letting go. Well, turns out Barton Crowley wanted that $4.5 million for his daughter, Jennifer, in the worst way imaginable and went out and had a funeral not a week after I turned up missing: closed casket, no body, of course, but with all the hysterics and regalia of a full-blown Catholic ceremony. Archbishop Salvatore Fazio from New York was even there! More to the point, Crowley was already petitioning the cops in LBI, along with the New Jersey courts, to have my status switched from "missing" to "deceased" with the normal seven year waiting period waived so Surety would pay the $4.5 million "forthwith and without delay."

Nice for Jen and Tiffany, but also good for me. There was a very real win for me if the Madson claim was settled—*if* it was settled—because outside of the local police and Coast Guard, who both seemed happy to get the case behind them, there was still you, Phials. And, yeah, I got caught up on your investigation through articles in the *New York Times* and *The Star Ledger*. Busy boy, you! Theories abound, but it seemed like you were stuck on the notion of suicide.

Odd, how wrong you were in your conclusion but how right in piecing together your argument for why it was not an 'accidental' death. Accidental meant Surety would be paying $4.5million. Suicide, well, we know about that from Granger Industries, don't we, Phials? In the case of suicide Surety was off the hook and wouldn't have to pay dollar one, but the logic behind the case you were building? Well, props to you, Old Boy, because whether you know it or not, you were hot on my trail.

From what I could tell, you picked up on the fact that there was one life vest in my Tanzer and none in the Soto's dinghy. You also must have gotten into the desktop computer I used at the Judge's compound because you knew I'd been checking the Coast Guard weather reports regular for most of that morning. My debt was a matter of public record. So was the fact I'd been drinking more than my fair share over the past several months. Maybe you got hold of that fisherman from Callahan's Bar to interrogate him about the drownings at Barnegat we discussed week before in Surf City over drinks.

But more than any of that, early along you picked up on my relationship with Tomi Fabri and though she wasn't about to corroborate anything you were selling about 'depression' or 'suicidal tendencies,' you never caught on to what was in front of your nose. Tomi and me and the meaning of our relationship. I wanted to escape, not only the debt and my work at NuGen. I wanted to escape Jennifer and her father. That, Phials, *that* should have been your greatest clue: I didn't want to die. After forty-three years of existence, *I wanted to live!*

So, okay, you came up with your suicide theory. You weren't quite there yet, but headed in the right direction except you didn't know two things I counted on all along. One, I'm smarter than you think and put a plan together that could survive my tumble overboard that day and police scrutiny afterward. Two, I understood how this society of ours operates and that the Judge still wielded a ton of power among the country club mucky mucks who called the shots in the justice system. I knew all along they'd never allow a ruling of suicide if only to protect the Crowley name, and get his daughter that money. Greed, Phials! Never underestimate its power among the non Puritans!

It is their Holy Grail. What they live for. Like in a game where the score is kept in dollars and to them that game *is* their life!

So now you're probably wondering what it was like for me to hook up again with Tomi Fabri in Ann Arbor. Well, let me tell you—since you'll appreciate this—it was crazy-wild for reasons you couldn't possibly imagine because it was there that I got to observe you up close and personal. That's right, that day in her apartment! And I'll bet that even today you don't know this. I was *watching*, Phials. Watching to see what you had on me up to that point, and just what made a man like you tick.

# Chapter 25

T hough my body still felt like it was on the rack in some medieval dungeon with Jen's father overseeing my religious conversion, it made me feel fucking-ay breezy when that Southwest 737 hit the tarmac in Detroit. Now don't get me wrong. Detroit's got to be — along with St. Louis, Toledo, and Akron — one of the most depressing cities outside of Calcutta, pillaged of jobs and industry as it has been over the past two decades. But it was the fact that I made it back home to the U.S. in one piece and was on my way to seeing Tomi Fabri that made my day.

Later, driving Detroit to Ann Arbor in a rented Ford Fusion (I left the Escape with the Blunts as payment for their help) I made it a point to go over my plan to get back East and what I'd do once I got there. *The Solow Building, 9 West 57th Street.* I tried to visualize the building: its entrance, its lobby, its fifty floors in my mind's eye much like a mountain climber might visualize Everest or a great fighter like, say, Duran or Pacquiao imagine themselves, hands raised in victory often enough so that it became fact, not fantasy. Like the only thing that stood between seeing it in my head and actually *doing* it was time, and all I had to do was show up.

I went through the exercise not just with the building but with the 47th, 48th, and 50th floors NuGen occupied, my old office, Corky's, and finally Lisa's, along with everything that was in it: desk, overhead fluorescent lights, photos of her father and mother Pat and Mike, now deceased, the books on her bookshelf—Jim Collin's *Good to Great,* Joel Osteen, *Your Best Life Now,* Jack Welsh's *Winning!*—and finally the Dell desktop with folders on 'Acquisition Candidates,' 'Acquired Companies' and 'Deals in Progress' such as the AvaTech IPO.

Within each of these were more specific files: 'Financials,' 'Legal,' 'Manufacturing Facilities,' 'Safety-Health-Environmental' (SHE) and, of most interest to me, 'Intellectual Property' (IP). Digging still deeper there resided the most valuable information of all and that was 'U.S. Government Issued Patents.' I knew from a meeting Corky held monthly with his Executive Committee (ExCo) that the formulas and back-up studies for AvaTech's 'human cell regeneration' (HCR) project was code-named **Genesis Too**, a name chosen by Nolan in finance after his favorite restaurant the Palm Too on 2nd Avenue. I also knew AvaTech was called **Novelis** (named after I don't know what!) to keep news of the IPO from NuGen employees outside of ExCo, so once I hacked into Lisa's computer the information I needed was there for the taking.

Clearly there were logistical problems just getting through security at 9 West now that I was presumed dead and no longer an employee, not to mention the time constraints I'd be up against, dodging the platoon of rent-a-cops paid to roam its corridors at night while I was navigating the firewalls and McAfee security blocks IT had installed to protect our desktops. But what they didn't know was I'd broken through those barriers to entry four years earlier with one simple insight: it was all about the person. The computer, itself, was a machine. It didn't know John Madson from Abe Lincoln or Lincoln from Jack the Ripper, but responded to the facts and bits of personal information only they supposedly knew: social security number, mother's maiden name, best friend in high school, favorite hobby, you know the routine better than me, Phials. And Lisa? Well, I had Lisa's life story down cold!

These were some of the thoughts that went through my mind that day, sluggish as glaciers and as dense in their gravity. When Bob Weir sang "what a long strange trip it's been" in the Dead's song *Truckin'* he could have been describing my existence I was thinking as I headed down Rt. 94 South on toward Ann Arbor because—Christ knows—it had been a strange fucking trip!

Oh, and just for the record, Phials. There's something else I want to explain, since by now I'm sure you got me pegged as some kind of rabid animal. You know that "Most Distinguished Alumni" award they gave me from St. Damian's? I know it was nine-tenths bullshit. And sure, it wasn't like there were five hundred candidates available to get it. But outside of that, outside the bullshit, there was something Tomasz Adamek, a Polish immigrant everybody picked on back then,walked up to the podium set up in the cafeteria that night and said.

Still a frail man with horn-rimmed glasses and short blonde hair combed like he just got out of bed, Tomasz stood up there at the podium nervous and fidgety. Then, stammering like it must have half-killed him to be talking to the seventy former classmates and priests who pretty much tormented him for four years, he said 'I know John Madson. You say you know him because you spent time with him in high school at football games, boxing matches, dances with girls, and bars drinking. I don't know him from those places because I was never there. But John Madson helped me when people here used to beat me up and make fun of where I came from. Back then,' he said collecting himself, 'nobody liked me, not even the priests. But John took me out to a bar with him. He bought me the first Pabst Blue Ribbon beer I ever had and told me "Tommy, you're okay. If anyone ever tries to hurt you, you let me know and I'll make them wish they hadn't." Back then I was always depressed and one morning I stayed home from school. I said I was sick so when parents left for work I could kill myself. But when I tried to hang myself my sister came back for a book she'd left behind and I decided not to do it. That day when I went to my locker, John Madson saw me and said "Tommy, you look sad. Come out with me after school today and I'll buy you a Pabst Blue Ribbon." Today I'm a chemist at 3M Corporation in Minnesota and, as you can see, I'm alive and well. That is why I flew back here to St. Damian's. That's why I came all this way. To tell this story and let you know that John Madson is the finest man I ever met.'

So that was what he said and guess what, Phials? That night in the cafeteria of my old high school when I got up to take that award I said to myself 'Fuck! Know what, I deserve this goddamned trophy!' Not for being a "success" in business. Shit, anyone can fire a bunch of people and steal the value others worked generations to create. But this guy, Tomasz. I'd forgotten that ever happened. Totally. And that's when I told myself 'You know, Jackie Boy, you are a fucking prince of a guy. You saved that poor bastard's life! So fuck all the rest of these people: the football bullies, the smart-assed class clowns, the guys bragging about getting in the pants of some love-starved Catholic girls from Sacred Heart Academy, and the monks able to "relate" to their students by making poor Tomasz the butt of their jokes.' It was me, Phials, who got that 'Most Distinguished' award and that's fucking why, get it? I was the only one ever took pity on that poor son-of-a-bitch and kept him from hanging himself!

Well, anyway, by the time I turned off Rt. 94, went past U of M stadium and parked in front of the South Fourth Street highrise where Tomi resided, I'd pretty much gotten all that out of my system and was ready to take my medicine for running out on her like I did. But just to be sure I took two Adderall tabs from out of my briefcase and swallowed them dry.

It was off to the races. I was about to see my 'Baby Luv,' Tomi Fabri.

# Chapter 26

If there was any lesson a man with a little experience with women should know, it's never to come calling at the door of a single lady unannounced. Especially one as comely as Tomi and who worked at an escort service like Head2Toe. Nevertheless, there I was standing in front of 7F, her seventh floor apartment dressed in jeans and a *N.Y. Giants* sweatshirt, feeling about attractive as an old gink in the Bowery with two black eyes and slits in his sneakers.

Summoning my courage I knocked and through the peep hole could see Tomi behind the door looking to see who might be a-callin' late morning on a Wednesday. My heart stopped as I held my breath then skipped a beat as I heard the door unlock then open.

'Jack?' she wondered out loud staring at me the way a schizoid must look at his first hallucination.

'Yeah, Tomi, it's me. I can't stay out here in the hallway. You need to let me in.'

Then she stood to the side and let me pass like the ghost she believed she'd imagined. Funny, but you'd think she'd be staring at me given the circumstances but it was reversed. Tomi stood still as a statue peering out into the empty hallway for a long moment, then closed the door as she turned slowly toward me, but it was me who studied her. Apparently just back from an all night outing with one of her clients, she wore a black sequined dress with hair up the way I liked it, one high-heel shoe on and one off, and drop-dead sexy as she gaped at me in shock and amazement.

'Did I get something wrong here, or aren't you supposed to be dead?'

'I'm not dead,' I said softly, approaching her and taking her into my arms. 'I am very much alive.'

And beyond the embrace I gave, her melting into my arms in something best described as 'splendor,' there was the matter of the erection I was suddenly sporting that pressed against the soft flesh of her abdomen. Blending, like me, into the moment, a spark of reality must have jarred her because she suddenly pushed me back, then held me at arms' length staring, eyes flinty with the wizened intelligence of a woman who'd been around and knew men all too well.

'So what's the deal, baby? Where the hell have you been?'

'It's a long story. Short answer is Mexico. Long one . . . '

I can't say exactly what happened just then but the room went blurry before my eyes, my knees went out from under me, and I fell forward, literally, into her arms.

*'Jesus, Jack!'* Tomi worried, hobbling with one high-heel on, the other off, as she helped me into bedroom and onto the DUX four-post bed.

I fell into it then, reflexively, tried to sit up but Tomi wouldn't hear of it.

'Now you just lay there,' she soothed, stroking my flushed face with her palm. 'Don't try to get up. I'm going to get you a glass of water.' She did. And I drank from the glass she held to my lips. 'Now what kind of pills you been takin'?' she asked.

'Nothing special. Speed. No booze. Not yet this morning. I think I'm just . . . spent.'

'And beat up,' she added, touching the gash on my forehead with her fingertips, looking soulfully at every scrape and bruise and cut like they were graffiti scrawled by vandals on a work of art she loved dearly. There was in her strokes and in her voice a kind of tenderness. 'Should I call a doctor, Jack? You look like hell, you know.'

'If I were bad off as you think, how could I have a hard-on so healthy?'

She smiled, still stroking, 'Sometime I think you'll have a hard-on in the casket at your funeral, Baby, so that don't mean nothin' to me. I need to know, you're all right.'

'And where I've been? And why I'm still alive?'

'No, Baby. I take you as you are, I'm just happy to see you. Now, come let me take your clothes off so you can get some sleep. We can do all the talkin' you like after that.'

Then she began unbuttoning my shirt, methodically, paying careful attention to each button like, to her, it really meant something.

'Tomi,' I said. She stopped unbuttoning and looked up to me. 'Thank you.'

'Now you can just close your eyes,' she smiled getting back to my undressing, 'while I take care of your other problem.'

I did as she told me and she did what she'd promised. Once I lay there naked, gentle as velvet I could feel her mouth envelop the head of my cock and then my balls, one at a time, until hard and ready as any man ever had been for a woman, she sat up then hiked her left leg over my torso. Eyes closed I could almost see the satisfaction light her face as she slid down, worked me inside her satiny wetness, and then rode me—gentle at first, then hard, and harder still—until we climaxed simultaneously and she slowly lifted that same leg up and over me.

'Now you go to sleep, baby. Ain't nobody gonna bother you here.'

# Chapter 27

From late morning to what seemed like early evening I must have been dead to the world. When I awoke, Tomi was sitting in a cushioned chair wearing a terry cloth robe smoking a Merit Ultra Light.

'Wow I must have really konked out. What time is it?'

She shrugged, taking a drag from her cigarette. 'Supper time. Seven o'clock, maybe. How you feelin'?'

I stretched, 'Not bad. I'm sure I look worse than I feel.'

Tomi half-laughed, 'You look fine to me, Sugar.'

My hand reached down to the bed frame as I sat up, ready to dress, and caught hold of a bolt with a stainless steel ring attached. My eyes darted to the bed's opposite side then down to where a pair of others just like them had been riveted.

'Learned some new tricks since I saw you last?'

Tomi didn't answer.

'Client?'

'I don't allow no clients into my home, Jack.'

'Ericka?'

'No,' she said taking a nervous puff from her Merit Ultra Light. 'She left me for a man.'

'Miss her?'

'Not anymore,' she said looking at me eyes glittering.

'Who then?'

'Nobody you need to know about.'

'A "he" or a "she"?'

'What's that got to do with it? You can't really be the one asking me questions, after all the worry you put me through!'

'No, I can't. I'm sorry. It's just that I missed you a lot and was hoping we still might have something between us.'

'What are you tryin' to tell me, Jack? You miss my lovin.' Well I missed yours too, but I know there's never gonna be more than that between us, is there?'

'Maybe I'm not so far away from all of that as you think. There's no Jennifer anymore, no Tiffany, not much of anything, really, except one last chance I have. This last one—the one in Mexico? I was supposed to come away a 'dead' man, get rich on a business deal, and start a new life but that didn't happen. Most believe I'm dead, but I'm sure as hell not rich, and until I get the money, I don't suppose I'm free, either.'

'What is it you're running from, Jack?'

'I don't know,' I confessed. 'America. Maybe myself. I just know I've got to start over. Do my life right this time. Away from the pressure. Away from the corruption and the feeling I'm worth less than nothing.'

Tomi strolled over to a portable bar she had set up in the alcove, poured two glasses of scotch and handed one over.

'Here, take this,' she said still listening to what promised to be a long night's conversation. 'I know we're just friends, Jack. You told me that and I believe you, but I want to help you. When I needed help—financially—you were there for me. So tell me. Just say the word, baby, and I'm yours. I'll do whatever you want.'

I took a long pull of scotch and it went down like something more than booze. More like a potion or elixir and, Christ Almighty, the feel of that liquor, smooth and crisp as it was going down, seemed to awaken every nerve-end in my body starting with my throat and brain straight down to my lower regions.

'*Jesus, I missed you, Tomi!*'

She put her bare arm around my neck and pecked me gently on the forehead near the wound that was still healing, but before I could say what I wanted, that I could never love her because of the way I was, who I was, the life I was living, a rap came at the door — *bam, bam, bam* — followed by three others each as aggressive.

'Who the hell is that?' I wondered aloud.

'Don't know,' Tomi answered. 'Why don't I let it go.'

'No, no,' I muttered, 'given my situation, I don't think we can afford that,' I added getting up off the bed and following her to the door.

Tomi looked through the peep-hole then turned back to me. 'It's a man I've never seen before, heavyset man in a three-piece suit. He's got a briefcase and is wearing a hat.'

'I know who it is,' I said, the full effect of the scotch and adrenalin suddenly pumping me wide awake. 'Answer it. That man is an insurance investigator,' I whispered with a trace of desperation as I pulled Tomi toward me. 'He's out to prove that my 'accident' was a 'suicide,' or that I'm not dead, or I'm not sure what, but I need to know what he has on me in case he takes it to the police.'

*Bam-bam-bam*, the rap came again, hard and persistent.

Tomi licked her lips nodding, 'Okay, baby. If there's one thing I know it's how to find out what's on a man's mind. I'll handle it,' she promised, straightening her robe and binding it at the waist as I crept from the foyer back into the bedroom and she opened the door.

I couldn't see, didn't want to risk giving myself away, but with the bedroom door opened a crack I could hear every word spoken between the two of you and steal an occasional glance when I thought it was safe.

'Yes?'

'Good morning, Miss Fabri, name's Phials, Martin Phials,' you said showing her your Surety ID. 'I'd like to ask you a few questions, so my company can pay out a claim to the surviving family of Mr. John Madson. We know this is a difficult time for friends and family. But the money, well, as you can imagine, Mrs. Madson and her young daughter could certainly use it. May I come in?'

'Sure thing, Mr. Martin. Sorry I'm not dressed. I just got out of the shower.'

'It's Phials, Miss Fabri, Martin Phials,' you said, no doubt observing the flat-screen TV, Apple MP3 player, Modani furnishings, and African art on the walls. 'Nice place you have here, Miss Fabri. Very stylish.'

'Make yourself at home. I was just pourin' myself a cocktail, wind down after work. Like one?'

'No, no,' you pooh-poohed, 'not at this hour, I never drink while on the job.'

A moment passed during which (not daring to look out so soon!) I imagined Tomi took a seat across from the couch where you were sitting, a glass coffee table between you.

'So?'

'Yes, Miss Fabri,' you began trying to appear discreet, 'through records I'm not at liberty to discuss just now, it's come to our attention that you and Mr. Madson were, shall we say, 'good friends' and had been for some time.'

'When you say 'we', you mean 'you', is that right?'

It was then I took a chance and peeked out from behind the bedroom door and, sure enough, there you were, across the room directly facing me! You held a hat in your hand—a dark brown Country Gentleman—toying with it as you leaned your broad frame forward to answer, 'It's true I am Director of Surety's Claim Investigation Branch so it is *my* investigation and yes *I* know that you and John Madson were in a relationship and seeing each other regularly. So my *real* question is this: has John Madson been in contact with you—by phone, e-mail, text message or any other way—since his boating accident?'

Tomi laughed out loud. I could hear the ice clanking in her glass as she shuddered with laughter, 'Jack is dead. If he was alive he'd contact me sure, but he's not and he hasn't!'

'And before that? Before the accident? When was the last time you were in contact with him?'

'I'm not that kind of person, Mr. Martin. I don't remember dates an' times. I just live my life as best I can. You're the one who'd know that anyway. You're the one probably goin' through his phone records, you're the detective!'

'Investigator, Miss Fabri,' you corrected, putting on your horn-rimmed glasses 'but let me help you out on that. John Madson made a call from his cell phone to your number here the day before his alleged drowning. It was 11:05 pm EST. The call lasted seven minutes and three seconds. What were you discussing during those seven minutes, Miss Fabri? Will you share that with me so my company can write that check to his survivors?'

'When Jack and me talked it was never about business.

You want to know, I'll tell you. Jack was a funny guy. He cracked me up regular. Not with jokes and such, just by the way he was, the way he looked at life.'

'And what way was that?'

'He made fun of things — his boss at work, politicians he knew through his father-in-law, even the Pope, people like that.'

'People in authority.'

'Yeah, something like that.'

'Was he depressed?'

'Jack? No!'

'Did he take drugs that you know of, prescription drugs, medication for an illness, let's say, or illegal ones?'

'Mr. Martin, you are an odd one, ain't you? You probably combed through his medicine cabinet found everything from KY Jelly to ExLax an' you askin' me a question like that? Anyone knew Jack intimate knew he drank scotch like he'd want to drown in it. Pills, too. Plenty of 'em. White, blue, red, some all three colors like an American flag. That was Jack. No one was ever gonna change him. Hell, no one wanted to!'

There was a lull, you jotting notes into the little spiral writing pad you always carry with you.

'Did he discuss the outing he planned with members of his staff at work?'

'No.'

'Did he tell you he was going out on a trial sail the day before when he spoke to you on the phone.'

'No, he didn't.'

'Strange.'

'Why's that?'

'You say he showed no signs of depression yet his

wife states just the opposite, that they'd just had a violent argument, that he'd been drinking non-stop and taking amphetamines for days prior to his disappearance and that her husband suffered from,' you flipped through your pad, 'here it is "dangerous mood swings." All of this was also observed by members of his staff and executives at NuGeneration Holdings. One man, a long-time personal friend who'd known him since childhood, a man named Daniel Brennan,' you added, 'swears that John Madson spoke to him frequently about taking his own life, about drowning, in fact. A fisherman on the Island we interviewed named Henry Swank claims Madson actually asked him about how he might do it. How others had fallen or willfully jumped from the side of a boat and drowned. So why wouldn't he mention anything at all about his intention to take his own life, Miss Fabri, when you spoke to him and spent nights with him in more intimate situations than any of the others?'

I peeked out in time to see you stick that bulldog face of yours out at Tomi across that glass table and it made my blood run cold as Tomi downed the last of her drink and slapped her glass back on the table.

'You are a good detective, ain't you, Mr. Martin? Got me all nervous and sweaty, me sittin' here, not a stitch on underneath this white robe I'm wearin'. Well, I guess he didn't say much about it 'cause our relationship was about sex mostly. Jack came to Ann Arbor for a good time. In a hotel room. In a motel room—never here—and I gave it to him. Sometimes we'd see a show, listen to some music at a club, sometimes we'd just fuck and suck 'til we couldn't see straight. But Jack never talked serious with me, just about money sometimes, but other than that it was a 'slam-bam, thank-you, Ma'm' kind of arrangement. He did the slammin', I did the bammin' and it all seemed to work out just fine.'

'Money? You said he talked to you about money, what did he say?'

'That he didn't have enough of it mostly, that his wife was spending him blind and he needed it,' she answered.

And from behind the door in the darkened bedroom I cringed when she said it. *No! No! No!* I was thinking, *I needed to be Happy Jack! Not desperate for money, Jack!* But Tomi must have realized that and so she stopped, probably to think of a way to throw him off the scent his pit bull instincts had already latched onto.

'Miss Fabri? Money. You said that he talked to you about money and that he didn't have enough of it?'

'Yeah, that's right,' she shot back, acting suddenly impatient with all your questions, 'and who the hell does these days? You seen Detroit lately. Like we live in a Third World country. Burnt-out buildings, empty manufacturing plants, see straight through 'em three, four blocks at a time!'

'But John Madson, specifically, Miss Fabri. What did he tell you about *his* financial situation and *his* need for money?'

'All right, all right!' she confessed. 'I never thought about it that way but maybe you're right. Maybe Jack did jump off that boat to die and leave the insurance money for his family. He may have hated that bitch wife of his but he felt sorry for his daughter. So maybe when he talked about his wife sayin' he wasn't man enough to provide right for 'em, well, could be he looked at suicide as the only way out. His only way to make things right, I don't know. I told you, it wasn't things like that, sad things, we talked about.'

'Did you know John Madson was an author, Miss Fabri?' Tomi shook her head.

'He was, and given the amount of time you spent together he must have shown you this,' you said holding up a copy of *CEO* magazine. 'It's a business article. No, I take that back, more like an article on *business psychology*. Fascinating, really, going back to your comment about Madson's cynicism toward authority. In this article he describes the innerworkings of the criminal mind. The minds of wanton killers like John Dillinger, even Jesse James,' you laughed, taking off your horn-rimmed glasses and putting them away. 'But, know what, Miss Fabri? You're lucky that Jack Madson probably is dead and that you probably are telling the truth about not having seen him because this article describes him. A dangerous man that boyfriend of yours, Miss Fabri, and maybe a murderer — or potential murderer — just like his friends here.'

'Well, like I told you, I haven't seen Jack since his accident and don't know anything about no article.'

'Very well, Miss Fabri,' you said, hat-in-hand, gathering your things, 'I can see you're tired and upset. I believe you've told me all I need to know.'

Peering into the living room I could see from your expression that you got what you wanted as you closed the spiral note pad with those stubby little hands of yours, nails polished like glass. But what had you gotten? The answers Tomi gave cut both ways. Being desperate for money could lead one kind of person to suicide, but could lead another type to do exactly what I had done. Which was it you'd come away with, Phials? Or was it both? Were you still investigating or had you actually developed a theory that you believed to a certainty? But then why bring up the article? To scare Tomi, make her doubt me, and drive a wedge between us? I wondered, anxious, as you lifted your heavyweight frame from the couch where you'd been sitting, grabbed your Samsonite briefcase in one hand while holding your hat in the other, and stood.

Tomi followed you out of the living room into the foyer and opened the door.

'Good night, Miss Fabri,' you said turning to leave, but she stopped you.

'Mr. Martin,' she said.

'It's Phials, as I've told you before, Miss Fabri, Martin Phials,' you corrected. 'What is it?'

'You are a very smart man, Mr. Phials, anyone can see that. Me? I'm not much of anything and sure no high-flyin' investigator like you. But I loved Jack Madson, if you can believe that, and like to know what you think happened that night.'

You thought about that for a long moment, Phials, nodded as if to re-confirm what you already suspected, then answered.

'In my opinion, John Madson's life got away from him, Miss Fabri. I've seen it dozens of times before. A man, or woman, doesn't understand that from God's vengeance, no man escapes. "You can run, but you can't hide," that's what the Negro boxer Joe Louis once said. That's what happened to your boyfriend, Miss Fabri, and that is what will happen to you. When God's justice caught up with him, Madson proved to be the morally weak individual he'd always been and couldn't face up to it. After that, no man—not his rich father-in-law, not his fancy Wall Street friends, and not the whore he lay down with—could save him. Your boyfriend killed himself, Miss Fabri,' you said, plopping your Country Gentlemen hat back over your meticulously coifed hair. 'He jumped off the side of his sailboat knowing the currents were treacherous, fully understanding he'd never come out of that water again. I think there's a lesson in what happened to John Madson for all of us, and especially a prostitute like yourself. Good night, Miss Fabri.'

With that you left, Tomi shutting the door behind as she turned around and leaned back against it. 'What kind of man is this, Jack? Who does he think he is, God? Talking to me that way? Judging me! He's not God, Jack, he doesn't know me! He doesn't know the way I think or what I feel!'

By then I'd crossed the room and felt her trembling body as she slipped into my arms like they were made to hold her.

'It's okay, baby,' I whispered. 'Phials is nothing, a nobody. You're worth ten Martin Phialses. Now, please, calm down. I promise the moral lectures are over starting now.'

Then she began to sob, slowly at first, and then full blown, like her tears were meant to wash away every mean thought and every mean word any man or woman had ever spoken about her.

# Chapter 28

For the next two days I mostly hung low at Tomi's place. She called-in sick to Head2Toe, a flu she said, which covers a lot of bases, I suppose. And it was fine being with her. I grew a beard and had my hair styled differently which seemed like a smart thing to do and maybe it pushed the envelope a bit but, dressed in military fatigues she picked up at the Army Navy Store, we shopped together at the grocery store, even went out to catch a movie one night.

All that being said, by the third day, with a plan beginning to flesh-out for traveling back to New York and gaining entrance to NuGen's offices at 9 West, I gathered what little I had and was packing when Tomi walked into the room and caught sight of what I was up to.

'You're leavin',' she said like this wasn't the first time something like this had happened.

'Yeah, I am,' I said continuing my packing.

'Where to?'

'New York City. Remember that opportunity I told you about. It's there.'

'You know life around here sucks, Jack.'

'Come on,' I said turning to her. 'You've got a nice place here, Tomi. A job keeps you living in style. Maybe a rich boyfriend from out of the dating service will take you away to an island.'

'It's not like that, Jack. Truth is, I got nothin'. I'm three months behind in my rent. No car. Hell, most of the furniture here is leased. Just look around. What do you see? Boarded up apartments, closed-down stores and factories. Detroit's a black hole, baby. The rich businessmen who were my bread and butter have lost their jobs or moved. My regulars don't talk about sex anymore, they talk about their kids' health care! It isn't like you think, Jack. It ain't the way I make it out. I got no reason to stay here or anywhere. I'm lost, baby, can't you see that?'

'Tomi, Tomi,' I said shaking my head feeling as sad for her as I was powerless to help. 'I got some money,' I offered reaching into my wallet. 'What is it you need? A thousand? Two? I got that to spare now that the money from China's come in.'

'It's not the money, Jack. I want to come with you.'

'We talked about that . . . '

'You don't have to love me. I know you like me bein' around. I know that from these past three days. I could come along. Nobody'd be lookin' for a married couple.'

'Yeah, sure,' I laughed. 'White guy with a black girl twenty years younger than him. No, no one's going to notice that.'

'We could go separate. Same flight. Different seats. You could go first class. Who could know if we know each other or not? Phials much as told us the cops think you're dead and he thinks you committed suicide, so what's to be afraid of?'

I looked at Tomi, *really* looked at her, maybe for the first time. I'd seen that look before, not in a woman, but in kids, the kind you see on TV who live in countries like

Africa, Haiti, or Kosovo, where all hope has died and yet it's that hope that keeps them alive.

'I could help, you know. If you're about to do what I think you are in New York, you're going to need somebody you can count on. Somebody to make phone calls to arrange things, to check things out so you don't have to do it yourself, to use as a kind of diversion, see what I mean?'

Thoughts like pieces of scrap metal tumbling in a washing machine clanked and clamored around in my head as I chewed on what she'd thrown at me. True, there might be some advantage in taking her along to help sneak me into 9 West when it came to that and the sex came along with a beauty like her was certainly no disadvantage, I reasoned.

'Okay, you can come along for now, but once I get what I want, you go your way and I go mine. One thing sure, you'll have the money to make a clean start of things and get the hell out of this city permanently, which is what I advise.'

'Oh, Jack! Thank you so much! I'll be the best fuck-buddy you ever had, ever *could* have!' she promised, hugging me so hard I could barely breathe for standing.

And it was then I noticed a burn mark. Like the kind a person might get from melting candle wax dripped on them. On her breast, exposed from her loosened robe, and others near the darkened areola around her nipple.

# Chapter 29

O nce I decided to take Tomi along with me things got easy. We blew out of Ann Arbor that night and checked into the Detroit Metro Westin. I knew we'd both need a new wardrobe and with my wallet fat courtesy of Wei Li, we were off to Saks to buy some upscale dresses and jewelry of the kind a Manhattan socialite would wear. Gorgeous as Tomi was, there'd be no doorman or house detective who'd ever suspect she wasn't a fashion model or wife of a prominent Madison Avenue attorney, and that's the way I wanted it. Then the two of us were off to Brooks Brothers to buy a top coat and three business suits, conservative as we could find, Breitling Avenger watch, ties, and two pairs of black lace Johnston Murphy shoes. All of this essential.

If shopping was easy, shopping with Tomi was even easier. The two of us—at least for the forty-eight hours we spent there—were like kids running around a play yard. Money was no problem. Never crossed our minds! We were too busy having fun, forgetting for those two days that I'd re-entered the U.S. beat-up and as close to 'officially dead' as any man could be, back to the very place I'd gambled everything I possessed trying to escape just ten days before.

But it wasn't about time (it seemed like a lifetime ago!) and it wasn't about money, either. Not really. What it was about was freedom and what I was feeling during that short break from grim reality when Tomi and me did whatever we felt like doing. Simple things like shopping for clothes, buying food at the grocery store, or watching a movie together in bed in our hotel room. And if we weren't totally free, well, we sure as hell tried to make ourselves feel that way. And it worked. At least until the morning we walked across the street to the Delta terminal and checked onto Flight 127 scheduled to leave Detroit Metro 8:45 am headed for New York's LaGuardia airport.

Tomi, dressed to the nines in a sleeveless black dress with a string of white pearls hugging her neck, boarded separately but—thanks to Mr. Li's generosity—traveled First Class like me. Once seated, and two vodka tonics into the flight, I couldn't help but notice Tomi flirting with the stewardess, talking her up, as I watched from an aisle away, then turning to me with a wink, sending over a napkin with the lipstick imprint of a kiss she'd left on it.

When we landed in New York, I made it a point to take separate taxis to the hotel just in case we were being followed. I decided on the Sherry Netherland opposite Central Park as a base of operations. For one, it was located just a few blocks from the Solow building. As importantly, the management there had a penchant for its guests' privacy. The hotel of choice for old school celebs from Barbra Streisand to Mick Jagger, its security staff waylaid curiosity seekers and the paparazzi before they made it past the signature sidewalk clock that marked its Fifth Avenue entrance. For guys like Jagger that meant keeping out middle-aged fans and drug-crazed groupies. For me it meant keeping out cops, detectives, and douche bag insurance claims investigators like you, Martin.

Once we settled into our suite, Tomi rested in a bedroom set on a landing above the dining area while I sat at a desk in another, drawing boxes with arrows of the Solow building's layout, trying to determine my best option for getting past security. The lobby was standard for an office building its size, wide and rectangular with a narrow apron leading to two banks of elevators positioned north and south that covered fifty-three floors if you counted P1, P2, P3 parking, all the way up to its top three floors—forty-eight through fifty—where NuGen's offices were located.

To the right of the apron as you entered from W. 57th Street was the Security Desk. Not really a desk, it was more like a counter with three guards who checked IDs and issued visitors badges with a bank of closed circuit TV monitors set below the countertop facing them. God knows what was on them but I know it wasn't porn because the guards paid no attention, at least for the eight years I worked there. But one thing I noticed was this: once the building closed and by that I mean once even the most fanatical workaholics that populated those fifty floors began to dwindle, say, around 9 p.m., the day shifts' security—which ran 6 a.m. to 2 p.m. and 2 p.m. to 10 p.m.—transitioned to a skeleton crew that held down the fort from 10 p.m. to 6 a.m.

To most, like me when I worked there, this meant very little. If you left an important presentation and were traveling the next morning, or if you forgot your wallet in your desk drawer, it meant you could call ahead or tap on the 2-inch thick, framed glass of the building entrance and a guard would come, have you flash your ID, and let you retrieve it. In other words, third shift security wasn't as rigid as the others. It wasn't three guards that manned the security desk, it was one. It wasn't a ten-man shift working the building corridors, it was more like three. *Night shift.*

Okay, so far so good, I was thinking, but this insight—significant though it seemed—wasn't getting me where I needed to be. After all, what was I going to do, tap on the window, overpower the sixty-year-old man once he let me in and race for the elevators? No, I thought, still scribbling boxes, still drawing arrows. The *best* time to get past security wasn't during any one of the shifts. It was in between, during the confusion while workers and visitors, maintenance crews and deliveries went on as normal but the guards themselves were in turmoil from one shift to the next, when they were most vulnerable. Hell, by 10 p.m., the hustle and bustle of a normal business day in Midtown Manhattan had already wound down, so that wouldn't do. No, I reasoned, it was at 2 p.m.—with everyone returning from lunch—when shift #1, working since early morning, turned security over to shift #2, that I saw my greatest opportunity, at the height of the business day and during that target period when shifts were in transition.

Moreover, who said I had to be a visitor in the first place? If there was any single thing my essay on criminal intelligence taught me, it was that these men—whether Dillinger or The Kid—never played by the other guy's rules, and society's least of all! For the most part the system counted on visitors to register voluntarily with Security, meaning it wasn't like they had ten guys with Thompson sub-machine guns lined across the apron leading to 9 West's elevator bank. Sure, there were three guards at the counter and maybe one or two more near the elevators, but they weren't checking on guys in two thousand dollar suits. They were looking for unshaven derelict types, stray bag ladies, guys talking to Jesus, or Middle Easterners, thin, swarthy, darting eyes, who they were probably going to stop and ask for an ID. Otherwise, odds were I could slip in — using Tomi as a diversion with one or two of them — hop an elevator and find myself at 2:05 p.m. standing with elevator door open at the entrance to the 50th floor where Lisa Ellison had her office and the AvaTech files waited.

With that realization branded white hot in my mind, my eyes dropped down to the sheets of Sherry Netherland stationery covered with boxes in the shape of the Solow building lobby, the rectangular apron where the elevator banks lay, the security station with arrows shooting through it, an unfinished Tic-Tac-Toe game, and scrawlings of men, their necks in hangmen's nooses with ropes attached to nothing but air.

I snatched those pages from the desktop and ripped them to pieces, tossing the shredded paper into the waste paper basket to the side of the desk.

*How could I know what a clever detective or forensic psychologist might make of doodlings like that?*

# Chapter 30

By the time I heard Tomi stirring in the bedroom, and the sound of the shower running, I'd already meandered to the hotel mini-bar and was scoping out what kind of booze they were stocking. Well, that got me thinking about my present situation, stuck in a room at St. Ann's Abbey, writing my so-called confession. My clock was winding down and I might need a jolt from the quart bottle of Chivas and another half-dozen 'mother's helpers' nestled in the med containers alongside it, I calculated, taking a break from my writing.

I obliged myself by cracking open both . . . pouring pills from the orangey plastic container, the other from the dark green bottle, straight into my mouth. That's when a gentle *rat-a-tat-tat* sounded at the heavy oak door to the room where I sat and Father Jeremiah walked in, this time with another priest, dressed in a white robe instead of the black habit worn by Jeremiah. His name was Brother Michael, the monastery's infirmarian.

"This is Brother Michael, Jack," Jeremiah said in a deferential voice.

"I know who he is." I answered, how could I not know? It was Brother Michael who used to write me infirmary notes to get me out of class when I was a student there.

Michael, now in his mid-eighties with snow-white hair

and ornery as a snake, strode across the room to me, his rangy body now stooped but his legs still long and his temperament unchanged.

"Let's get a look at you," he said prying his fingers beyond the brown crust of dried blood into the bullet hole in the left arm of my shirt then tearing it open to expose the wound.

He looked around to Jeremiah who hovered behind him, "Hand me my medical bag," he ordered, rummaging through it for a jar of liquid soap and a bottle of Poland Springs water.

"Where's the basin?" he asked. Jeremiah handed over a finger bowl, the kind priests used to wash their hands before blessing the Eucharist during Mass.

The infirmarian, who was a trained nurse, mixed a solution and washed the wound, nodding as he studied the spot where the .32 slug had entered the fleshy part of my lower bicep, near the armpit. "You're lucky, Madson, the bullet passed clean through," he said as much to himself as to me as I watched his clear blue eye focus, taking a pair of tweezers from the medical bag, as he examined the hole more closely, "though pieces of fabric from your shirt entered along with it."

Brother Michael was insistent as he inserted the tweezers four, maybe five times, directly into the wound (and it hurt like hell!), finally pulling a tiny circle of blood-soaked cloth out and proudly holding it up for me to see.

"How badly is he injured?" Jeremiah ventured.

Michael didn't take the time to answer, cleaning out the wound again—blood, old and new, along with spidery nests of crimson tissue drenched in the yellowish fluid associated with infection.

"When was your last tetanus vaccination?" he asked looking me straight in the eye.

"I don't know. When I was a kid, I guess."

He grunted, "And aside from the booze, what is this crap you're taking?" he demanded, examining one of my prescription bottles, then another. I snatched them from him. He looked at me stunned momentarily, and nodded slowly, "I see . . . " he said, turning to Jeremiah his cold, clear old man's eyes still on me. "Your friend here is lucky. The gun was a small caliber semi-automatic, .22 or .32 caliber. The puncture is small because of the bullet's size and velocity. He's also lucky it passed straight through," he added smearing Neosporin over it as he prepared a dressing, "so he hasn't lost much blood though infection has begun to set in and he's a candidate for lockjaw unless he gets a tetanus booster within the next eight hours. That's the good news."

"And the bad?" I asked taking a swig from the open bottle on the desk in front of me.

"The bad is you're an alcoholic and addicted to amphetamines. Beyond that, it looks to me like you've been up for three days and nights now so—if you don't have a heart attack or stroke first—you'll be crashing, *massively*, and could lapse into a coma. But that's not the worst of it, Madson."

"Yeah, what's that?"

"The worst of it is you passed through St. Damian's preparatory school with the Brothers as teachers. The worst of it is you've turned out to be this piece of shit I'm looking at."

"So how come you know so much about bullet wounds, Father? Bob Gallagher from East Coast Securites, he was never shot, was he?"

Michael secured the gauze and cotton dressing with adhesive tape, got up off his knees, and stood, "This is still Newark, Madson, not Short Hills, not Summit. Can you remember what that's like, or do money and amnesia always walk hand-in-hand? But it's worse now than it was then — Latin King, Bloods, Crypts, MS-13 — civilization's falling apart around our ears. Gun shot wounds, knife wounds, wounds from glass bottles, ice picks, bottle openers, I see them all. Why do you think we sequester these kids in dormitories away from their friends and families? It's the gangs! To them it's what boxing or baseball was to you, but there are no more gyms, no baseball diamonds, and they wouldn't care anyway. Gangs are what the Catholic Church once was, or corporate America, or the city, or state, or federal government. With all of those a shambles, it's gone native out there, Madson, it's gone tribal."

"I don't have any money," I apologized.

*"No one wants your goddamned money!"* he said angrily as he re-filled his beat-up black medical bag and turned to leave.

"Brother Michael," my voice trailed behind him.

"No, you don't have to worry," he groaned anticipating what I was about to ask him like the wizened old Irishman he was. "Something else you learn working with these kids and the street gangs. I'm no 'rat.' You'll be the one calling 911 and the police, or Father Jeremiah here, but not me. Never me."

Then he left the room opening the heavy wood door by its old-fashioned black iron handle and shutting it behind him with a *whooshing* sound like he'd just re-sealed a vacuum.

"How do you feel?" Jeremiah asked.

"Exhausted."

"Do you want to rest? I could take you back to the dormitory and find you a room."

"Not necessary. Not now. I need to finish this, what I'm writing. After that I might sleep," I said clamping my eyes down like pulling the blinds over the two lone portholes of a ship at sea. "After that I might sleep forever."

Jeremiah appraised me, nodding doubtfully, "Okay, Son. At least Michael has examined you and your wound is treated. How much longer? How much time do you need to finish this 'confession' of yours?"

"Don't really matter. Schedule's not up to me, Father. It's up to Martin Phials, the death claims investigator from that insurance company I told you about. See, I'm expecting him to come knocking on the door any time now."

And that's how it went, Phials, my third encounter with Jeremiah along with Michael, the monastery's infirmarian, who dressed my gunshot wound. But notice even then I knew how, like a bloodhound, you'd gotten my scent and were hot on my trail. Well, you've got to admit, I never underestimated you, Phials, got to give me that much.

But I digress. Where were we? That's right. The suite I'd checked into at the Sherry Netherland, with Tomi getting out of the shower, entering the room naked as a jay bird, drying her hair with a thick white Turkish towel as I looked up from my 9 West diagrams gawking at her.

'*What?*' she asked.

# Chapter 31

O nce Tomi got dressed—down, like me, in jeans—we discussed the plan I'd laid out for us. Tomi sat on a lounge chair, feet up on a coffee table, with me still at the desk, wood chair turned toward her.

'Idea's simple,' I began. 'First, we go to 9 West, dressed up like on the plane, exactly 1:55 p.m. Why? Because Security changes shifts at 2 p.m., that's the most chaotic time for them and the best for us. Second, at 2 p.m. while the shifts are changing, you'll go to the Security Desk and ask for the offices of Gaylord & Fitch. It's a law firm at 25 West 57th. Now, if you're sweet, like I know you can be, one—maybe two—of the guards, seeing a chance to flirt with a sexy sister like you, is going to take the time to look up the address, probably go to the front of the lobby and point out the building. That's what we're counting on 'cause by then, say 2:03 p.m., I'll have moved to the south side of the building, past the single guard left there, to the elevators on my way to the 50th floor.'

'What about after that? Once you get what you want up there? What then?'

'Then I leave, but not right away. We don't want to take chances, understand? Even with this beard and haircut, people at NuGen know me so I've got to wait on the 46th floor, which is vacant, for every nerd in accounting, every

185

wonk in IT, and every boot-licking middle manager to leave before I can move up to NuGen's offices on the 50$^{th}$ to hack into Lisa Ellison's computer. That's going to take time.'

'So, what are you sayin'? You're gonna hide there 'til everyone leaves?'

'You think I *want* to? Hell, I'll hide out out a couple hours until the graveyard shift takes over to get what I'm after, but don't think I like it! You ever been in a building like that once everyone leaves? Dead as a mausoleum. I can tell you 'cause I checked it out once after a few too many at Alfie's. But know something? There may not be anyone in the building except a few security guards and maintenance workers, but around 1 a.m., you can still hear the sounds the people make left behind—laughing, arguing—I tell you it's spooky.'

'You're a funny man, know that, Jack?' Tomi said shaking her head and laughing. 'You're so afraid of that man, Phials! Let me tell you somethin', men like that, I seen 'em before. I been with 'em before. Somethin' seriously wrong with a man like that, Jack. Somethin' too much in him or not in him enough, I don't know. But one thing I can't figure is why you're so terrified he's gonna find you. He ain't gonna find you, lover, because he thinks you dead!'

'You don't know him the way I do,' I said getting up from my chair, pacing. 'You've never seen him on a case. Like a pit bull once he gets his teeth sunk into it. Got no wife. No family at all, way he tells it. But when it comes to sniffin' out the truth, what's going on *beneath* the things cops see, he'll get there, baby, you can count on it.'

'Didn't seem so great to me,' Tomi snapped, 'but plenty nasty, I'll give you that.'

'I saw him in action. Place called Granger Industries, Ohio. A guy tried to get away with killing himself, leave some money behind for his wife and kids. Didn't fly. Not with Phials. Detectives? They stood around like kids listening to a rock star. 'Guys,' he says, 'like you, the first thing that hit me about this case was that it was a car accident, but then I went to where it happened. Skid marks on the highway? There were none because he never hit the breaks! Damage to the guard rail? Total because I'd estimate that car was traveling at seventy miles per hour when it hit. And then there's the rest . . .' 'Sir?' someone in the group asked. 'Check his appointment book for the past ninety days,' Phials suggested. 'Seems like Mr. Slezak had a long psychiatric history that his wife, Doris, knew nothing about. And there were drugs: prozac, elavil, tofranil. Go ahead, check it out, you'll see. This was no car accident, it was suicide. In fact, you fellas ought to take a look at the statistics sometime and learn a little about the insurance business from our actuarial tables. I've got ten volumes on murder,' he chuckled good-naturedly. 'More than that on accidental death. And suicides? Guess you could call me an expert on the subject. Suicide, by category: race, gender, occupation, season of the year, time of the day,' he rattled-off. 'Suicide, how committed: firearms, hanging, poison, leaps, drowning; Suicide by poison, sub-divided by types of poisons: pesticides, drug overdose, carbon monoxide, household chemicals, natural toxins. Suicide by leaps sub-divided: leaps from high places, under wheels of cars, under wheels of trains, under the hoofs of horses . . . you get my point, don't you, fellas? Tom Slezak was a nut job. Psychiatric reports say as much. It all fits into the same set of statistics once you've see enough of them.

Slezak drove his car full speed through that guard rail on Rt. 516, never touching his breaks, at 70 miles per hour because he wanted $100,000 for his wife who had MS and their three kids. Sad, yes, but accidental death? No way, boys, no way possible.'

'But you didn't commit suicide, Jack, you're alive and standin' right here in front of me!'

'Okay, sure, it's his job to sway the authorities so his company doesn't have to pay out on life insurance claims, but that's not what it's about for him. For Phials it isn't the satisfaction he gets proving Surety's not liable for the money. No, he's got what you might call his own peculiar set of principles. For him the satisfaction is bringing people to justice like God's avenging angel. For him, it's about catching guys who live in the shadows, like me, and dragging them into the light of day. That's what gets his cock up. Shit, that's what he lives for, baby.'

'So you think he's pretty smart, do you?'

'Fanatically so.'

'And he always gets his man because he can see through his bullshit straight through to what's really going on in his mind, that right?'

'Yeah, something like that, what of it?'

'Your inspector friend called you a murderer, Jack. You heard him call you that, didn't you? You could hear it from the bedroom, right? 'Murderer, or *potential* murderer,' that's what he said, Jack. So why didn't you show me that article you wrote? The one about outlaws and killers, the way they *really* think, and what goes on in their minds? Why did you hide that from me?'

'Hide it? Have you gone crazy?' I asked. 'I wrote that piece for a business magazine *three years ago*, Tomi. Three years ago or more. It was *CEO* magazine, baby, do you have career plans I don't know about? Do you want to be a CEO?'

'CEO, FBI, CIA, what do I know about any of that? I just know that somethin' important, somethin' got published and other people read, you shoulda told me about that, Jack,' she said, more upset than I'd ever seen her. 'I know you don't love me,' she added, head bowed then looking straight ahead at me, 'but least you should treat me with some respect.'

Well, I have to tell you, Phials. What Tomi said that day really took me by surprise. My days with Jennifer showing, by instinct I nearly lobbed the grenade of her own sexual secrets back at her but thought better of it, held her in my arms, and told her I respected her more than she could know. 'Really?' Tomi asked like a little kid would. 'Really? Do you mean that?' And I swore that I did, not lying, either. Tomi was a stand-up lady, no question. Hell, I took her with me, didn't I? She was 'aiding and abetting' my crime, as they say, wasn't she?

So, we left it at that for the moment though like an echo, the sound of her words stayed with me reverberating like a shout in an empty cavern, the words evaporated into space but the echo still there in my head. I said nothing more about it and neither did she, until a moment later a thought flashed through my head concerning the visit I wanted to make to 9 West that afternoon. 'Hey,' I told her just before we left to case out the Solow building, 'that wig you bought, the Afro? Wear it today while we're checking things out at 9 West, will you?' Eager to help, Tomi nodded and the storm clouds passed us over. Then, I kissed her on the forehead and we left for West 57th Street, notepad in her pocket book, camera bag with Nikon COOLPIX dangling from the leather strap hung over my right shoulder.

The Solow building is famous, if not for its architecture which is better than average, then for the over-sized red "9" that stands in front of its entrance to mark the address' importance as a New York City landmark. In fact, there's a fashion brand built around it—shoes, dresses, coats—so it wasn't unusual for tourists to cluster around it's signature number "9" peering into its lobby, as Tomi and I did that afternoon.

Of course, I did my best to go unnoticed among the hundreds of people entering and leaving but I can tell you that as fall began to recede and winter's cold crept into Manhattan, along with the chill that day came a hollow sort of feeling. Like I was there *but not there*, like I was alive *but not really alive.* Kind of eerie, I remember thinking and maybe just another strain of the viral paranoia I'd come to expect waking up each morning a dead man since my boating "accident" three weeks before.

Looking through the plate glass into 9 West's lobby Tomi and I confirmed that, like clockwork, the shifts did transition at 2 p.m. and that it was done with no small amount of confusion. Guards talked and joked, signing in and out as they exchanged rosters and timesheets with schedules of visitors and deliveries for the day. And why not? From the guard's point of view, what were they really protecting? Nine West offered no money to steal like a bank and wasn't seen, even by Homeland Security, as a prime target for terrorists, like the Empire State Building or Wall Street or the Twin Towers before they were decimated. For them it was a job, plain and simple.

It was then, while peering into the window to the lobby,

that I noticed the reflection of someone, or something, else. It was me, of course, staring back in the building's plate glass—much thinner than I remembered—a man I barely recognized, dressed in a topcoat and dark suit with a beautiful African American woman, wearing a wig, clinging to his arm. *Who was he? What had he become?* I asked myself. *How could things have gone so fucking off track?* The thought made me dizzy like I had too much to drink and the city was spinning around me. The whirlies, we used to call it back in high school. And I didn't want to think about it anymore. Not even for a second. Like they tell circus acrobats when performing their high-wire act, 'Just keep on going and don't look down!' Well, that's what I was like, Phials. I didn't want to know how high up I really was or how far out I'd really journeyed because, truth be told, I knew there was no turning back. Not now. Not ever.

And, man, if ever I craved a stiff drink and a hit of meth it was then, I thought as I turned to Tomi, beautiful as ever.

'Hey, babe,' I said, 'what say I take you to Babbo tonight. All the celebs go there: Jay-Z, Brad Pitt, Jaylo, you name 'em!'

'Is that true, Jack, *really?*'

'You stick with me, pretty lady,' I said taking her by the arm, 'and you're gonna find out for yourself!'

# Chapter 32

Thing about popular restaurants in Manhattan: unless you're Beyonce or Derek Jeter, reservations can be a bitch to get on short notice, but we got lucky. I called ours in for Mr. and Mrs. Barton Crowley and, miraculously, we had a table for two, 9 p.m, at Babbo!

The cab ride there wasn't long but gave me a chance to take the fragments of thought that fluttered through my head like moths and pull them together so they became coherent again. Near the edges were the abstract ones—more philosophical than concrete—that had nothing to do with the technology theft at NuGen. Like why was I back in New York about to put my ass on the line yet another time? Of course, the short answer was money (wasn't it always?) but, more, why had I gotten involved with Johnnie Eng and the Chin Chou to begin with? Then, back like a pendulum, my alcohol-drug-drenched brain would swing to the more practical aspects of the break-in. Like how was I going to navigate the security blocks in Lisa Ellison's computer, knowing that if I didn't get Wei Li what he wanted I was a dead man sure.

'How you doin', babe?' I asked Tomi, who was in the back seat beside me, visions of celebrities dancing in her head.

'Just fine, Jack. You sure know how to treat a girl!'

I smiled as she slipped her hand in mine, then returned back to my world, the grim one, as she returned to hers, our hands entwined but our thoughts hurtling in opposite directions.

And it was those moths fluttering on the periphery of my consciousness that I chose to grab hold of and secure first. Upon reflection it all came back to that article I'd written, my time at St. Damian's, Barton Crowley and his daughter, the havoc I'd presided over at NuGen and the contamination — some flaw or original sin — that infected my soul. That was what my clenched fist held once I'd captured those moths, opened it up, and looked into it.

See, even with these outlaws I'd written about in my *CEO* article, there were facts people didn't necessarily know but must somehow understand, so even though they committed horrible crimes — robbed, murdered and, in the case of Jesse James, burned entire towns to the ground — history forgives them. The reason is that each had his story, I theorized, his reasons for becoming the outlaw he became.

Billy the Kid was just that: a loopy kid orphaned at a young age. His first crime was stealing a block of cheese. They arrest him. He escapes. Now, suddenly, he's a fugitive from justice! After that he takes to horse stealing to survive until he meets John Tunstall, a rancher who's on the verge of being wiped out by two cattle barons named Murphy and Dolan. Tunstall takes Billy under his wing. Teaches him to read and write. Reads the Bible to him and becomes a kind of surrogate father.

Well, life being what it is, the Murphy-Dolan gang murders Tunstall in cold blood. Enraged, The Kid rides to town and swears-out warrants for their arrest, but what

Billy doesn't know is that the Sheriff and his Deputies are all in Murphy's and Dolan's pockets. When Billy and his 'Regulators' track them down and bring them to justice, there is no justice. Sheriff Brady releases the murderers and arrests Billy!

Now, one thing that all of these guys—Dillinger, Jesse, and The Kid—have in common: they don't like being fucked, particularly by authorities who are supposed to be upholding things that are 'right' against things that are 'wrong.' So, pissed-off as he is, once he's released from jail, The Kid shoots Sheriff Brady and his Deputies dead and becomes a cold-blooded killer, on the lam, with a price on his head.

The story of Dillinger isn't much different. Buddying up with a life-long criminal named Ed Singleton, as a young man Johnnie steals $50 from a local grocery store. Cops catch them. Singleton, who has a history of arrests, pleads innocent and gets two years. Dillinger, advised by his father to 'take his medicine,' pleads guilty and winds up with 10 to 20 on a first offense. By the time he leaves Indiana State Prison ten years later, a reckless teenager is turned into Public Enemy #1.

And Jesse James? Every school kid knows that Jesse derived no small amount of joy robbing banks and trains, but did you know that while he was nowhere near his mother Zerelda's farmhouse in Missouri, Allan Pinkerton sent a gang of thugs to surround the place? With his family still in it, the Pinkertons set the house ablaze then threw a bomb in the kitchen killing his young half-brother Archie and blowing off his elderly mother's arm! So okay, Phials, you tell me, who's the 'good' guys and who's the 'bad?'

Well, I'm not exactly sure why—with Tomi's hand

between my legs, stroking my cock in the back seat of the cab—I'd be thinking about The Kid, Dillinger, and Jesse, but I was. Could be it was to divert myself from thinking too much, getting jumpy about what was about to go down at 9 West. Or maybe I was feeling a little like they must have felt before one of their bank jobs or train robberies, trying to figure exactly what it was brought me to this point. And to me that was exhilarating because, like them, I'd peeked behind the curtain to see the hypocrisy that was there and decided I wanted no part of it. Fact is, I wasn't afraid anymore, can you understand that, Phials? I was no longer intimidated, or infatuated, or just plain bought-out by greed. I had graduated mentally and emotionally. I had become, and was never more than at that moment, an outlaw by choice!

'You okay, sugar?' Tomi asked, my cock firmly in her grasp as she massaged my balls with her long thin fingers.

'Never better,' I lied, pecking her on the lips.

She smiled as a car horn blared on Sixth Avenue, content to stare from the backseat window, watching pedestrians as they bustled along the sidewalks or threaded between vehicles frozen in traffic.

Not so for me. Time was running short and I knew it. It was time now for me to seize the legion of thoughts—the moths—that fluttered near to me to examine them. And what I discovered, held tight in my clenched fist once it was opened, was my most obvious concern, the only one, really: on the night of the theft, once in Lisa Ellison's office, would I be able to hack into her computer and get access to the AvaTech files? That was my problem, Phials, not in a general way, but in a very specific one.

See, there were two approaches I'd narrowed it down

to. The first was the easiest: use the right password and I was home free, simple as that. Problem was, though I'd become an expert on the details of Lisa Ellison's narrow little existence and knew everything from her shoe size to the name of her pet papillon, a hacker had only three tries to hit paydirt or NuGen's Dell computers would automatically shut down. Further complicating my chance at even a well-educated guess was the fact that users needed to change their password every 90 days. True, after that time an employee could use the same password again (something someone as unimaginative as Lisa was sure to do!) but who could say when it would drop off and be replaced by a new one? No one could know, not to a certainty.

That left me with my second approach, again not fool-proof, but one I'd been using to tap into NuGen employees' expense account for years. The scam came to me while on a business trip to Fargo, North Dakota. I'd been out late drinking the night before our meeting with the CEO of a company we were planning to buy, hadn't done squat in the way of research, and had to make a presentation to their Board the next day with no time left to prepare. Now, my first thought was to hop on the internet, install 'Edgar On-Line' to round up analyst surveys, write something plausible up and print it that morning on the hotel printer. But that won't work, not from a remote location, I realize, so unless I can figure out a way to install that software, I'm totally fucked.

That's when I get a bright idea that comes in the form of an Indian guy in IT owes me big time. 'Suresh, Old Buddy,' I say calling him from my hotel that morning, 'you know it was me recommended you for your job in

IT, pushed hard to get you out of that mailroom. Now I need a favor, or Corky's gonna fire my ass sure.' 'Yes, you sure helped me. No doubt about that.' 'So what can you do for me, Buddy, I'm desperate!' 'Well, there is an 'administrator password' that allows us to log-in to the network from employees' laptops in case of an emergency, but I don't think I can give that to you, Jack.' 'Suresh, you don't know how important this deal is to me, *to our company*.' 'Will you promise never to use it again?' he asks. 'On my mother's eyes!' I swear. 'Well okay, Jack, but never tell anyone I gave this to you.' 'I will. I mean, I won't. I give you my word, Suresh.' There was a long silence. 'ANG-001-1764,' he said. 'That's the number. Use it and you will have access to the network so you can install Edgar On-Line or whatever software you need.'

And that was all I needed because that password, the administrator password, was not re-set every 90 days. Moreover it gave me access to every laptop and desktop operating in our IT network. As valuable as gold, diamonds or hard cash, that day I realized I'd gained entrance — with absolute impunity — into every personal expense account, department budget, and corporate credit line in the entire NuGen system!

But even this triumph that had me surfing the perfect wave of white collar larceny for years now left me riddled with anxiety that night. Everything I had — my life! — was riding on me either hitting Lisa's password tries number one, two, or three or scoring with the password Suresh had given me. But that was four years ago and for every month of every day since I'd sweated NuGen's IT director switching it to a new one or — given the recent financial audits Lisa had clued me into — launching a 'corrective action' in response to a cited violation based on tighter security that changed the administrator password every 90 days like all the others!

Well, that gave me something to ponder straight through to the moment the cab pulled up to the entrance of Babbo. And this is what I came up with. My first two tries before resorting to the info Suresh had provided would be based on a clue Lisa herself contributed to the cause once when I complained to her about having to create new passwords every three months. 'Do what I do,' she advised then. 'Use two or three passwords that you'll always remember and alternate them: your name and date of birth, the name of a pet or, in your case, the latest cocktail waitress you've been trying to seduce. That way, even if you forget which one is current, you always know it's one of the other two!'

Of course, I understood whatever approach I decided upon was no sure bet but I knew then I had a starting point, and that gave me at least some fleeting sense of accomplishment. I looked to my Breitling Avenger, 9:00 p.m. Seventeen hours to 'go-live,' I calculated, as I took hold of Tomi's hand and we entered the restaurant.

'Hey! I'm in the mood to celebrate,' I told her once we'd been seated and ordered a bottle of Dom Perignon. 'Let's have a toast, "To success and happiness!"' I proposed.

Then we clinked glasses and drank, Tomi letting loose the tiniest belch afterward, giggling as she covered her mouth with her hand.

'I never been to a place like this before, Jack,' she said taking in the restaurant's décor and its patrons—men in custom-made Italian suits making deals, lovers sharing intimacies across a table, all impeccably coiffed, faces bright and shiny with success.

'Not with clients?'

'Motel rooms, mostly. Dinner at the hotel's restaurant, sometimes room service. Got so those rooms was more like prison cells to me, baby.'

'Seems like most of our time together was spent in rooms like that,' I said taking down a second glass and pouring her another.

'Maybe it was, Jack, but you took me to New York,' she answered proudly.

'Yeah, I did.'

'And you're happy for it, ain't ya, Jack?'

'Sure thing,' I said, wondering why champagne glasses were always so fucking small as I waved down a waiter to get menus and another bottle.

Dinner was as good as advertised and, believe it or not, we did catch sight of a celeb or two, if you consider Matt Lauer from *Today* and Lindsay Lohan, fresh out of rehab, celebrities. But they were enough for Tomi who, after we'd eaten and were on to after-dinner drinks, got serious as she was prone to do in the final stretch of a night out.

'So what is it so important up there in that building with the big red "9," Jack? What is it worth all this worryin'?'

I smiled confidently, contemplating Tomi's question. *So, what is it so important up there? How about potentially the most important bio-medical breakthrough in human history.* And I'd done some research on my own to back that claim up.

For centuries human beings had dreamed about regenerating the body from its own cells, but humans—unlike certain animals—have very little regenerative capacity because of an evolutionary tradeoff: suppressing cell growth reduced the risk of cancer, so humans lived longer. A person could re-grow his liver, and re-grow a fingertip while very young, but not much more. AvaTech scientists had found a way to 'silence' genes known to suppress tumors, isolate them once they reverted to a stemlike state, then allow them to multiply to create new muscle, cartilage, bone, even nerve cells so they could be transplanted into injured patients. Research studies had already demonstrated the technique's near limitless possibilities: advanced treatments for wounded soldiers—burn patients, amputees—victims of heart attacks, liver and kidney disease, even Alzheimer's. *So, yeah, Tomi, getting my hands on these studies to sell to the Chin Chou was worth all the worrying!*

Of course, she didn't need a dissertation, I was thinking as I downed the last of the Dom Perignon, but to me it was important for her to understand the magnitude of our endeavor, 'Let me explain,' I answered as patiently as I could tell it. "What we're taking out of those offices at 9 West tomorrow night could change medicine forever, Tomi. It's a technique that uses RNA to reprogram cells so that they multiply into healthy tissue or muscle or whatever an injured body may need to heal faster, or simply replace whatever organ may have been damaged.'

'Tissues? Organs? I don't know nothin' about that, Jack,' she said, taking a sip from her champagne glass, laughing.

'Look, you see that man over there?' I said motioning two tables away. 'Would you say he has a lot of money?'

'Sure, why not?' she answered.

'What if I told you he had three months to live? How much do you think he'd pay to have those cancer cells that are eating him alive from the inside stop multiplying and have normal, healthy ones take their place?'

'I don't know, Jack! I'm no doctor!'

'All right, take that woman,' I said, motioning to a second table across the room. 'What if I told you she had a son, a nineteen-year-old son just come back from Afghanistan, second and third degree burns covering his face and arms and legs. Burns that would scar him, turn him into a freak for the rest of his life. How much do you think she'd be willing to pay to see those burns healed and what would have been scars too hideous to describe replaced by new skin, fresh and healthy and normal?'

'A lot,' Tomi uttered.

'How much?'

'I don't know,' she stammered.

'No, seriously,' I insisted, looking deep into her ebony eyes. 'How much would you pay to repair burn damage that would make your son, who came back to you body covered with burns, healthy again, so he could be proud of himself, get a job, find a girl, and live a normal life?'

'Anything. Everything. I would pay all that I had if that was my chile!' she answered, as ardent as I had ever seen her.

'That's right, Baby, anything and everything,' I said, stroking her cheek with my fingertips and gazing into the most soulful eyes I had ever encountered. 'Wait here, I've got a phone call to make.'

Then I walked into the bar, buzzing with laughter and conversation, through to the doorway just outside the entrance to Babbo where I dialed an international number.

'Speak,' the voice of Wei Li demanded.

'This is Madson. We get your recipes tomorrow. I'll be at the Hong Kong Hilton day after next. *Zhiao*, Mr. Li.'

The next thing I heard was a click at the other end. The deal was on. Tomi and I would be making our move on the AvaTech files, 2 p.m. tomorrow.

# Chapter 33

Tomi and I got back to our room early a.m.,
sleepwalked through our sex, fell asleep in a heap,
and that was that, lights out. Not a word. Not even
a glance at one another. Like we were drugged, only it
wasn't the kind of drug you take externally. More like the
internal kind, say adrenalin, except it had the opposite
effect like we were marionettes and Gepetto had just cut
the strings.

We slept in and didn't get out of bed until near 10 a.m.
From there it was coffee, strong, a discussion about how
dressed up Tomi should be to catch the guards' attention,
with my wardrobe consisting of an ultra-conservative Brooks
Brothers suit and blue power tie. During that time and for
the rest of the morning, Tomi and me, we were awash in
tension, silent and pervasive, the words between us terse,
near military in cadence, about the most basic kind of
logistics. 'Where would we eat?' 'For how long?' 'Weren't
there alternate scenarios to the break-in still to be gone
over?' This was the day all right, no doubt about that.

At 11:45 a.m., we took the walk from the Sherry
Netherland to the Plaza Hotel where we had eggs Benedict,
juice, and mimosas, two each 'to fortify our backbones,' I
told her. Fact is, I never worried about Tomi's drinking,
even that day. She could put them down all right, but

sexy as she was without two or three drinks, she was a lot sexier—eyes large and fluid with that big lazy grin of hers—after a couple stiff ones: right out of central casting for her role as seductress at the Solow Building.

'You're awful quiet,' Tomi said.

'You, too,' I answered sipping from a cup of espresso. 'Guess we both got a lot to consider.'

'You more than me, lover.'

'Yes,' I answered solemnly.

'Sorry you brought me along?'

'Nah, you been great, really.'

'What then?'

'I know it's not likely and, Christ knows, I've studied blueprints of Number 9 West 57th from the internet, even made drawings of my own from memory, but I've got some serious time to kill up there on the 46th floor, maybe six or seven hours. Afterward, once everyone's left the building, I've got to take the stairs up to the 50th, undetected. No sure bet since there'll still be maintenance workers and guards around from then 'til morning.'

'You ain't losin' your nerve, are you, Jack?'

'Not my nerves I'm worried about, Baby. It's my freedom. Ever been to a maximum security prison?'

'Just the local lockup in Ann Arbor. No big thing, but what about me? What happens to me after you come down off that mountaintop on 9 West?'

'Look,' I said leaning across the table to take her hand, 'you just take care of those guards. Get them talking, the way I know you can, and once you see I'm on the elevator headed up, go back to the hotel and wait for me there. After that the only thing you need to think about is how you're gonna spend the $250K I plan on forkin' over to you once this is over. That's not so tough, is it?'

'No, that ain't so tough, Baby. I'll be there waitin', you can count on that.'

I smiled when Tomi said that, so matter-of-factly and determined. Then our eyes met and, yeah, I almost said it, almost said 'I love you' and she almost said 'And after this is over? Then what?' But neither of us said a word, though our fingertips touched if only for a moment. And just then I felt like a Little League outfielder running to catch a fly ball calling 'I got it!' along with a teammate, only to watch the ball drop onto the grass between us.

'Yeah,' I said, 'it's already 1:20.'

The walk to 9 West 57th was second nature to us by then. We'd done it physically three times earlier but dozens of times in our heads. But unlike the clothes Tomi wore that day, we never debated what we'd do once that big red '9' came into view. Synchronized like clockwork, we'd enter the lobby as strangers—me behind her—separated by mere seconds. Her first, to engage the guards at Security. Me afterward, moving toward the elevator banks swift as a bullet the minute Tomi engaged them.

Then, there it was. Jesus, Phials, even now I can see that oversized red '9' like it's been branded onto my brain, such was its impact on me that afternoon.

'1:58, Baby,' I said glancing at the face of my Avenger.

'I love you, Jack,' Tomi whispered. I started to say something but she touched my lips with her fingertips. 'You don't have to say nothing, lover. Just know that deep in my heart I do, no matter what else happens.'

I nodded my understanding if not my acceptance

and she was gone, a Burberry raincoat swept away toward that gaudy red number as she blended into the river of pedestrians and street vendors toward our destiny, me about to follow, only a few seconds behind.

Through the plate glass, I observed 9 West's security guards, three of them, positioned just beyond the lobby's entrance, watching like hawks as the flood of secretaries, managers, senior execs, salesmen, corporate lawyers, and maintenance workers bustled through the building's main entrance on West 57th Street, Tomi Fabri among them. A short line had already queued in front of the Security Desk, north side of the lobby, but it was moving fast, I took note, heart pounding like a timpani as I caught sight of Tomi pulling off one of the ballsiest stunts I ever saw. Once a place in front of the desk opened, she pretended to turn her ankle when she stepped forward lunging to her right and away from the elevators, holding onto the marble countertop for support as she hung over it, breasts presented like on a silver platter, eyes staring vulnerably and helplessly into those of the Solow Building's Head of Security.

Having already entered the lobby (looking all business with briefcase in hand), I'd have no better opportunity than this, I was thinking, as I heard a man's voice say, 'Are you all right, Miss?' and another 'Here, let me help you!' and watched as even the guard stationed mid-lobby in front of the elevators gravitated from his post to see what was happening. 'It's my ankle!' I could hear Tomi gasp in a sultry Marilyn Monroe voice. And as I darted toward the alcove, carved like a cave into the lobby's center, from the corner of my eye I could see Tomi surrounded by adoring men all in blue security blazers as she hiked up her dress to her thigh to reveal a shapely ankle and exactly where it hurt.

And it was with that not unpleasant image that I slipped into Elevator #3, floors 25 through 50. I pressed the button to the 46th floor—the vacant one—at the last minute hoping no one would notice, careful to keep from giving the security cameras anything more than my back and a sideshot of my face.

Eyes glued to the elevator floor, the chime sounding at each stop rallied a strange sense of pride like the bell signaling the end of a round in a boxing match. Round 1, '*Yeah, I made it and was winning!*' Rounds 2 and 3, '*Still on my feet, motherfucker!*' Rounds 4, 5, 6, '*Yeah, I'm cruising, baby!*' Until the last and final bell, the one for the 46th floor and '*Yeah, right! It was me! I am the last man standing! A solitary warrior on my way to $5M and the Heavyweight Championship of the World!!*' the voice in the back of my head bellowed, my body taut, my heart pulsing as I exited the empty elevator into the darkened corridor, finally allowing myself a sigh of relief.

From there I slipped off to the right, beyond the glass doors, into what used to be the offices of Schwartzcroft & Stern, an investment firm gone belly-up during the '09 recession. The offices were not heated, I noticed shivering, as I moved swiftly past what was once the reception area. The shadowy dim of emergency lights revealed discarded magazines and corporate brochures strewn around like the skulls of dead cattle bleached white in the desert. My eyes scoured the rows of empty offices to my left and right, deciding (why the hell not!) to head for the one far back and in the corner. The one with the view of Central Park, office of the Chairman and CEO, I concluded, an ironic smile passing over my lips. I plunged on through the Park-side corridor past deserted cubicles, huddle rooms, the board room with its enormous Sony flat screen TV monitor, simultaneous translating equipment and U-shaped configuration of seating, then paused at its entrance.

'Must have been some hot shit, these guys Schwartzcroft and Stern, at least until fourth quarter 2008 and the collapse: "Schwartzcroft & Stern! We've Got Your Best Interest at Heart!" the advertising slogans went. "Worried About Retirement?? You Can Count On The Expertise Of Schwartzcroft & Stern To Guide You Through Life's Unanticipated Bumps!" "Schwartzcroft & Stern: Integrity! Sound Business Judgment! Years Of Experience!" '*Well, fuck them all! Fuck them all and their penny stocks, ponzi schemes, complex investment instruments, and financial derivatives! Fuck all their bullshit!!*' I solemnly reveled, marching beyond the offices of Schwartzcroft & Stern Business Managers, Directors, VPs, and CFO into the inner sanctum of Chairman and CEO, Arnold Schwartzcroft.

Even empty as it was, I had to concede Schwartzcroft's digs were impressive. Big modern desk, flat screen TV monitors, bookshelves that covered an entire wall (were the books *real?*), I observed as I walked through it like a kid whistling past the graveyard, in awe of the ghosts that swirled alongside me in an office dimly lit with bright city lights reflecting through the plate glass windows.

I entered the private lavatory, glanced to the mirror on the wall, my eyes drifting to the commode and porcelain sink with ornamental faucets, wondering how much a guy like Schwartcroft left with after the catastrophic failure of his company. $100 million? $200 million? Who the fuck knew? Not me. I didn't know and didn't want to know, I was thinking, as I floated—a spectral spirit myself—to a world globe that, sliced in half and held together by a stainless steel hinge, might open to reveal Tiffany glassware and an ample supply of liquor. I tried my luck. Had workers or security or the jackal executives themselves beaten me to it? I wondered, a large grin expanding from the corners of my lips when I saw it had somehow remained stocked.

Never one to miss an opportunity for celebration, I helped myself to a bottle of Chivas (not my label!) along with a half dozen Ritalin tabs taken from my trusty briefcase and poured myself a scotch, neat, slugging the pills down, then drifting—drink in hand—toward the plate glass window to take in what was a fucking-ay spectacular view of Central Park and its surroundings.

From that vantage point, understanding that sooner than I could imagine I'd be up on the 50th floor in Lisa Ellison's office, I studied the Sherry Netherland Hotel trying to calculate the window to the room where Tomi was waiting, then stared at it until my eyes watered.

In a matter of hours, I'd be back there, flash drive in hand, and $5M richer.

# Chapter 34

Can I begin to describe the dread I was feeling as darkness fell over the city and the tide of commuters withdrew like the sea before a tsunami, and I realized the moment of truth had finally come? Yeah, Phials, I was plenty nervous as I took my last pull from the bottle of Chivas, stuffed it in my briefcase, and started retracing my steps out of Schwartzcroft's office through the empty corridors back to the lobby.

The emergency lights cast a saffron glow on everything—office furniture, wall clocks, even the cubicles—illuminating the edges so they looked more like the outline of things than the actual physical objects. And as I'd suspected, feeling my way along the corridors of the deserted office that night was creeping me out big time, but I stayed the course! Once I got to the lobby, I moved to the door and cracked it open to check out the main hallway, relieved to see it was desolate: nobody and nothing. I pushed open the glass door to the entrance of Schwartzcroft & Stern, then crept cautious as a B&E artist toward the heavy metal 'EXIT' door leading to the emergency stairway.

I shoved the door open and entered the concrete landing (it reeked of cigarette smoke) careful to hold onto it an extra couple of seconds so it shut without a sound, then turned toward the staircase rising up in front of me. I took a deep breath and began climbing, understanding that time was not on my side. The longer I stayed in 9 West, the greater the odds of being discovered. That basic understanding, the thought of $5M and a second chance at starting my life over, was all the inspiration I needed as I arrived at each landing — 47, 48, 49, and 50 — the thought of prison or, worse, the total failure of my plan and my life jabbing at me from behind like the sharp point of a saber. '*Move your ass, Madson!*' the possessor of that long sharp saber was screeching, red-faced as he poked me. '*You know you're a loser. Always have been! So move your ass and move it now! Show us what you got, Kid!!*' And I responded (as I always did!) not bothering to catch my breath as I stopped at the landing and reached for the steel handle of the emergency exit door marked '50.'

I jerked the heavy metal door one-quarter of the way open and poked my head out to look for guards or maintenance workers. I saw no one and was about to make my move — landing to hallway — when I heard the sound of a man's voice

'Hey! We still got work to do!' he called out to someone across the corridor from him.

Then, summoning every ounce of restraint in my body, I pulled the door back toward me, inch by inch. The voice, *that voice*, I realized, wasn't far from me, a suspicion confirmed by the squealing sound of wheels turning and the clanking of metal on metal: the sound of a mop and bucket being pushed to a spot just beyond the door where I stood.

I pressed my ear against the metal door, gradually easing my weight from it, allowing it to close, and finally shut with a 'click.'

'*¡Eh! ¿Has oído lo que te dije? ¿Estás descansando de nuevo?*' the man just beyond the door called out again.

A faded response coming back this time, '*¡Estoy cansado! ¡Estuve toda la noche con mi novia!*' the second man called back to the first, with me so near the maintenance worker beyond the door that I could hear him sigh, then mutter, '*Lazy bastard!*' before finally walking away.

Then the two of them, I imagined, took the elevator down. I couldn't say to what floor but if I was lucky all the way down to the building's basement where "maintenance" had its office and the workers' lockers were housed.

After that I can tell you, my heart was racing and even with that saber beginning to prod me again, I rested the side of my face on the cool metal of that red door, eyes wide open, feverish with anxiety, as I began to read the graffiti disgruntled office workers out for a smoke had scrawled on the walls with black markers, spray paint, even lipstick. 'WHERE'S MY BAILOUT, MOTHERFUCKER?' asked one. 'FUCK CORKY IN THE ASS!' wrote another. 'ALL BANKERS ARE FAGGOTS!' wrote another. 'CAPITALISM EATS ITS YOUNG!' And as I stood there, collecting my nerve in that stinking concrete stairway, I actually wondered, 'Have I died? Am I in Hell?' But that saber, it wouldn't leave me alone or give me time to think or time to rest and like a soldier responding to the calvary call something deep inside me rallied and I was back at the top of my game, perspiration running down my face and armpits as I pulled at the steel door handle, opened the door again, and made my move out into the hallway of the offices of NuGeneration Holdings, Inc.

Through the soundless corridor I darted, through the glass doors with the Remington Rider Logo emblazoned on them, past the reception area—clinical as a surgeon's operating room—beyond the admin's desk and business managers and sales offices, through to the executive wing and straight as a rifle shot into the office of Lisa Ellison, VP-BioTech Division. I stood just beyond the doorway, eyes scanning the business and self-help books, faux art, the half-dozen or more photos of 'Lisa with Dog,' 'Lisa with Parents,' 'Lisa with Nephew,' 'Lisa with Nieces,' finally coming to an abrupt stop at the Dell OptiPlex desktop that was standard issue at NuGen these days.

This was it, the moment I'd obsessed over since leaving Mexico and I was not about to blow it, I swore to myself. And from the second I laid eyes on that computer, a sense of manic efficiency seized me like I was possessed by Satan himself. Like I was a kind of automaton, especially after I sat behind Lisa's desk and got to work in front of her desktop switching it on, having already decided on my approach to getting beyond the firewall and personal security blocks, which passwords I would use, and my fallback position if I guessed wrong twice.

The screen lit up with the sound of wind chimes and the configuration of Window 7 Professional's multi-colored logo coming together, then switching to a second screen bearing the words, 'Press CTRL+ALT+DELETE to begin the log-in process. And so I followed instructions, eyes like needle points glued to the screen. 'CM/npx1e11i' were the letters that popped up on the next screen, Lisa's operator ID, just above the white blank space, cursor within it, flashing 'password.' *Yeah, password,* I was thinking, the thumping pulse sent from my heart to my temples beating a steady, elevating rhythm as the blood rushed through my veins and I launched my first attack on NuGen's security block.

Employee passwords consisted of four numbers followed by letters, no fewer than six and no more than eleven. I remembered (if you could call the eruptions bursting into my brain "memories") that in choosing the first of the three tries I'd considered everything important to Lisa Ellison: her mother who she idolized, her Porche 911 that she pampered like a newborn, even her nephew whose photograph with her (both wearing a white jiu-jitsu gi) I was staring at across the desktop but, in the end, it was all about her, wasn't it? 'Use your name and date of birth, or the name of a pet,' she'd told me in a conversation months before. No husband, no kids, no real friends—deep in her heart she understood that—and so my first choice was easy: Lisa's date of birth ,1976, followed by her name written in eleven consecutive letters, *1976lisaellison.*

My mouth was dry and I could hardly swallow as I entered the four digits, pecking them out one at a time on the keyboard. Then, 'lisa,' I tapped out. And finally 'ellison' I typed, staring at the screen and the white box now filled with my first choice number-letter combination, nodding my head with conviction and pressing the computer's 'ENTER' key, eyes closed and praying.

When I opened my eyes it was like someone punched me full-force in the solar plexes with an impact that actually threw me back in my chair. '*Shit!*' I swore under my breath, the resolve for an attack with my second choice of passwords gathering like a tumultuous storm inside me. '*It's the dog!*' I swore, eyes locking on the color photo of Lisa smiling with that little white faggot papillon she was always gushing about wrapped in an 'oh-so-cuddly' embrace. '*It's got to be the dog!*' I affirmed and this second choice should have been my first, I was thinking, having heard a dozen times a dozen that 2010 was, as she put it, 'the grandest year ever' since it was in April 2010 that little dog-monster Oliver came into her life.

The rest was logic, if not science: four numbers '2-0-1-0,' six to eleven letters, 'o-l-i-v-e-r.' The password I was laying my second bet down on, far and away the best choice after tipping a hat to Lisa's own vanity, and one I knew in my heart she had used and was using, but once the 90 day mandatory password switch was added to the equation, well, who could know if that particular day *2010oliver* was 'on' or if it was 'off?'

So I went for it, Phials, full bore this time, pounding the number-letter combination out on the keyboard in a blind fury of optimism, hoping to somehow will it to be correct, then staring at that tiny rectangular box, moving my hand toward the 'ENTER' key and plunging my finger down on it.

'*Fuck! Fucking bullshit, motherfucker!!*' I seethed. "*You lousy bitch! You don't even know how to pick a fucking password!!*' I was ranting as the little 'x' and the words 'the user or password is incorrect' blinked back at me, cold and unemotional, a machine after all, that had the power to make or break me.

I took a deep breath then blew the air out of my lungs, knowing I had to get centered, *focus*, and it was like I was at a craps table in Atlantic City or Vegas. Everything I had, my very existence, was on the line and totally dependent on a single roll of the dice or, in my case, a set of three letters followed by seven numbers, the administrator password given to me by an Indian kid named Suresh nearly four years before. The odds? I just didn't know, I had to admit, my confidence fading in the welter of two miscalculations in a row. '*Okay, okay,*' I tried to calm myself. '*No reason to believe the password's changed. You tried the others, saving the best for last, a safety net, so here you are, no better or worse than you calculated,*' I reasoned, literally talking to myself as I typed the letters 'A-N-G' in caps, followed by a dash and the numbers '0-0-1,' followed again by a dash and finally the four digits '1-7-6-4,' *ANG-001-1764.*

I studied my handiwork. There it was, everything I'd dreamed about, everything I wanted, in the white box. I glanced at the face of my Avenger, seeing that it was already 10:15 p.m., understanding fully that this was my last and only chance at breaking through NuGen's security block to gain access to AvaTech's **Genesis Too** file and the freedom I'd spent my entire adult life trying to find. Then, without another thought, I punched the 'ENTER' key and— *bang!*—that was it! With wind chimes sounding, the screen reformed a new configuration as apps, one after the other, popped up on the screen like rabbits from a magician's hat, '**Novelis**,' '**SHE**,' '**Legal**,' '**Manufacturing**,' '**Financials**,' and finally the file I'd been waiting to see, been dreaming about for probably longer than even I knew myself—'**HCR**,' the 'human cell regeneration' file and with it the business life of Lisa Ellison, VP-BioTech Division opened up before me in its entirety, the entrance to a new and wondrous world materialized with me standing at its threshold!

Frantic with excitement, hands trembling, I reached into my briefcase for the Iomega flash drive. Then, as efficiently as Suresh or any computer geek in NuGen's IT Department, I attached it to the adaptor and then into the USB 3.0 portal. With adaptor installed, I made the connection and watched it link with the desktop's motherboard, streams of sweat wending their way from my temples down the sides of my face as a stunning series of letters, numbers, and scrawlings like hieroglyphics flashed at blinding speed across the desktop's monitor.

Within seconds, the files had transferred. The AvaTech research was mine, a wave of satisfaction warm as mother's milk passing over me as I meticulously closed each of the open files, logged out, and disconnected the 250 GB flash drive to cover my intrusion. About to slip the device into my open briefcase, I suddenly felt the odd sensation of someone staring at me and stopped to look up. Standing, flashlight in hand in the doorway to Lisa Ellison's office was Sgt. Cephus Jackson, security officer in charge of the Solow Building, floors 35 through 50.

'*Mr. Madson, what in God's name you doin' here?*'

# Chapter 35

I know what people mean when they say 'caught red-handed,' though I never stopped to consider from where the expression derived. But one thing certain, that night—at that moment on the 50th floor of 9 West in Lisa Ellison's office—I knew I'd been caught 'red-handed' as Sgt. Cephus Jackson stared me down and I secured the flash drive that contained the secrets to human cell regeneration in my briefcase.

'Cephus, that you?' I asked stupidly, pretending the flashlight's glare had me struggling to see.

'Yeah, Mr. Madson. It's me, Cephus. What you doin' here? What you doin' in Miss Ellison's office, Mr. Madson? What you doin' alive at all since you supposed to be . . . *dead.*'

I grinned about the phoniest grin I'd ever mustered, clasping the briefcase handle in my right hand as I rose from the chair behind Lisa's desk.

'No, I'm not dead,' I laughed. 'In fact, I'm very much alive, haven't you heard? Didn't anyone tell you?'

'Nobody told me nothin',' the tall, rangy black man answered eyes turned suspicious. 'But that aside, why you in Miss Ellison's office? And why you operatin' her computer in the dark?' he continued, his train of thought carrying him to a most unfortunate conclusion as his hand dropped slowly toward the .38 Smith & Wesson he carried in a holster hanging at his hip.

'No need for that, Sargeant,' I temporized, palms held in the air, still grinning like an idiot. 'If you think something's wrong here, that's fine. That's your job. But there isn't anything wrong here. I'm just taking back some work Lisa took over for me while I was away. She knows about it, so does Mr. McCorkle.'

Jackson's hand pulled up from his weapon as gradually as it had lowered, his wary eyes locked on me, a predator studying his prey, calculating the odds of pursuing his first instinct which was to arrest me at gunpoint or mitigate his stance, allow me the benefit of the doubt by taking the matter to a higher authority.

'You know, I'm really sorry about this confusion. I can't believe they didn't tell you I was in a hospital and got released yesterday. Clean bill of health,' I went on moving around the side of Lisa's desk toward him, 'though I got to admit I took a terrible konk on the head during that boat accident.'

'Stay there where you are,' Cephus demanded.

I stopped dead in my tracks, not five feet from him.

'Hey, Cephus, how long we known each other, five years? What say you and me head down to the first floor Security Desk and straighten all this out. It's you I'm thinkin' about, Buddy,' I told him re-calibrating my steps more toward Lisa's open door than him. 'It's good you're doin' your job here, my friend, but let's don't get overexcited. Let's go see the Lieutenant, he'll tell you. He'll show you I'm security cleared and a bona fide NuGen employee, alive and in good standing.'

'Seems reasonable,' Jackson said, still suspicious and now resentful at the complexity that confronted him.

'Yeah, that's right! That's the ticket! So let's go,' I said, proceeding as he reluctantly followed me out of Lisa's office, through the lobby, and into the hallway.

'Wait a minute,' Cephus said, stopping as sudden and intransigent as a mule. 'I'm goin' to radio Lt. Evans, make sure he's back at the Desk from rounds.'

'Suit yourself,' I said turning to face him, watching, the paranoia building up from the soles of my feet like a storm rising into my torso and heart, hands and fingertips, face and brain as Cephus took his Motorola two-way in hand then raised it up toward his mouth, me knowing that if I allowed him to start that transmission it was all over, I was good as dead.

As if in slow motion, my eyes followed every millimeter of his movement—radio to lips—finger to 'transmit' button and then that energy, all of those thousands of thermal units of energy churned up and funneled from the storm raging inside me seemed to purify into a single thought and that single thought like a lightning bolt leapt from my brain into my fist as I struck Cephus Jackson a massive blow to the side of the head that sent him reeling backward into the corridor's wall where he hung momentarily until his legs gave way beneath him leaving him semi-conscious and sprawling on the floor.

The suddenness and violence of the punch left me nearly as perplexed as he was and I stood there (staring quizzically at the hand that did it!) watching as he gathered his wits, soon understanding what had happened to him and started to reach for his holstered weapon.

His eyes and my eyes stared into one another's, both of us realizing at the same moment that we were indeed locked in a death struggle that one or the other of us would not survive. Then with instincts running rampant through me, I searched that dimly lit hallway for a weapon of my own, eyes falling upon the mop and bucket left behind by the night maintenance workers.

Cephus sprawled as he was, long arms and lanky legs scattered in different directions, attempted as best he could to grab hold of his gun, and after several false starts managed to clasp it in his hands. He was pointing it at me, about to shoot, when I reached down to my left, seized the steel mop wringer from out of its galvanized steel bucket, and swung it blindly around like a baseball bat, coming down hard on top of the security guard's skull an instant before he pulled the trigger!

The mop wringer was a hideous weapon, a weapon of mass destruction at least when it came to the skull and face of Cephus Jackson, the first of which caved-in like a rotted Halloween pumpkin, the second of which seemed frozen like a clown's mask, two dollops of red blood pooled high on his cheekbones wending down from the frontal part of his skull to his forehead, onto his face.

*What had I done?* a part of me shrieked in horror at the sight of him. No subtlety here, the corpse at my feet told me in no uncertain terms as I returned the mop wringer back into its bucket and the pool of soapy water submerging it again. My eyes shot up and down the hallway, it was vacant but wouldn't stay that way for long, I knew. At my feet directly across from Cephus Jackson's body sitting as grotesque as a ventriloquist's dummy—reduced so cruelly from person to thing—was my briefcase and within it the flash drive I had done all this to possess. The question before me at that moment, I quickly concluded, was not 'what had I done?' I understood what I had done and would spend the rest of my life contemplating 'why I had done it,' the problem staring me in the face in the corridor that night was 'what to do with the body?'

The answer came to me with surprising ease. I was on the 50$^{th}$ floor already. With Cephus dead and his head bashed-in (but with remarkably little blood) there was only one course of action for me to take: carry it to the roof and toss it over before rigor mortis set to make it look like suicide!

I glanced to the mop bucket and mop wringer making the quick calculation that to leave it there and let the maintenance men mop the floors with its contents as if nothing had happened was better than trying to improvise a cover-up that seemed sure to backfire. 'No,' I thought then, trying my best not to panic, 'you need to move now while you can, before the maintenance workers return.' And so I did, jerking Cephus' blue security blazer over his head from the back to stem the flow of blood, then throwing his 6-foot 2-inch, 170-pound body over my shoulder marine-style, as I took my briefcase in my other hand, opened the emergency exit door, and began my trek up from the 50$^{th}$ floor to the roof.

How bizarre was it then when as I lugged my victim's corpse up that last flight of steps, he began talking to me through the bloody fabric of his blue blazer? 'I ain't dead,' I heard the muffled voice say and I swear to Christ, Phials, I almost had a coronary right there, right on the staircase as I approached the maintenance door leading to the roof. 'I ain't dead,' Cephus Jackson repeated, the irony of one supposed dead man speaking to another inescapable as he continued. 'Don't worry,' he said talking from the left corner of his mouth like a stroke victim, 'Don't matter anyways. Got cancer, bad cancer.' 'I'm not going to kill you!' I told him, pushing open the maintenance door with my free hand. 'Broke for bills. Wife gone. Kill me. Gonna do it myself anyways,' he muttered, 'but you still a murderer.' 'I'm going to take you up on the roof, then call an ambulance once I'm out of here, *you got that?*' I hissed back over my shoulder at the half-dead man. 'I be dead soon,' he insisted as I took him down from my shoulder and pulled the blue blazer that hooded his face back over his head again, 'but you got to live with it. That some heavy liftin' for a man to carry. Some mighty heavy liftin'.

I positioned his long limp frame sitting on the ground below the ledge of the brick safety wall and looked down into his bloody face, a mass of skin and tissue pushed up above his forehead like a king's crown. I turned, ready to walk away, when from the corner of my eye I could see that like a cadaver risen from the grave, Cephus had propped himself up against the safety wall and was standing dazedly, a Ruger LCR revolver in hand.

'I carry two guns, Mr. Madson, didn't think about that, did you?' he asked, half laughing, eyes lit bright as candles. 'Now, I'm gonna shoot 'cause I don't think I'll live long 'nough to arrest you.'

Then his glazed-over eyes narrowed and I lunged toward him, right shoulder hitting him hard at the waist. The gun went flying into the air and he stumbled back as if in some final stage of his death throes, twisting furiously to escape my grip—then he did—falling backward over the wall. His body spiraled in semi-circles as he fell those fifty-one stories down onto the plaza with a sickening *thwomp*, his brains and guts and innards spread across the concrete not twenty feet from the big red '9.'

# Chapter 36

I didn't take time to watch the spectacle caused by a body hurtling to the ground from the roof of a New York office building, but it wasn't hard to imagine as I raced off the roof back into the stairway: business types hanging around after hours, entering and leaving bars; shoppers hailing taxis on their way back to hotel rooms; tourists rushing to pre-theater dinners. Everyone's attention would instinctively go to the body, but seeing the bloody remains of what was once a human being splattered on the concrete, they'd be forced to turn away, repulsed.

The 57th Street traffic would stop as drivers leaned from car windows to get a better look. Security guards would come running from out of 9 West's lobby. They'd crane their heads up, eyes combing the fifty-one stories to try to discern what floor the guy on the ground had leapt from, realizing finally — since the windows were sealed — it could only be the roof. But by then it would be too late. The roof would be empty and I'd be long gone, I calculated barreling down each of those fifty-one flights that night. Before the security guards realized what happened and called 911, and the cops arrived on the scene, I'd be on my way out one of 9 West's emergency exits set between 57th and 58th Streets, headed for the Sherry Netherland where Tomi waited.

And that was exactly how it happened. Like my thoughts had become author to my reality, police and ambulance sirens screaming through the night as I made my out of the Solow Building's emergency exit into the urine-soaked alleyway, and blended into pedestrian traffic on West 58<sup>th</sup> Street, briefcase in hand.

Could it be I'd lucked-out, downloaded the AvaTech files, and was going to make it out of New York, hide intact? I marveled at my good fortune, walking briskly toward Central Park, the Sherry Netherland Hotel where Tomi waited. The amphetamine fix from hours before was wearing down like the spring of a wind-up watch, but the rest of it, the effect of the other factors: the excitement of the theft, the rush of my death-struggle with Cephus Jackson, and the thrill of escaping 9 West undetected, well, how could I be anything but wired, amphetamine fix or not?

My thoughts, admittedly rambling then, touched next on the subject of Tomi and what to do with her. Sure, she'd done her part—such as it was—and next morning I'd make sure she got the money I promised. But then, for me, it was over. I'd be leaving New York and Tomi was on her own, albeit $250K richer. Enough money to change her life, help her snare the guy or gal she seemed so intent on finding, though in my heart of hearts I doubted that would ever happen. More likely she'd go back to Motor City, rent a fancy apartment, throw money around like it was confetti, and get ripped-off by some smooth talker somewhere along the way, but that was her problem, not mine.

As for me, once I made it to Hong Kong to collect the $5M I had coming from Wei Lee, I'd head back to Mexico. Why the hell not? True, I was a little worse for the wear, but nothing fundamental had changed. Queretaro hadn't changed! It was still the tranquil oasis amid a world of violence and corruption, a world 'untainted by the tawdry affairs of men' as the poets say. So far as my situation, that too was basically unaltered by everything that had happened since I first left the U. S. I still had the money, $50K in my pocket with another $5M on the way, roughly double the stash I originally planned to take with me first time around. So what had really changed, I asked myself, except for the one thing I never counted on . . . the murder.

Manslaughter, at best, murder, at worst, I conceded darkly, as I cut across Central Park South toward the Sherry Netherland, something cold and shadowy rustling within me as I pondered the man I'd become since leaving my family, my job and my life behind, reluctant to contemplate the stark fact that on this night I'd become a killer, without explanation, in fact, with very little in the way of forethought at all. With horrifying detachment I wondered what being a killer of men meant to the way I would live my life from that night forward, the way I would see myself, who I was as a person. *Was I a bad man?* I asked myself, since bashing another human being's brains in? *Had I become evil?* Or was I, like the others I knew—and had known—a man of indeterminate value?

I raised my right hand so near my face I could see the glint from the headlights of passing cars reflecting in the tiny ruby set in the center of my St. Damian's graduation ring and read the Latin words inscribed in each corner of the pyramid around it: *scientiam, fiden, humilitatem*, the words read, *knowledge, faith, humility*, the three legs of the stool that, if followed, would keep a young man on the path to a moral life. *'How could things have gone so terribly wrong?'* I asked myself then. And you can believe me, Phials, I agonized over that question, nodding a distant greeting to the doorman as I entered the hotel, recognizing for the first time that there was something deep inside me that loved Death.

Truth be told, I didn't know who Jack Madson was anymore. Like I possessed an identity, or believed I possessed one, but had somehow lost it along the way. Like the pinions that held my life together and the compass that once directed it were suddenly missing, leaving me adrift. And know something, Phials? That was what terrified me more than anything. See, from that night forward, I knew the life that lay before me, my future, would forever be a blank white slate of nothingness.

Those were the thoughts that occupied my mind as I entered the hotel room that night, closing the door behind me, walking into the living room, and stopping dead in my tracks. It was Tomi standing there on the landing above the dining room wearing a red dress with stiletto heels, sexy as ever, a Bell .32 Ultra-Lite clutched in both her hands pointed directly at me.

'Guess there'll be no "Welcome home, dear" tonight, will there?'

'Shut up, Jack,' she told me, her two hands shaking as she trained the gun on me.

I didn't react, didn't blink, but continued taking off my suit jacket, hanging it over the back of a dining room chair set behind the mahogany chiffonier filled with glassware and china.

'You know you're not going to use that gun, so why point it? You're no murderer. You could never shoot me. Hell, you couldn't say "No" if I asked you to suck my cock right now.'

'I told you to shut up!' Tomi insisted.

'Yes, she told you to shut up, Jack,' a second woman's voice, throatier, more authoritative, chimed in.

It was a familiar voice, I realized, eyes traveling up the landing beyond Tomi to find Jennifer standing outside the entrance to the bedroom.

'I might have guessed it was you behind this. What kind of bullshit she been filling your head with, baby?' I asked accusingly.

Tomi tried to respond but couldn't hold a candle to Jennifer's sense of timing, or treachery, and it was Jen who answered.

'Tomi and I are a couple, Jack. I think it's time you knew that. It began innocently enough. I was naïve . . . '

'*You, naïve!*' I scoffed.

'I was *naïve*,' she insisted, 'perplexed as to why you were cheating on me and with whom. I'd always given you what you wanted sexually, was even willing to petition Father on your behalf to help finance that ridiculous crusade you were planning to become a Congressman or Senator, or whatever it was . . . '

'And the AvaTech files? I suppose they had nothing to do with any of this?'

'Father's detectives never lost track of you, Jack. Not in the United States and not in Mexico. They told us you were still alive and back here, if that's what you're getting at?'

'That is what I'm getting at!'

'But then I met her — *Tomi* — the woman who'd taken you from me,' she soldiered on. 'I wanted to see for myself what kind of woman could steal you from me, so I asked father's detectives for the address, told them I wanted to confront her, and so I did,' she affirmed, casting a fond glance in Tomi's direction. 'Turned out Tomi Fabri wasn't anything like I'd imagined. She was . . . beautiful . . . perfect in mind, spirit, and in body. And, Jesus, she had such tits! A tongue on her that could . . . well, suffice it to say the attraction was immediate and mutual.'

'But that kind of sex, even lesbian sex, couldn't put you over the top anymore, could it? You were way beyond that, weren't you, Jen?'

'I don't know what you're talking about,' she snarled.

'I saw the steel 'O' rings on the side of the bed,' I told her. 'And those tits, magnificent as they are, were too perfect for a freak like you, isn't that right, Jen? And so you got your kicks the only way a twisted bitch like you could, chaining her to a bed, dripping candle wax on her chest, torturing her with shocks from electrical wire, to make her, what? Less "perfect?"'

'Shoot him. Kill him now, my love,' she growled. 'Let's get out of this hell hole!'

Tomi turned to Jennifer then back to me, hands still quaking, eyes narrowing to slits as she took aim with the Bell revolver.

'You're not going to shoot,' I told her.

'She loves me, Jack. Can you understand that? *She loves me!* Nobody never said that to me before. Not even my Old Man before he'd stick his thing in me. *In my ass, Jack! Into the ass and mouth of a twelve year old girl!* And I believe her, Jack. I believe that she loves me!'

'Oh, I do. I do love you, my angel!' Jennifer swore.

'So now I'm going to pull this trigger and, I'm sorry, Jack, but you're gonna have to die, baby.'

And I believed her. I believed Tomi was going to pull that trigger, if not at that exact moment, then soon, once

I'd run out of diversions, once I'd run out of bullshit to throw her way.

'*Shoot him! Shoot him now!!*' Jennifer screamed at her.

But like those outlaws of old, my brain suddenly kicked into overdrive, into that zone of resourcefulness that comes during a man's most lonely, torturous moment when there appeared no way out, and that's when an alternative to getting my brains blown out burst like a lightning flash into my brain. The six-shooter I smuggled out of Nueva Laredo. I'd put it in the bottom drawer of the chiffonier behind me for safekeeping, I remembered. A gun, *the gun*, was there for the taking just three feet behind me!

'*Shoot him! For Christ's sake, what are you waiting for? If you love me, you'll shoot him! Think about your father, Tomi!*' Jennifer was shrieking, '*Think about your father and shoot that bastard of a man now!*'

And with the word 'now,' two things happened: the first was a sound like that of a bull whip cracking ringing out through the room. The second was that upon hearing that word, 'now,' my legs went out under me and I crumpled to the floor beneath the dining room table, a stab of pain to my shoulder, shot through the arm!

I could hear Jennifer screaming instructions to Tomi, wild and maddened, like a bad dream unfolding, but couldn't make out the words, couldn't understand what she was saying, as I rolled on my side and Tomi, realizing I was still breathing, took aim at me again. With body turned toward the chiffonier and mind focused like a laser on the drawer and the gun it contained, I flung it open and reached for the Remington, blood streaming down my arm to my hand onto the white carpet where I lay. But before I could take aim with the Remington, or even raise it, the sound of a second '*crack*' thundered through the room, shattering the continuum of Jennifer's ravings, filling it with the smell of gunpowder, and causing me to wonder 'had I been hit again?' But I didn't have long to wonder because in that briefest of instants the .32 slug whistled past my right ear forcing me to lunge to my right, six-gun in hand. And it was there that I remained, set and ready to fire, studying the position of Tomi's legs from beneath the table.

'Don't shoot, Tomi.' I warned her, gun trained on her abdomen.

'*Kill him, Tomi! Kill the motherfucker!!*' Jennifer was wailing as Tomi's eyes, gleaming with panic, looked to Jennifer and back to me again.

And amid the chaos, in some measure of time incalculable to the human senses, I noticed the subtle movement in Tomi's knees that I never wanted to see. Then as we stared into one another's eyes—her standing above me on the landing, me peering out from beneath the table—and me begging, 'Don't shoot, baby! Don't shoot the gun!', Tomi bent her knees forward ever so slightly to brace herself in the meteoric second before pulling the trigger, warning enough for me to get off a single shot of my own that ripped through her red dress and into her belly, killing her instantly.

A pang of deep sorrow seized me then, Phials, choked the breath out of me, in fact, as I watched Tomi Fabri collapse onto the floor and saw Jennifer rushing, not to her, but to my briefcase with the flash drive in it, ripping it away as I tried to take hold of it.

'You are a stupid man, aren't you, Jack?' she said standing over me.

'Maybe,' I said, 'but I'm not evil.'

'So you say, my love.'

'But *you* are.'

'When it suits me,' she said turning to leave as I tried to get to my feet.

'Then why not shoot me?'

'In case you haven't noticed, you've already been shot.'

'A flesh wound,' I taunted.

'Wound enough to tie you to Tomi's death and that's enough for me. Bye, Jack,' she said leaving for the door as I struggled to my feet. *'Couldna done it without ya!'* she laughed, her cackles flooding the Sherry Netherland's corridors as she ran for the elevator.

# Chapter 37

O nce I got to my feet I realized I was lucky at least when it came to the .32 slug that had passed clean through the bicep of my left arm. The wound was bleeding steadiy but didn't look serious. 'Lucky me!' I was thinking as I walked across the room to Tomi, who I knew was dead before she hit the floor.

I know you've probably seen a dozen bodies in your line of work, Phials, but not so with me and like some kind of religious supplicant before a saint or prophet, I got down on my knees and stared deeply into her face, and her ebony eyes, still wide-open. 'I'm so fucking sorry, baby,' I whispered, touching her cheek. Her skin was still warm but set like the porcelain of a China doll and it looked to me then like she wasn't dead at all but simply resting, like an angel, as I reached forward to close those lifeless eyes, now staring out into oblivion.

Odd, but I started to explain myself to her, telling her I never intended to kill or even hurt her, but stopped short realizing the only thing left behind was a body, the shell of a person, not Tomi. The *real* Tomi was gone, left for God knew where. Heaven? Hell? Purgatory? The only thing left in front of me was the corpse of a sweet love-starved girl. But wherever it was the souls of people like Tomi Fabri wound up, I prayed she'd finally be happy and finally be loved by someone, maybe Jesus Christ.

It was from that point—understanding that you'd probably already heard from a cop buddy about the jumper at 9 West and decided something didn't smell right—that I realized even a stupid bastard like you must have puzzled things out. *Corpses!* Corpses showing up by land (Tomi), by air (Cephus), and by sea (Soto) so that for me it was a foregone conclusion you'd finally seen me for who I was. Not a 'suicide' as you wanted so desperately to prove, but a murderer, or something damn close to it.

So, wounded, and desperate as I was, I hopped a cab from the Sherry Netherland in search of sanctuary. The only place on earth I figured might take me in. My old prep school where there were priests who I believed might see me for the man they knew, not the criminal I'd become. Through the tunnel back to Jersey, I was off to St. Ann's Abbey where the Brothers resided. But I wasn't the only one thought like that, was I, Phials? And if you think you know me, guess what, I know you at least as well and knew you'd eventually find me here. The cops, they'd buy into suicide when it came to Cephus Jackson, but not you. Not with that Eagle Scout-on-steroids brain you got. There was no fucking way you were going to believe two employees from the same building hadn't died under suspicious circumstances in less than a month!

See, the guys dressed in blue uniforms see life as one awesome coincidence like what happened to those Japs tossed and tumbled by that earthquake, swept away by a fifty-foot high tsunami that carried trucks and ships and trains and houses and finally irradiated with plutonium gamma rays or whatever the hell it was. But to cops, it's not just Japan. To them, it's the entire human population that's totally fucked and doing somersaults in black water rushing over people at sixty miles per hour, them with their guns, badges and batons tumbling in that rolling wave of radioactive shit along with everyone else.

But you, Martin, you are a special case. The worst kind of sinner because you think the people tumbling in that washing machine of shit are there because they deserve it, that somehow they went to the wrong school, or wrong church, or made some fateful miscalculation at a crossroad in their life. You think you're outside of all that, that you're cleaner, better, smarter, more disciplined, and that somehow you can be society's high priest who judges others and exacts revenge on behalf of some lunatic God that despises his own creation.

In your mind, I may be a killer, psychotic as you, but at least the people that died I'm sorry for hurting. Fact is, one morning I woke up and came to the conclusion I wasn't the only one who was totally fucked up, that most everything around me was equally hollowed-out, rotted, and falling apart, and that the earth itself was in open rebellion against us. I'd become poisoned by the fallout, Phials. Like the radiation in the air I breathed had gotten into my blood and organs and given me a kind of spiritual cancer. So, to save myself, I made a run for it. But you, you're far worse than me because your pride wouldn't allow you to admit the disease that's infected us could even exist, and so you've succumbed to it. It's like you boxed everything around you up into neat little packages and then shoved every living soul into a world of your own creation. That's vanity, Phials. And like the Bible warns against, you created a false image of God before man, and that phony God is *you!*

Anyway, that's the way I figured it as I took a pull from my near-empty bottle of Chivas, then turned to find my supply of amphetamines equally exhausted. But I didn't have to ponder your situation much longer, thank God, because that's when I heard the gentle tap of Jeremiah Cullinane's knuckles on the door to my sanctuary-prison, the large door creaked open, and there you were standing sober as a judge, eyes cruel as an executioner's, the priest standing behind you in the doorway.

"Welcome! I've been expecting you, Martin," I said, toasting the occasion with the last drops of liquid in my bottle. "What took you so long?"

"Still think this is a game, do you, Madson?"

"If it's a game, I must not be too good at it. You see, Jeremiah," I said turning to the priest, "Mr. Phials and I have been engaged in an intimate game of chess for the past five weeks and it looks like he's got me checkmated. So how'd you find me, Martin? How'd you know I was here? How'd you know I was still alive?" I roared, bottle in hand, the decibels getting away from me. I was raving.

"It wasn't difficult because you're nothing special to me, Madson. A spoiled, high-strung New York exec who's gone off the deep end. If I've seen it once, I've seen it ten times since the Crash. You're just a little more violent than most. You shot your girlfriend dead, didn't you Madson? Offed that guard at 9 West, too, I'd lay odds. But since you asked, I'll tell you because you're not so hard to figure out as you think. I knew you would be here because in the course of your miserable existence no one's ever 'honored' you for anything, except here at this Catholic monastery built brick-to-mortar with stolen money stolen from Gallagher's East Coast Securities penny stock scam. Must make you feel real proud getting a trophy like that for 'Most Distinguished Alumni' from a crew like that! With no family to return to, no friends or colleagues to rely on after you'd robbed technology from NuGen and they thought you were dead, I knew you'd eventually go back to get the girl. What I couldn't predict is that you'd kill Tomi Fabri and the guard along with her! So where to now? Just one place. The only place that would consort with a low life like you, Jack. The monks at St. Ann's Abbey, the Catholic monastery, Central Ward, Newark that helped create someone like you."

"All that energy for lil' ol' me! It gives me goosebumps! And the other question? What made you think I was still alive?"

"It was the missing life vest for one. I knew you never drowned. I knew right off that someone engaged in a struggle with Soto and wound up with the jacket that was supposed to save him. Besides, the whole scheme was too pat. Too perfect. Like the pieces of a puzzle they fit together in a way that to me could never be genuine. Your plan was as phony as you. Like the life you lived. But more than any of those things, it was your profile. Any number of statistics would support the case that this was fraud, plain and simple. High achiever, hard drinker, drug addicted, used to getting his way all through life then the bottom drops out. Everything you knew and everything you thought you knew was suddenly in jeopardy. Your entire identity about to disappear before your eyes and you cracked. Simple as that. You might glamorize it, call it what you want, romanticize it for all I care. But in the end, you are a coward, Jack. You couldn't stand the heat but you sure did enjoy the excitement of the fire in the kitchen! And when you did crack, it all came pouring out, putrid as a lanced boil. All of that anger and hate. All of that self-loathing. No, you weren't a suicide, but you were the closest thing to it. A reckless killer whose only motive was the basest kind of rage. A baby without his bottle!"

"Guess you got me figured out pretty good, don't you, Phials?"

"It's my profession, Madson. The innerworkings of the criminal mind, what you wrote about in that article of yours? That's my end of the business. Been at the top of my game for thirty years now, Madson, and if I have my way there'll be thirty more because I like what I do. To me it's a public service I perform, cornering rats like you and throwing them back in the garbage heap." Phials stepped toward the black phone cradled by the side of the desk where I was sitting. "I'm going to call the Newark branch of the Federal Bureau of Investigation now, Jack. I hope they like wise guys in Rahway prison because if they don't I'm afraid you're in for the shock of your life."

It was then that I slowly raised my right hand from under the desk, the Remington six-shooter held firmly in it.

"Even you can't be this stupid, Madson," Phials bluffed.

"My God, son, think what you're doing!" cried Jeremiah as a tight grin crossed my face.

"You don't even have a gun with you, do you, you stupid bastard?"

"I don't carry a weapon, no need, not in my line of work. Mine is an investigative role. It's the FBI and police who do the arresting."

"Shut up, you bag of wind, and give me the keys to your car! Now!!"

Reluctantly, with his eyes locked onto mine, Phials tossed them to me.

"I'm going to walk out of here now, Jeremiah," I said holding Phials at bay with the gun, "and you're going to come with me. Then you're going to lock that door behind you and give me the key. I don't need much time. Fifteen minutes, that's all I'm asking. After that you can call the FBI or the cops or the Sisters of Charity, I don't give a damn, got it?"

"You'll never make it out of here, Madson. Not even out the front door. Look at you!" he jeered. "White as a ghost! Still bleeding!!"

"Shut up!" I roared back at him, slamming my six-shooter into his head. A crack split open above his left eye, blood cascading down the side of his face.

Phials touched the gash with his fingertips then brought his hand down, studying the blood like nothing like that had ever happened to him, like he'd never contemplated the thought of someone hitting him in the face.

I laughed, a thin rumble of a sound that escaped through my clenched teeth, "So, you're not so tough after all, are you, Martin?"

"Tough enough," he said wiping the blood away with a handkerchief. "They're going to get you, Jack," he swore then. "They're going to arrest you and when they do I hope they try you in court for homicide and then they kill you by lethal injection like the mad dog you are."

"So long, Martin. Jeremiah, you come with me," I said waving him forward with the Remington.

But then the lights in the room went funny in front of my eyes and I felt like I was on a merry-go-round gone wild. And that's all I remember. They tell me I passed out. In a heap, they said, right there on the floor three steps into the hallway.

# Chapter 38

Who can say how long I was out? Certainly not me. And when I awoke from what I'm told was a coma, I had only a vague recollection of where my mind had been or for what length of time it had been there. It was like I'd been in a dimly lit room, an ante-chamber of Hell, having been engaged in a long discussion with a shadowy figure who fled the room the moment my eyes opened.

"Am I dead?" I remember asking.

There was no answer only a fluttering sound. Had my dark friend of before come back to pay me a visit? I wondered but then a voice did come. It filled the room which was flooded with fluorescent light.

"No, Mr. Madson, you're not dead. You were never dead and the doctors tell us your prognosis is excellent."

"Where am I?"

"Beth Israel Hospital, Newark, New Jersey. That priest friend of yours called an ambulance. You've been here three days."

"Jesus," I said rubbing my eyes and, indeed, I realized I was in a hospital room bright, white, and reeking of antiseptic.

"Who are you?"

"So you'd like to have a talk?" he asked moving from

the far corner of the room to a chair beside my bed as he spoke.

"Who are you?" I asked more emphatically, staring into his face as he settled himself in the chair. He had an angular face with probably the clearest blue eyes I'd ever seen, cool as ice.

"I am a missionary on the capitalistic highway of life, Mr. Madson. My name is Roberts, Norman Roberts, but that's irrelevant. I work for your father-in-law, Mr. Barton Crowley, and that is very relevant."

"What do you want? I feel like hell," I said swallowing twice to get the saliva in my mouth flowing. "My head feels like a cannon ball, can you call a doctor?"

"Vision a little blurry? Thoughts a little muddled? Having trouble putting your words together in a sentence?"

I nodded to all three.

"Good, that's the way we want it. Let's talk, Mr. Madson. Let's put our pistols on the table, shall we?"

I shuddered, leaning back in my bed to get a better look at him, more than just his eyes and face. Roberts was wearing a custom-made Italian suit and looked like he could be a high priced lawyer though his language and demeanor hinted at something rougher, less refined. Even through the fog of medication, I could see his physique was athletic but not muscle-bound, agile and strong as an MMA middleweight. All put together—face, eyes, body—I had him pegged as head of personal security for Team Crowley *aka* the detective who'd been following me around for the past two years or more.

"You want to talk? Sure you can talk but don't expect me to say anything. You may wear expensive suits, Norm, but you've got cop written all over you."

Roberts was altogether calm as he spoke, but a vein in his forehead gave a jump and began to pulse, "That's good to hear, Mr. Madson, because what I have to say, well, if I were you I'd listen carefully."

"The girl—Tomi?"

"Yes, that's right, she's dead. You killed her."

"Jennifer? Tiffany?"

Roberts pulled his face closer to mine. His expression, I noticed, had traveled a good distance between from indifference to a kind of menacing petulance, "Also dead. At least to you. That's what I'm here to tell you, Mr. Madson, so please knock off the questions and get this right. There's a reason you're in a private room in Beth Israel and not under arrest and recovering at Lenox Hill or Bellevue for that matter. Call it fate or blind luck but you've walked into a miracle. The police had you dead to rights, Madson. The fisherman, Soto, no case, not really. The two others, Jackson and the girl, *dead to rights.*"

I started to say something, but the look in his eyes shut me up and it occurred to me that this man was awfully good at intimidating. Once he said something even with just those cold-blooded eyes, you may as well have been an insect on a pin.

"I don't care if you killed them or why, that's not why I'm here. Why I'm here is to give you this," he said drawing a white envelope from the inside pocket of his suit jacket and handing it to me. I looked at it like it was a dead rat he just put in my hand. "In that envelope is the beginnings of your new life, Mr. Madson, do you hear what I'm telling you? One hundred-fifty thousand cash, a driver's license, and an American Express card all in the name of Jesse J. Martin. That's you, do you understand me?" he asked pushing his face forward to within inches of mine, staring deep into the pupils of my eyes. "So far as NYPD is concerned, Jackson was a suicide and Tomi Fabri a high priced hooker who met her match four days ago at the Sherry Netherland, her killer still at large. That makes you either a free man or her killer, partner. All you have to do to stay free is take that envelope, get as far from New Jersey as that money will take you, and never be in contact with your wife or daughter again. *Never*, you know the meaning of that word, Madson?" He took hold of my wounded arm at the bicep and gripped it powerfully. "*Mr. Madson?*"

"Yes, I know its meaning," I uttered, suddenly scared as well as bewildered. Where was I really? I wondered. Who was to say whether this was a private room at Beth Israel or a room of torture in the bowels of Crowley's estate? "*Never, I will never be in contact with Jen or Tiffany again!!*"

"That's right, Mr. Madson . . ."

"But the press? The media, they must be all over this," I wondered out loud as Roberts rose and started putting on his overcoat. Then he turned to me, the faintest hint of a smile crossing his taut lips.

"It doesn't matter what's done in private, in sessions like the one we've just had. What's important is the public show, Mr. Madson, and we control that. The show must be flawless because the public show, the one we give the media, is the language we use to tell our friends and enemies that we still have order enough to make a public display. That's not so easy if you consider the general insanity of the world these days. You see, it doesn't matter if you murdered Tomi Fabri or twenty security guards. What matters is that you and I came to an accommodation. What matters is that the

Crowley name stays intact, that you leave forever, and that Mr. Crowley stays happy."

Roberts turned to leave, putting on a gray fedora, and stepping to the door.

"Phials? What about Phials, he'd never let you . . ."

"Phials was taken into custody yesterday, Mr. Madson. Oh, that's right, you've been in a coma, haven't you? Awful man, all over the television news! Horrible what he did, profiting from the death claims of thousands of military families, investing the payout and taking the interest! The flower of America's youth, Madson, the young patriotic men and women who gave up their lives for the struggling peoples of Iraq and Afghanistan. Shameful! Absolutely reprehensible that friend of yours, Martin Phials!" Roberts turned to leave, but thought better of it. "Oh, and one more thing," he said, his back still to me. "Your computer, the one with that novel you were writing about the boating accident and murders? It's there on the sofa. Phials told me to tell you that he read it and that you were right."

"Right about what?"

"'Entropy,' that's what he told me to tell you. He said you were correct 'It isn't about evolution anymore, it's about entropy,' that's all. You can make out of it what you like, but that's what he said. In fact it's the only thing he has said since they arrested him."

"So Crowley's people set him up to shut him up," I whispered softly as the door to the room opened.

"All done in there?" the stern, cheerful voice of a robust man in his late seventies inquired.

"Yes, Sir," Roberts shot back with an efficiency that gave me pause as I looked beyond the door, cracked open several inches, to catch a glimpse of my father-in-law.

In the instant between their exchange, our eyes met. Crowley's eyes were dark and black as a terrier's eyes in the heat of a hunt. Racing and intense, wild and yet contained. An animal's eyes to be sure, the vanguard to a soul capable not merely of killing but tearing the flesh apart and feasting on the entrails. The look lasted so short a time before those eyes became jovial again that I was forced to wonder if I'd seen it at all or if my mind, swarmed by the damp and fog of three days of unconsciousness, had somehow super-imposed my own night terrors on his eyes before they had withdrawn back into the dimly lit chamber where I'd spent the past three days and nights conversing, I concluded now, with the Devil, himself.

The door shut soundlessly behind Roberts, but I could hear his voice like a yapping mutt at the feet of its impatient owner as they made their way down the hallway. 'Yes, Mr. Crowley.' 'No, Mr. Crowley.' 'To be certain, Mr. Crowley.' *Ad nauseum.*

I looked down to my hand (it seemed like someone else's!) that still held the bright white envelope, and opened it, rummaging through its contents. It was true what Crowley's detective had told me. In it was one hundred fifty thousand USD in five hundred dollar denominations along with an American Express Platinum card and Oregon state driver's license. The credit card carried the name 'Jesse J. Martin,' but the driver's license bore my full identity, 'Jesse James Martin.'

'Imagine,' I summoned the scattered forces of my drug-numbed mind to appreciate, 'Jesse James Martin, a modern day outlaw,' I ventured visualizing the words as a *NY Post* or *NY Daily News* banner headline. Even my harshest critic would have to admit it had a certain ring to it.

# Epilogue

The trip out west to Oregon is about twenty-five hundred miles. Now I know that sounds like quite a haul but in a way it made the perfect end to my personal journey through Hell — traveling the landscape of Super-America, coast-to-coast, on an interstate so proud and new in former times, now pock-marked as the carpet-bombed air strip of a Third World city.

I guess I forgot or maybe never knew that once you got out of the tri-state area a hundred-fifty grand still gets you places. True, I wasn't driving my Jaguar anymore, more like a 2010 Mustang convertible, but once you tore yourself from the ghouls that populated Wall Street, everything settled down to what they'd call 'Nowhere USA' but many believed was America's heartland.

From Jersey to Pennsylvania, Iowa to Wyoming, then on to Utah with its Great Desert Basin so flat you can see the curvature of the planet, so barren even the simplest life forms can't survive its desert bake. It was just ten miles northeast of here mid-1800s that the Donner party tried to cut time from their trek from Illinois to California. Forgetting what every other creature had learned over the millennium, they failed to take enough water. Twenty-two of their oxen died of exhaustion before they made it out, forced to leave four wagons behind in the salt flats where the temperatures soared to one-twenty by day then dropped to sixty by nightfall.

Eventually they made it to the Sierra Nevada Mountains but it was Utah's Great Salt Lake Desert that decided their fate. By winter they were starving to death with no chance of surviving the freezing cold without resorting to cannibalism. Men, women and children reduced to the lowest form of humanity. Of the eighty-seven in the party, forty-one died from exposure or disease. Some, who'd lost their minds, simply leapt from cliffs and killed themselves or wandered aimlessly into the maw of a mountain blizzard never to be seen again. Not so pretty, I thought grimly as I plowed ahead still deeper into Mormon country, wondering if this was the real America, an endless strip of uninhabitable desert that stretched between New York and Los Angeles.

By early evening as the sun set over the Rockies I decided to cool my heels in a city of 85,000 called Ogden. Truth be told, once released from Beth Israel Hospital I took Norman Roberts' advice to heart. It wasn't difficult. I knew my father-in-law well enough to understand my days were numbered if I lingered in the Garden State, that it was him who got the AvaTech files, and that he'd probably already parlayed them into millions. But none of that mattered to me anymore, not where I lived, how much money I made, or what equity investments I favored. To me it was all bullshit, part of the public show Crowley and men like him had staged since the rise of the robber barons, and even before that I suppose.

For starters, I was alive! No small matter given the events of the past month, or five years, if you chose to see it that way. Crowley and his henchmen were off my back if I stayed away. Mr. Li and the Chin Chou had little hope of finding me with my new identity and relocation out west. And during that trip for the first time in my life, I wasn't afraid anymore. Like the dread had diluted and was being absorbed by the open space around me. Miles upon miles of farmland in Illinois and Nebraska, flat as a schoolmarm's ruler, and mountain ranges that rambled high and far, a molten ocean frozen fast in time, majestic I suppose you could say. But unbounded, free as the men and women I encountered at road stops and motels along the way. Hardy, clean-living folks, most of them: mothers with little kids in strollers once I entered the small towns and 'C' cities scattered like Monopoly pieces across the American landscape. Dads, as I neared the county line into Ogden, fixing tractor engines off the side of the highway, some riding horses, waving a greeting along the way, me saluting back, bewildered by the notion that anyone in Utah or anywhere else gave a damn whether I lived or died!

Of course, there were stores and restaurants, schools and churches as I took my Mustang downtown looking for a hotel. Some of the stores were privately owned but most stood like monuments to the reach of the large chains that stretched like long cold fingers out into the west. Stores like Walmart, McDonald's, Target and KMart. The schools and churches stood in stark contrast to those chain stores that enveloped the kids and families that attended them like a hangman's noose. Modest people dressed in denim jeans and button-down shirts in modest buildings, practical and sturdy, 'Made in America' before the marketers had surrounded them, promoting globalization and credit cards by the dozen issued by banks like Wells Fargo, Bank America, JP Morgan Chase and Citibank. Banks on top of banks, I observed as the Mustang glided down Main Street. And I wondered, if even now I had escaped the tentacles of Super-America or had the hype seeped so deep into our souls that even the people in a place like Ogden needed the reassurance of its credit cards, banks, chain stores, and fast food restaurants to feel they were Americans.

Later, after I'd checked into the Marriott and walked around town before taking down a steak at Applebee's, I wandered into the Glory to God Catholic Church in Downtown Ogden. It was early afternoon on a Sunday I realized and a baby was being baptized. Of course, no one knew who I was when I walked in to see the family gathered around the baptismal font as the mother, a sturdy looking woman, handed her baby over to the priest. She smiled at me as I stood watching, proud it seemed that a stranger took an interest in the ceremony. I nodded a friendly acknowledgement as her husband glanced toward me, my eyes catching his long enough to see that he seemed a decent enough fellow who probably worked a trade, a carpenter, if I had to guess. 'I baptize you, John Matthew Brady, in the name of the Father, the Son, and the Holy Spirit . . . ' the priest proclaimed as he lowered the baby into the water and brought him up again, screaming his little lungs out, wet, cold and terrified. 'I pray for you,' I whispered as I left the church. 'I pray for all of us because it's you we're counting on now. It may seem like a lot to ask but we blew it, and if the world is going to be saved it's going to take your intelligence and humanity to see us through.'

Afterward, I ate that steak with a cold bottle of Sam Adams, got back in my Mustang convertible, and started driving down the interstate headed for Idaho. A short way into the drive, my mind began to wander and I got to thinking about Tomi Fabri. And maybe it was the terrain around me, mountainous and mystical, with the deserted four-lane spread out in front of me far as I could see, but for a time that night I felt like Tomi was very near me and I could hear her voice in the wind as it whistled by. '*Are you happy?*' I asked her. And she answered that she was. '*Is it lonely being dead?*' And she told me that it wasn't, that there were lots of others there like her. '*Do you forgive me?*' I finally asked and she assured me that she did. '*Then I guess it's okay for me to try to be happy, too,*' I told her. But to this there was no reply.

Early that morning, it was lonely as I crossed the state border into Idaho and I thought then about leaving this mess of a country with its flags and its debt and eternal optimism to go back to Mexico or another country, but decided against it. See, in the end, I'm an American, a coalman on a train trundling down the track in search of a new day.

Coming soon
From Barricade Books

# The Kafka Society

The next Jack Madson

Series crime thriller

By Ron Felber

*(Turn the page for a preview of Chapter One)*

# Chapter 1

It was Christmas week and it may have been snowing but you couldn't prove it by me, locked up at the Metropolitan Correctional Center in Lower Manhattan. Like it or not, I was here at least until my sentencing, then off to a penitentiary; most probably Lewisburg, or if things really went south, the Fed's Supermax in Florence, Colorado. No "Season's Greetings" card in that image, I don't suppose, with the population restless, me, beside myself, waiting for celebrity attorney Jimmy Bryant to show up, and a rap version of "Silent Night" sweeping through the Tier's concrete and steel like a powerful wind set over the lesser winds of television voices, screams of inmates arguing, clanging of metal bars slamming shut, and a thousand other sounds.

Originally it was my pal Vicky Benson who was supposed to defend me but she got pulled because of what they called "tangential complicity" in my case so they gave me a court appointed *pro bono* type named George Shapiro—fat, lazy, and about as interested in keeping me off death row as my ex-wife, Jennifer. But then Vicky got me lined up with Bryant. Jimmy Bryant's birth name was James Delaney O'Brian. He started his career that way but once he got involved with acquitting a slew of Hollywood-types on drug charges, became uneasy with the implications of his

County Cork background and Americanized it to Bryant. He even landed a reality TV show out of it back in '09 called *The Defense Never Rests* for a season or two and was now a frequent guest on *The Chris Matthews Show*, *O'Reilly Factor*, and *Meet The Press* on Sunday mornings.

Of course none of that made me feel any less anxious, *or angry*, about him being late, I thought miserably. But in the end, the back story to the state's charges against me— ranging from murder to conspiracy to commit terrorist acts against the United States of America had little to do with Jimmy Bryant or Vicky Benson. No, everything, *all of it*, had to do with just one person, and that was Havana Spice. *"Naughty but nice, Havana Spice,"* I sang in a whisper to myself. It was about her then. It's about her now. And I guess you could say our relationship was written in the stars. In fact, I'm sure you could say it.

But I digress, which I hope is not so difficult to understand. You see, for me, the past three days have been a kind of "home coming." Initially, they put me in solitary confinement for "my own protection" and I suppose there was some wisdom in that. Having been a cop myself for a few years after I'd dropped out of Georgetown University in D.C., I knew how the story played: put the wrong guy in the wrong cell block and the inmates in the zoo would tear him apart with the ferocity of primates on red meat. Of course, it didn't always go that way, my racing mind reminded, though in my case, in the case of Jack Madson, it worked out all right so far.

Besides, I hated the "hole," who wouldn't? Only the craziest psycho would like it there. They called it the hole because it was put away below the Tier and off by itself. There was no place to put clothes or personal belongings.

Hell, there wasn't even a loo because they thought you might beat a guard to death with the toilet seat or try to drown yourself in the bowl! No, there was just this hole in the center of the concrete surrounded by steel bars. No window. No toilet. No nothing.

Used to be you could only keep a guy in solitary for twenty-one days consecutive by law then take him out for three days before you could lock him back in there again. Now, with the Religious Right spewing all of their faith, love, and charity throughout the universe, the authorities can keep a prisoner in solitary near forever like at Supermax in Colorado, or Pelican in Florida, those 'special' places where they kept guys like Mafia Don John Gotti — men the law obsessed over and wanted basically to drive to madness, if they chose to do so. And, believe me, even I could see it. The madness, I mean. After four, five days — which is the period they kept me in — never seeing a soul, never knowing if it was daytime or night, you could look down into that black hole like it was the gullet of the Devil's throat leading one-way straight to Hell with every swinging dick God had damned to perdition cursing, crying, or just smiling like "We'll see you down here soon enough, fucker," staring back up at you.

I sniffed at the foul prison air and looked around edgy as a cat on a hot tin roof, studying the wending path of a cockroach scurrying on the bare concrete floor into a jagged crack in the wall of my cell. Even for me, a veteran of calamities, my present circumstance seemed grim, I brooded, taking note of the neighborhood: across from me was "Doctor Mopwringer," a body builder who beat his brother-in-law beyond recognition with a galvanized steel mop wringer while high on Angel Dust; to my right, Bryce

"Bad Boy" Horton, a methamphetamine-addicted Mongol biker who propane-torched-to-death a fourteen year old girl he'd chained to a tree for the fun of watching her burn; to my left, Dimitri Salitas, Odessan-born Russian mobster who poured hydrofluoric acid into the boots of a half-dozen rival gang members, dissolving the bones in their feet and ankles before drowning them in a boiling vat of the stuff.

So, why do I tell you this? Is it to kill time while I chew the tips of my fingers raw waiting for my interminably, chronically, ever-annoyingly late hot shot attorney, James O'Brian—sorry, re-boot and Americanize—James "Jimmy" Bryant? Or, maybe, it's just a way to let some steam from off of the roiling miasma that had begun to churn inside me and not stopped since my arrest for a movable feast of capital offenses three weeks ago? Hard to say, except that after becoming an expert on the intricately jaded subject of myself over the past twenty-seven days, I'm proud to announce that my ramblings are not without their method. *Item One*, they are to show you that I am not such a bad fucking guy. *Item Two*, they are to demonstrate my point about how perverse life in the underbelly of "The Empire in Decline" can be. *Item Three*, they are to show you that John "Jack" Madson—yes, all six foot and one inch, one-hundred seventy-eight pounds of him—understands the difference between coercion and choice, logic and insanity, and what is right and what is wrong.

Booze? Drugs? Crazy-assed sex? Guilty as charged, but I swear to Christ if ever there was anything true about my life and constitution, it is that *I do not belong here locked up with these monsters!*

# Author's Biography

Ron Felber is a graduate of Georgetown University and Loyola University Chicago, where he earned his master's degree in English.

After graduation, he worked as a deputy sheriff, transporting federal criminals. His writing career began with articles based on his experiences for *True Detective* magazine. His recent book *Il Dottore: The Double Life of a Mafia Doctor* was the basis for the popular dramatic television series *The Mob Doctor.*

He lives in New Jersey with his wife, Lorraine, and their three children.